SHERLOCK HOLMES
The Legacy of Deeds

SHERLOCK HOLMES
The Legacy of Deeds

NICK KYME

TITAN BOOKS

Sherlock Holmes: The Legacy of Deeds
Print edition ISBN: 9781785652066
Electronic edition ISBN: 9781785652073

Published by Titan Books
A division of Titan Publishing Group Ltd
144 Southwark St, London SE1 0UP

First edition: October 2017
2 4 6 8 10 9 7 5 3 1

A CIP catalogue record for this title is available from the British Library.

Printed and bound in the United States.

What did you think of this book?
We love to hear from our readers. Please email us at:
readerfeedback@titanemail.com, or write to us at the above address.

To receive advance information, news, competitions, and exclusive offers
online, please sign up for the Titan newsletter on our website.
www.titanbooks.com

SHERLOCK HOLMES
The Legacy of Deeds

CHAPTER ONE

A NIGHT AT THE BALLET

There can be no doubt concerning the genius of Sherlock Holmes. His cognitive acumen and mental acuity are so well developed that most humble professors of Oxford or Cambridge would appear lack-witted by comparison. I have seen him often make them appear thus. But, during my years as his companion and friend, I have learned that such a gifted intelligence carries with it a most debilitating burden. For Holmes's mind, arguably his greatest virtue, is also his gravest curse. It hungers for knowledge, sated only by the sustenance brought by cases. Indeed, whenever Holmes found himself without problems to solve, he would descend into the most profound malaise of spirit, one that often saw him reaching for the cocaine syringe.

It was in the winter of 1894 that such a bout of melancholy led me to procure two tickets for the Royal Opera House, in the hope that a cultural distraction might at least prove briefly diverting for Holmes. Two seats in the gods was the best my modest purse could afford, but our opulent surroundings more than made up for a slightly compromised view of the stage, which presently was obscured from view by a red velvet curtain bearing Her Majesty's royal crest.

"Ballet, Watson," remarked Holmes. "Had I known this was the planned diversion I should have locked myself in my room and not emerged until this farcical notion of yours had run its course. At most I am in the mood for opera. Something German."

"Had I not, Holmes, you would be embracing oblivion in your dressing gown and slippers, bemoaning the stagnation of existence and ruing the distinct lack of mental stimulation that has seen you not leave our lodgings for these last three weeks!"

Holmes turned sharply, his eyes alight with indignation in the gloom. "There is nothing wrong with my dressing gown and slippers!"

I sighed deeply, ignoring the frowns and mutterings of nearby patrons. "Ballet might not be the diversion you crave, but it has got you out of Baker Street, man, and therefore I shall consider it a success!"

"I shall judge its success upon the interval, Watson," said Holmes. "*Swan Lake...*" he muttered, narrowing his eyes, "... oblivion would be preferable."

"Holmes, could you please at least—" I began, exasperated, only for a gentleman in a gaudy maroon jacket and a shirt with attendant silk puff tie to glare at my half-formed outburst.

"Yes, Watson," Holmes chimed in, glancing at me askance with his attention now on the stage, "do be quiet. The performance is about to start." He leaned over to address the unhappy gentleman. "A surgeon," said Holmes, as if it were sufficient explanation, "too used to hearing the sound of his own voice," to which the gentleman nodded, favouring Holmes with a smile and me a remonstrating shake of the head.

As the lights dimmed, I sat back in my seat and thought that oblivion would indeed be preferable. For whom, however, I had yet to decide.

Mercifully, my irritation at Holmes was short-lived, thanks in part to the fact I am used to such bouts of "playful" humour from my companion, especially during his less genial periods of inactivity, and because, unlike Holmes, I found *Swan Lake* to be amply suited to my tastes and current mood.

I have no musical acumen per se, as opposed to Holmes who is an excellent violinist. Nor am I a follower of the ballet, but the art and narrative certainly ushered my thoughts towards a pleasant fiction.

Holmes, it seemed, had settled into silence at least, though I suspected his mind was engaged in analysis and observation rather than simple enjoyment of the arts. The tempo insisted by the conductor, and the adherence to it by his orchestra; the precise number of steps in each balletic movement; the true natures of the dancers, their relationships and vices; Holmes had an eye for such things, all of which would provide greater entertainment than the spectacle itself.

It was about halfway through the second act, and Prince Siegfried had encountered the Swan Princess Odette, when during a set transition the evening took a most unexpected turn. As the lights faded and a veil fell across the back half of the stage, there arose an almighty clatter. I thought at first I had imagined it, for the orchestra continued unabated, but when the veil began to lift again I saw the truth of it.

A woman, the White Swan herself no less, lay face down on the stage. Her limbs were splayed indecorously, and a slew of sand had spilled over the body from a burst hessian sack.

A steadily increasing hubbub took hold, until the orchestra fell silent by degrees and a stagehand who had run into the spotlight to investigate declared, "She's dead! Miss

Evangeline is dead!" prompting a rash of sudden exclamations from every onlooker.

In moments, the curtain descended so as to block the terrible scene from view.

Holmes had risen to his feet, a thin but certain smile turning his aquiline features. "Watson," he proclaimed, "I do believe you were right about the ballet after all." Then he shouldered his way towards the stairs.

I followed, as eager to lend my assistance in any way I could as Holmes was to learn of how such a tragic event could have come to pass. I suspected he hoped for something more heinous than simple misadventure. It is not that Holmes is a sadist, far from it—for he is as committed to justice and law as any man I have met—rather he anticipates the prospect of mental taxation succeeded by an act of foul play.

The backstage was in quiet uproar by the time Holmes and I had reached the stalls from the loftier heights of the gods, and we were only granted passage by the burly usher on duty by the virtue of my medical credentials.

"A doctor, man!" Sherlock Holmes exclaimed to the stunned usher. "Stand aside, sir!" Holmes gave me a near imperceptible wink, to which I could only sigh, as we passed beneath the curtain and into the shadows beyond.

A grim scene greeted us on the other side. A circle of performers, as well as numerous stagehands and hangers-on, partially surrounded the girl, who still lay prone. Her head turned slightly during the fall, I could see the poor girl's face was decidedly slack and ashen. I needed neither my years of medical training nor my experience as an army surgeon in Afghanistan to know that she was almost certainly dead.

Once I had established my credentials I managed to breach the cordon and knelt down by the girl in the slimmest hope that

I would detect some sign of life still clinging to her. Alas, the caved skull I felt beneath the scalp was as sure a testament to her demise as the lack of breath or a heartbeat. She could have been no older than sixteen.

As I did my perfunctory work, Sherlock Holmes observed from the shadows, both the body and those surrounding Miss Evangeline. Upon entering the circle, I had made my own cursory examination of the closest onlookers, for spending so much time around a man like Sherlock Holmes breeds almost subconscious observational habits. Three stagehands, I saw; two were younger men, one perhaps a suitor of the departed Miss Evangeline, for his face was whitest of all and riven with grief, and an older man who had clearly experienced such calamity before in what I assumed were many years of service to the house. He had an ill-favoured look, I thought, hard-bitten and inherently shifty. Also amongst the most immediate mourners were fellow dancers, those who had been about to take to the stage.

"She is dead," I confirmed, somewhat unnecessarily, and yet still it drew gasps from the crowd, all except for the hard-bitten stagehand who could only muster a sneer. "A blow to the back of the skull," I added, indicating the fatal wound. "Holmes…" I said, but when I turned to enquire as to his opinion my companion had already gone.

It was sometime later as the audience were sent on their way, in light of the tragedy that had taken place, that I came across Holmes again, waiting for me at a stage exit, smoke pluming from the bowl of his briar pipe.

"Murder, Watson," he told me as I approached.

He leaned one foot upon the wall to support him, in quite the insouciant manner.

"Good lord, Holmes, should we not—" I began, half turning

on my heel before Holmes raised a hand to arrest my return to the opera house.

By now, the well-heeled patrons were spilling out onto Bow Street, disgruntled at the impromptu curtailing of their evening's entertainment but also titillated by the sudden macabre turn.

"I have already spoken with a passing constable who is," and here Holmes made a show of checking his pocket watch, "I believe about to reprimand the culprit."

Not a moment later, a constable ushered out the pale-faced young stagehand I had seen only a few minutes ago and escorted him into the back of a waiting Black Maria.

"Jilted lover," explained Holmes, as he took a deep draw of his pipe before releasing a heady grey cloud of smoke.

"But the lad looked grief-stricken," I replied, unable to countenance that this poor soul had committed such an act.

"And was," said Holmes, "but unlike his fellow theatricals, our man here was not in the least surprised. He was grieving before that sack of ballast ended the life of Miss Evangeline."

"But how can you know that, Holmes? We arrived after the deed had been done."

"A supposition, I'll admit, but one supported by fact." Here, Holmes's eyes appeared to flash as if some fire within had been briefly rekindled. "His hands, Watson, in the course of wringing them together, I saw a small nick between thumb and forefinger, the kind of insignificant wound one might suffer by the blade of a blunt knife, especially if said blade was being used to cut a rope. Further, his grubby shirtsleeves were up around his elbows and upon his left forearm I noted a long red weal, a recent injury I judged, and one brought about by a rope burn. Consider also the small amount of sand that had accumulated in his turned-up trouser legs. I can therefore only conclude that the lad laid a hasty trap for the object of his former affections in reply to some perceived slight or rebuttal."

"Remarkable," I said, impressed as ever by my companion's swift deduction. "I did, I admit, notice the cut rope and considered foul play but I thought surely—"

"The old stagehand," Holmes replied. "A grim and embittered individual, of that there can be no doubt, but hardly proof of guilt. However, did you notice the way he slightly favoured his left side in the sloping of his shoulder? What about the way he held his left leg rigid as a board, whilst he gave a slight bend of the knee in his right?"

"A leg injury," I realised, recalling now what Holmes had seen instantly.

Holmes nodded. "Just so, Watson. Something related to his profession, I'd warrant, since I cannot imagine anyone hiring a stagehand that was unable to perform every conceivable aspect of his duties. To climb a ladder and cut the ballast rope, the saboteur would need to be agile, quick and certainly foolish. Hence our young hand." At this last remark, Holmes detached himself from the wall and appeared to slump. "You were right, Watson," said Holmes, heading towards the nearest hansom, "a fine distraction, but all too fleeting and with little in the way of mental taxation."

I made to reply, but Holmes had already boarded the hansom and secreted himself within the cab. I opted for silence, since I knew no further words of mine could lift my companion's self-inflicted torpor.

It was not to last, however, for the coming days would bring sufficient intrigue and horror to engage even the mind of Sherlock Holmes.

CHAPTER TWO

THE HAUNTED GUEST

Despite the excitement of the previous night, I slept soundly. My only concern was for my erudite colleague who, upon turning in, had appeared to still be suffering from the malaise of inactivity that had precipitated our visit to the ballet in the first place.

Any hopes I had harboured, however macabre, that the death of the young ballerina would stir the mental weariness of Sherlock Holmes were quickly dashed by my companion's swift deduction and the matter's almost perfunctory resolution.

It was, then, when I was roused from slumber by a hammering upon the street door that my hope for a mystery to dispel the enervation of my friend was rekindled. I caught snippets of a muted conversation from below between Mrs Hudson and whoever it was at our door, before emerging from my room in my dressing gown and slippers, only to find Holmes sitting in his armchair, pipe in hand, seemingly in anticipation of the visitor.

"Good morning, Watson," he offered genially. "I trust I did not wake you. It appears we have a guest. I have already instructed Mrs Hudson to send them up."

"Am I to greet him in my dressing gown then, Holmes?" I asked, gesturing to my attire.

Holmes smiled, but despite his bonhomie, I saw the yearning for a case that would stimulate his cognitive faculties. After the previous night's disappointment I shared my friend's fervent desire. "Why, Watson, you are the very picture of refinement!" he said, and signalled for me to take a seat.

I heard muffled footsteps ascend the stairs and a few moments later there came a second knock.

"Would you mind, Watson?" asked Holmes, looking at the door through a heady plume of smoke.

I would have scowled in Holmes's direction but for the fact that his attention was fixed solely on the identity of our mysterious guest outside. I did as requested, admitting a short, thin gentleman wearing a smart grey suit and bowler hat, which he removed when Holmes beckoned him to enter.

"Good morning, sirs," he began, and I could tell from his demeanour that whatever he had come to impart was of some dire import. In fact, so shaken and haunted did the man appear that I immediately suggested he sit down.

"No. Thank you," he replied with a shake of the head, and a slight tremor of the right hand as he smoothed his tie.

"A cup of tea then?" I asked, about to call for Mrs Hudson.

Again, he declined.

"Please, my name is Edmund Garret, and I am in need of assistance. A matter grave and terrible, to be treated with the utmost discretion and tact."

"A matter your patrons would find alarming if news of it were to get out," said Holmes, his eyes never leaving our guest.

The man looked agog at this, but recovered his composure sufficiently to reply, "Indeed. It is quite delicate."

"Tell us then, man," I urged, sitting down on the settee. "What is it? From where have you come?"

Holmes answered, cutting off poor Mr Garret before his mouth had formed the words. "A Covent Garden establishment, and a cultured one at that." Holmes set down his pipe and leaned forwards, an alertness in his expression the like of which I hadn't seen for some time. Even the brief flash of interest I had seen outside the Royal Opera House could not compare.

"Forgive me, Holmes, but how could you possibly have known that?" I said.

"It is simplicity itself. Are you paying attention, Watson?"

"Enrapt, Holmes."

"First, attire. For the apparel oft proclaims the man, wouldn't you say so, Watson?"

"I would, Holmes."

"Shakespeare."

"*Hamlet.*"

"Quite so. Here," said Holmes, returning to the matter in hand, "our subject is wearing a smart suit so I can safely assume he is not a member of the working classes, thus eliminating several professions in one fell swoop. But he isn't gentry either. Look at the tailoring, Watson."

I did. "It seems competent enough. A fine suit, Holmes."

"It is too narrow across the shoulders, resulting in the fact that Mr Garret's sleeves ride a little high above his wrists. The skirt of his coat is also high, and from this I can discern that Mr Garret did not, in fact, purchase this suit for himself. Note the seams, Watson."

"Stitched competently. I see nothing untoward."

"A tiny darkening of the fabric, just above the hemline where the jacket has been let out. Still a little too short, though. Your wife's handiwork, I presume, Mr Garret?"

Mr Garret could scarcely respond, as paralysed as an insect under a microscope.

"Note a slight squint about the eyes," Holmes went on, "indicating many hours spent scrutinising objects of great detail and complexity." Here, Holmes got to his feet and turned to me as if I were his student and he my mentor. "A paleness of the complexion suggests he spends much of his time indoors. There is a stretching of the top pocket, where no doubt he puts his eyeglasses where they are to hand. Taken with the suit, this could suggest a bank clerk. But note, the absence of a writer's pad on the finger and no trace of ink under the nails of either hand. And, finally, observe the package he has tucked under his left arm. A flat brown paper bag."

"I confess, I had not really paid it much notice, Holmes."

"You see, but do not *observe*, Doctor. There is a tiny slip of coloured paper poking from the top; bright, gaudy and with the slightest suggestion of a design one could only associate with a very specific establishment. Pollock's."

"I beg your pardon, Holmes?"

"Benjamin Pollock's."

"Ah, the toyshop."

"The very one."

"Located in Covent Garden market."

"Indeed, Watson. I would posit Mr Garret combined several errands this morning. First, he purchased a gift from Pollock's. Given the urgency of the matter before us, it is highly unlikely he did so on his way to Baker Street. This then suggests he visited the toyshop before he went to his place of work, which, in turn, must be nearby or Pollock's would not yet have been open. So then, a profession that requires the wearing of a suit, but isn't well paid, one located in the vicinity of Covent Garden and during which he spends a great deal of time indoors and requires such scrutiny that the man has a squint and wears glasses. Given the location, I would suggest an art gallery. A small one, as befits such modest trappings. The Grayson Gallery of Wellington Street."

Edmund Garret nodded to my companion.

"Indeed, I do, sir. I am an assistant to the curator."

"Remarkable, Mr Holmes. Truly. But there must be several galleries within a reasonable distance of Pollock's," I said. "How could you possibly know it is this one?"

"Chalk dust, Watson. See here," said Holmes, pointing at Edmund Garret's shoes. "The finest feathering of chalk dust around the edges. A cart carrying builders' chalk upturned on Wellington Street only a day ago. Though the spilled cargo has since been removed, the chalk dust remains, transferred to Mr Garret's shoes."

"Bravo, Holmes," I said.

"Mere logic," Holmes replied with a dismissive flourish as he returned to his seat. "A simple assimilation and analysis of salient facts. So then, Mr Garret, to your business with us this morning. The hour at which you arrive at our door certainly suggests some urgency and I assume because it is you, Mr Garret, standing here before us and not one of our associates from Scotland Yard, that you have yet to inform the police. That makes robbery unlikely. Kidnapping then? Ah ha, but wait! You said yourself that this was a delicate matter. I doubt a kidnapping would provoke such a reaction. The same is true of simple misadventure. Therefore I can reach only one conclusion as to the reason for your visit. Murder."

At the mention of the word, Edmund Garret seemed to pale further. "Murder, yes, but one so foul and repellent as to make all of London shrink in fear."

"Tell us then, man," I said, hoping to arrest poor Garret's decline with a short, sharp instruction.

"I cannot. I dare not. Even to speak of it… You must see it for yourselves. Please, I beg of you, Mr Holmes."

Holmes took a pull on his pipe, and through the pall of smoke I swore I saw my friend smile. "Very well, Mr Garret, we shall bear witness to this unspeakable horror and cut to the truth of it," Holmes declared, to which the man responded with a prolonged and profuse bout of thanks.

"Be off then, man," Holmes told him when Garret's gratitude began to wear thin. "We shall meet you at the gallery. Watson and I shall need to attire ourselves appropriately before we can be abroad in London," and here he glanced at me with mock resignation, "even if my companion thinks it acceptable to meet our guests in his slippers."

I bristled at the remark but held my tongue as a relieved and still shaken Edmund Garret left our rooms and headed down the stairs, bound for Wellington Street.

"Ready yourself, Watson!" Holmes proclaimed, almost leaping from his chair in that mercurial manner of his.

"I see your mood has improved, Holmes," said I, somewhat ruefully but inwardly relieved about the lifting of his malaise.

"Indeed it has, Watson. Indeed it has. Quickly now!"

CHAPTER THREE

THE THIEF OF REGENT STREET

I dressed hurriedly, and soon a cab was taking us to Wellington Street and the Grayson Gallery.

"What manner of travesty could have befallen the place, Holmes?" I asked as we left Baker Street behind.

"A better question is how it could have gone unnoticed," Holmes answered, staring into the shadowy confines of the hansom as if a secret would be revealed to him if only he looked long enough. "Wellington Street is less than two hundred yards from the Royal Opera House and yet no commotion, no indication of murder or horror of any stripe manifested yesterday evening, or, evidently, this morning. So, the question is, how does an act so heinous as to paint a man white and render him quite unable to relate the particulars of the deed not at least arouse some concerned curiosity?"

I had no answer, save to say that we would perhaps be wiser once we had reached the Grayson Gallery and the scene of the alleged crime.

Holmes sat back in his seat, preferring his thoughts to

my attempts at conversation. I returned to staring out of the window, noting the passers-by going about their daily business—the coalmen with horse and carts, drunks staggering about, vendors selling trotters and eels, and the usual profusion of beggars and urchins.

On the corner of Weymouth Street I heard one young newsboy flogging to all and sundry, some story pertaining to a foreign dignitary having arrived in London. Intrigued, I rapped my knuckles on the ceiling of the hansom to instruct our driver to slow down so I could procure a broadsheet, since my companion evidently had no interest in conversation.

As I was fishing around in my jacket pocket for a penny, Holmes smacked his cane against the edge of the window and I recoiled from the shock.

"Good God, Holmes! You could have struck me."

Holmes then thumped the cane twice more upon the ceiling for our driver to apply the whip.

"I was after a broadsheet, man. What was all that about?"

"A waste, Doctor," said Holmes, without so even favouring me with a glance, "especially when we are about to run into the object of your curiosity. And we need to make haste while we are still able."

At these remarks, I could only look at Holmes dumbfounded.

"The *velikiy kniaz*," he added, as if this explained all. "His royal carriage was amongst the traffic on Regent Street this morning."

"I beg your pardon, Holmes?" I asked, as our carriage came to an abrupt halt. "What's all this hullabaloo," I muttered, half to myself, half to Holmes, and stuck my head out of the window. We had not long turned into Regent Street and barely made it a hundred yards when a large crowd that stretched from colonnade to street corner barred any further progress.

I turned back to Holmes, intent on further enquiry, only

to find he had hopped out of his seat and left the hansom to proceed on foot.

"Holmes!" I called after him, having to raise my voice above the excited hubbub in the street around us. "What the devil?"

"Come, Watson," Holmes called back over his shoulder. I swore I saw him grin as he near vaulted atop a goods crate bound for one of the many shops on Regent Street. Thusly elevated, Holmes stood astride his new vantage point and extended his cane across the masses that now thronged the street.

Never have I witnessed such crowds, and was sure to cling tightly to my wallet as the fine ladies and gentlemen who frequented Regent Street rubbed shoulders with every enterprising dipper, tooler and sneak of the West End.

Scrambling a little, I joined Holmes at the summit of the goods crate and tried to ignore the disapproving glances directed our way. For his part, Holmes appeared to have no trouble feigning ignorance.

From this precarious perch I had a better view of the crowd, and in addition to the gawkers and filchers I noticed several men and women angrily jeering at some hitherto unrevealed objection.

"Your idle curiosity, Doctor," said Holmes.

Still none the wiser, I followed the direction indicated by Holmes's outstretched cane and my gaze alighted on a large entourage leaving Hamleys. I could only assume that this was to whom the protestors were directing their ire and the reason why there was a sizeable police presence on Regent Street. The entourage was led by six dour-looking men, whose long green velvet uniform coats embroidered with regal livery, taken together with black wool tricorns and high leather boots, marked them out as Russian Life Guards. A livelier man followed these grim wardens, his own attire altogether more vibrant. Both he and a young boy—whose close resemblance to him led me to conclude he was his son—wore red wool suits with light golden braiding at the cuffs and shoulders. Father and son's hats were fur-trimmed with sable and fashioned of black wool.

"The Grand Duke Konstantin," said I, recalling the headline if not the body of the newspaper article Holmes had denied me earlier, and with not a small measure of awe at seeing such a royal personage in our midst. I realised belatedly that this was whom Holmes had been referring to when he had used the Russian, *velikiy kniaz.* I turned to my companion, whose gaze I noted was not on the grand duke's entourage but instead followed the myriad urchins moving like eels throughout the crowd.

"Visiting Regent Street," said Holmes. "Though a father buying a gift for his son would not usually bring all of London to a halt," he added with disdain.

"As well as draw out a few firebrands," said I, referring to the rowdy protestors.

"There!" Holmes suddenly announced, and practically leapt from his vantage point to delve into the masses all eager for a glimpse of Konstantin.

"Holmes?" I asked confused, scrambling down after him.

"Come, Watson, don't dawdle," I heard him cry above the din of the crowd. It was only by virtue of my companion's height that I was able to track him through a mob so dense that it took me several minutes to make any headway moving perpendicular, as I was, to the general flow.

Ignoring the muttered insults and defamatory invectives, I began to elbow my way to the other side of the street and was roughly halfway across when a young woman barrelled straight into me.

Fearing she might be a finewirer, I recoiled and took a firm grip of my wallet, but upon seeing her and the obvious distress she was in, I realised my error.

"Miss…" I began, catching the slightest glimpse of a pretty face, blue eyes and blonde hair, before she bolted past me with scarcely an acknowledgement, let alone an apology. I was about to turn and remonstrate with the young woman, when out of the corner of my eye I saw the cause for her apparent anxiety.

A stern-looking thick-jawed man, his eyes narrow and close together, and wearing a dark jacket and woollen cap, appeared, clearly giving chase, his gaze fixed on her retreating form. So intent was he on his pursuit that he barely spared me a glance until I seized him by the forearm and brought him to an abrupt halt.

"See here, sir," I said. "What's the meaning of all this?"

The man turned sharply, but found my grip strong enough that he was forced to answer my question.

"She's a thief!" he snapped, a feral look in his eye that I didn't favour at all. "She stole my wallet," he added, a slight accent to his voice that I couldn't quite place.

"Well, I advise you find the nearest constable, sir," I told the man, releasing my grip. He snarled something at me as he resumed his pursuit of the woman, whom I noted, with some satisfaction, had made good her escape.

I watched him disappear into the crowd too, before Holmes hailed me with growing impatience and I continued across the street. Upon reaching the other side, I made a swift check of my wallet and, to my utmost relief, found it present and unmolested.

"Making friends, Watson?" asked Holmes, poised at the entrance to Orange Street. "Why I endure your indulgences I shall never know," he added, turning on his heel.

"Should we not alert someone, Holmes?" I asked, referring to the plight of the young woman. "He had a rough look about him that fellow."

"I think not, Watson," Holmes replied, walking away swiftly.

"I believe the constables present have enough to contend with without concerning themselves with petty theft. We don't have time to go around chasing every young lady who steals your pocket watch."

"My what—?" I patted down my jacket and to my dismay discovered Holmes was indeed right; my pocket watch had been stolen! "Good God, Holmes," I began, about to head back into the crowd.

"A matter for another time, Watson. Fear not, we shall see you reunited with your father's watch. For now, we must be on our way."

"I hope you are right, Holmes. It is very dear to me."

"Then hope your scoundrel reaches your lady thief and justice is served. The Grayson Gallery awaits!"

CHAPTER FOUR

A GRUESOME EXHIBITION

I was still annoyed about my pocket watch when Holmes and I finally reached our destination and were met by Edmund Garret at the threshold of the gallery. Rather than enter through the main entrance, the tremulous assistant took us around to a side street and a shadowy back door.

"I warn you," he said, fumbling nervously with his keys as if the mere proximity to this place eroded his resolve, "it is a grim sight."

"I expect it is a good deal worse than that, Mr Garret," said Holmes, intent on the door and doubtless already calculating what might lie within, "for why else come to us before notifying the police. I assume Scotland Yard are on their way?"

"Yes, sir," said Garret, paler now than when we first met the man in 221B. "I had hoped to keep it from public knowledge a little longer, but there was nothing for it. I dread to think what it'll do to the gallery's reputation."

"If there is one thing that is ever certain, Mr Garret," said Holmes, "it is that Londoners have an insatiable yearning for the gruesome and the macabre. I fully expect the gallery will thrive. Now, onwards, Mr Garret."

Edmund Garret nodded and at last managed to open the door. A dingy corridor beckoned, little more than a preamble to the gallery proper, and Garret escorted Holmes and me through several smaller rooms. Finally we arrived through a stout-looking door and then under a high archway into a large chamber with a vaulted ceiling upon which was a fresco in the classical style, depicting a scene from *The Odyssey*. There were comfortable benches down the centre of the room intended, I assumed, for the prolonged admiration and observation of the various landscapes and portraits hanging on the walls. But however fine the art, my eye was drawn to something even more arresting and entirely more unpleasant.

Dressed in their finery but lying in disarray and death were the patrons of the Grayson Gallery, both men and women, their faces contorted in fear and agony. I counted over thirty dead, mostly clustered around the exit, as if a stampede had been brought to an abrupt and terrible halt. A faint waft of decay had begun to emanate from the bodies. I had noticed the tang of it before we entered.

"The sheer horror of it…" I remarked, and covered my mouth at the sight.

As an old campaigner, and a doctor besides, I am no stranger to death, but there was something altogether aberrant about its presence in a place such as the Grayson Gallery rather than a battlefield or hospital.

"What do you see, Watson?" asked Holmes, as seemingly unmoved by the grim scene as the portraits looking down on it.

"A sight at which my mind recoils, Holmes. It's almost as if—"

"They were clamouring to get out," said Holmes. "Observe

the smashed champagne flutes underfoot, the general panic and disarray. Art appreciation has never been so deadly." He paused then added, "A brisk morning, is it not, Watson."

"I'd say so, yes."

"And yesterday evening? Wintery, would you agree?"

"Rather bleak, I seem to recall."

"Quite so, but bleak enough to warrant coats and scarfs indoors?"

"I'd say not, Holmes. But why the enquiry?"

"A coat rack in the corner of the room, heavily burdened," he said, drawing my attention to it. Holmes turned to Edmund Garret. "Tell me, sir, is it usual for your guests to need outdoor attire?"

Poor Garret could scarcely take his eyes from the horror of it all to answer my companion.

"No, sir. It had been requested. The exhibition was to celebrate British Antarctic exploration, the southern continent, the pioneers and so on. The patrons were to feel the cold as they entered."

I had read an article about a lecture given in 1893 by Dr John Murray about renewed interest in Antarctica exploration. Given the sprawl of the British Empire, the southern regions of the world were one of the last few uncharted territories, and had captured the imagination in certain quarters.

"To enhance the experience," said Holmes.

"I assume so, sir."

"And yet a fire has been lit," added Holmes, gesturing to a soot-blackened hearth and chimneybreast. "Can you explain that?"

"I can, sir. We did not want the guests to catch their death."

"So the cold was temporary," Holmes added.

Garret nodded.

"I see," said Holmes. "Tell me, Mr Garret, was this room locked and secured when you opened up this morning?"

"It was, sir."

Holmes paced over to one of the victims. "This man, I assume he was a colleague of yours?"

The man in question wore a suit but was not dressed so finely as to be mistaken for one of the guests.

Here the poor assistant looked close to tears as he clapped eyes on his erstwhile colleague. "Arthur Mabbot, yes, he's the curator."

"Tell me, Mr Garret, where might your superior keep his keys? I note the room has no bolt and in order to access it you must have used a key of your own. Arthur Mabbot would have his own keys, would he not?"

Edmund Garret scratched his head. "He kept them in his breast pocket, sir." Holmes checked, but found no keys. Garret frowned. "How peculiar."

Holmes checked every one of Arthur Mabbot's pockets but none yielded up any keys. "Watson, you have keen eyes," he said, "do you see any keys lying about that the deceased Arthur Mabbot might have dropped or absent-mindedly discarded?"

I looked, but found none and informed Holmes of the fact. He turned his attention back to Edmund Garret.

"I put to you, Mr Garret, that Arthur Mabbot did not have his keys, and furthermore that they were used by another person, as yet unknown, to lock this room from the *outside*."

"You think someone stole his keys, sir?" asked Garret.

"Precisely."

"And trapped everyone within."

"They knew they were going to die," said Holmes, grimly, before producing a magnifying lens and conducting an examination of every detail of the crime scene, during which process I watched him touch, taste and sniff a variety of seemingly innocuous items that he no doubt considered vital to the case at hand. In fact, so fervent and exacting was he in his actions that when he came to a sudden and certain halt in front of one of the paintings I wondered if he had done himself some injury.

"This one, Mr Garret," he cried, at which the assistant shuffled over.

I followed, to find Holmes enrapt by a most macabre piece; a skeletal figure, encrusted by ice, perhaps a depiction of Death itself, for many had lost their lives to the Antarctic. It struck me, as I looked closer at this and several of the other paintings, that rather than a celebration of explorative endeavour, the exhibition felt more like a warning of its perils.

"That's the *Undying Man*," Garret explained, suppressing a mild shiver. "I've never liked it, and like it even less now. It's one of the grimmer pieces."

"Frozen in death. And the artist?" asked Holmes, his gaze fixed on the painting.

"A gentleman who goes by the name of Ivor Lazarus, but I don't know who that is, nor have I met him. Please, Mr Holmes, can you find who did this?"

"I would be delighted to, Mr Garret," said Holmes, turning his gaze to the room's entrance, "should Scotland Yard prove unfit for the task."

I turned, and saw a familiar figure standing beneath the archway. When I looked back I noticed Holmes had just snapped shut his pocketknife and was returning it to his pocket. The newcomer said, "Ain't this a right mess."

"Inspector Gregson," said Holmes, genially, affording the inspector a mildly deferential nod. "It is indeed a most grisly tableau."

"I do hope you've not solved this one already, Holmes," said the inspector as he approached.

"All in good time, Inspector. Perhaps you would regale us with the skilled deductions of Scotland Yard?"

I have often suspected Holmes held Tobias Gregson in some small regard, for the man was not without intelligence in spite of some of his less desirable qualities.

"Very well," said Gregson, running his thick fingers through his fair hair. Not one to shirk from a challenge, he began to assess the scene. Most men, even those of Scotland Yard, and certainly the two police constables who now appeared behind the inspector, would pale a little at the sight of so much death and horror, but Tobias Gregson was inured to such things.

Just as Holmes had done, Gregson paced the room, inspecting the bodies, taking account of the broken glasses and even feigning interest in the odd painting. Holmes keenly observed him throughout, betraying no hint of his thoughts on his face or his demeanour, as unreadable as Horatio Nelson in Trafalgar Square.

Having finished his tour of the macabre, Gregson stopped in the middle of the room to proudly announce, "Poison, Holmes."

"Indeed," said Holmes, but elaborated no further. "Go on, Inspector."

"It's as plain as day," Gregson replied, and gestured to one of the victims. "No wounds, collapsed in disarray, heaped atop one another like marionettes with their strings cut." Gregson smiled, and I thought it a self-aggrandising, ugly gesture. "Am I warm, Mr Holmes?"

"Positively stifling, Inspector," said Holmes. "And through what means?"

Gregson frowned. "I don't follow."

"The *means*, Inspector. *How* were they poisoned?"

"Ah," said Gregson, "the flutes," he pointed out the glass underfoot. "Champagne flutes."

"Indeed, indeed. A fact to be confirmed by autopsy, of course."

"Of course," said Gregson.

"And what would you make of this?" asked Holmes, turning to regard the painting he had been examining before Gregson's arrival.

Gregson appraised the piece for a few moments, before deciding, "Firewood, I expect. It's hideous."

I could not disagree.

Holmes smiled. "Well, I believe the inspector has matters here well in hand. I have only one further question, then we shall be on our way…"

"Oh yes, Holmes?" said Gregson, looking quietly pleased with himself.

"For Mr Garret, if he is amenable," Holmes replied.

"If it'll bring this terrible matter to a conclusion, I should pledge my service in any way I can, sir."

"Nothing so dramatic. I merely wish to know who commissioned the exhibition in the first instance."

"I fail to see how that's relevant, Holmes," said Gregson.

Holmes ignored him, his attention on Garret.

"It was a Mr 'D.G.' of Mayfair. I don't know any particulars other than that, I'm afraid."

"Not to worry, Mr Garret. It shall suffice. Amply so, in fact." Holmes smiled. "Good day, sir. I have no doubt we shall be in touch again." To Gregson he added, "Inspector. I assume you are bound for the police surgeon after you've gathered your evidence?"

"And I assume you'll be joining us, Holmes?"

"Well," said my companion, "since you asked it would be rude to refuse. Good day."

Once we were back on Wellington Street, having passed a constable on the way out of the Grayson Gallery, I turned to my companion and asked, "D.G. of Mayfair. Are we to pay this fellow a visit then, Holmes? I can think of no other reason for your interest in him."

"Indeed we shall," said Holmes, stepping out onto the street to summon the nearest hansom.

"Where then, Holmes, in all of Mayfair, will we find him? I assume we shall not be going door to door?"

Holmes gave me a smile that suggested if required we would knock on every door of every Mayfair residence.

"I have eyes and ears everywhere, Watson, as well as making it my business to know whom from whom."

"In all of London!"

Again, Holmes replied with that same smile. I do believe he enjoys mildly torturing me in this manner.

"And I also assume the painting is in some way significant," I said, "though I cannot fathom how."

"Perceptive as ever, Watson."

"So has Gregson cut to the heart of it then. Poisoning?"

"Amongst his colleagues at Scotland Yard, Inspector Gregson is singular," Holmes conceded. "A man not without intelligence, even if he is quick to grasp at the obvious."

"So it wasn't poison then?" I asked as the hansom pulled to a halt and Holmes and I climbed aboard.

"Baker Street, my good fellow," Holmes shouted to the driver, and gave the ceiling of the cab a solid thump with his cane. "It was indeed poison, Watson," said Holmes, answering my question.

I frowned, confused. "So, Gregson…"

"Was mistaken, yes."

"Holmes, I have no idea what you are talking about."

"Alas, Watson," said Holmes, narrowing his eyes, "I fear your state of confusion shall last a while longer yet."

"Confound it, Holmes!" I cried. "Must you be so cryptic?"

"Only if you insist on being so obtuse, Watson," he replied mildly.

"Very well then," I said, deciding to admit defeat. "Are we not to Scotland Yard then?"

Holmes shook his head. "In the absence of the living, we shall look to the dead to lay the accusing finger. The Scotland Yard morgue, Watson. Inspector Gregson will have much for us to review. But first to Baker Street. I suggest you fetch your medical bag." Holmes then shouted loudly to bring the cab to a sudden halt, at which point he sprang out and headed off down the street at a brisk pace.

"Holmes?" I called after him, leaning out of the window.

"The Scotland Yard morgue, Watson. I shall meet you there."

"And where are you going?" I asked, having to shout.

"Eyes and ears, Watson. Eyes and ears."

Shaking my head, I instructed the driver to avoid Regent Street, and realised Holmes had been headed in that very direction.

CHAPTER FIVE

THE MYSTERIOUS DEMISE OF
REGINALD DUNBAR

By the time I had finished my errand at Baker Street and made my way to Scotland Yard, Holmes had already arrived. I found him waiting pensively in the morgue, his fingers steepled and pressed to his lips in a manner I have regularly seen him adopt when contemplating the nature of a particularly obscure problem.

So engrossed was he in thought that I had to practically announce myself before he showed any awareness of my presence.

"How long have you been down here, Holmes?" I asked, suppressing a slight shudder. I am most familiar with death, having seen all too much of it during my lifetime, but it wasn't the sense of the morbid that caused my shiver but rather the bone-aching cold that pervaded the Scotland Yard morgue.

"Not as long as this fellow," uttered Holmes, only half listening. He gestured to a figure lurking in the shadows, the police surgeon. I knew him as Roper. He was a portly man, and possessed little to no good humour. Not that Roper was particularly unfriendly but instead he carried a sort of blandness about him, due, I expect, to spending so much of his time with the dead. Despite his shortcomings, this was Roper's domain and he ruled it like a jealous king, eyeing me suspiciously as if I had trespassed across his borders without permission.

"Doctor," I said by way of perfunctory greeting. He gave me a shallow nod.

The morgue was a large but dingy space, made to appear smaller by the gloom and the fact that little outside light could penetrate through the thick frosted glass of its few windows. An air of decay was present, only partly masked by a chemical acerbity that bit at the nostrils. The tiled walls had once been white but had been turned grimy yellow by the slow attrition of years.

Gregson arrived soon after I did, his grim burdens in tow, carried by many sweating constables. It took almost an hour to ferry the dead into the morgue, which, despite being large, was soon beyond its capacity—it had only twelve slabs—and many bodies had to be laid upon the bare floor. There were thirty-seven victims in all, the majority of whom were guests, the remainder made up of Arthur Mabbot and two waiters.

With Roper and his assistants, as well as Holmes and me, there was little room to move. Gregson had dismissed his constables, but stayed behind to ask questions and have a closer look at the victims, who appeared to have no obvious connection other than a predilection for art.

"Not an easy task getting through Covent Garden with this lot. The hoi polloi are still up in arms about the grand duke," he said as I was examining one of the victims, a man, around early fifties with a slightly Slavic cast to his features.

"We saw protestors amongst the crowds on Regent Street," I said.

"Been keeping us busy ever since he arrived. One half of London wants to catch a glimpse of royalty, the other half wants to see it brought down a peg." Gregson leaned in. "And by that, Dr Watson, I mean stripped of their wealth and brought down to the common man's level. It's given rise to several groups known to Scotland Yard who are firmly against the idea of a decadent few." He sighed then, regarding the bodies. "Thirty-seven men and women, poisoned in an exclusive London gallery," he said. "Somebody is trying to say something."

"Indeed they are," uttered Holmes, at last emerging from mental solitude, "but perhaps they are shouting it loudly so we fail to hear what is being whispered beneath."

Gregson frowned. "As usual, Holmes, you have completely lost me." He moved on to speak to Roper, either genuinely losing interest or tired of my companion running intellectual rings around him.

"Tell me, Watson," said Holmes quietly. "Does this one have a name?"

Prior to autopsy, I had watched as Roper's assistants removed the man's clothes, and his belongings sat on a tray nearby. "He carried an engraved cigarette case," I said. "I believe—"

"Reginald Dunbar," said Holmes, having found the item and opened it to the engraving.

"Yes, that's the one. What of it?"

Holmes regarded Dunbar intently, but did not elaborate. "A theory, Watson, nothing more. I would prefer to keep it to myself until it has had time to develop."

I was about to answer when Gregson gave a raucous bellow of delight from across the room.

"I knew it!" he said. "Poisoning. The whole sorry lot of them, I'd wager."

"And who would bet against him," murmured Holmes as he and I went over to join Gregson and Roper.

Holmes leaned in close to smell the dead man's lips. "Quite

right, Inspector. And the facts at hand suggest cyanide. Not for the layman," said Holmes, with a quick glance at Roper, "discerning one poison from another. See here," he added, gesturing to the fingers of the man's right hand, which had curled into a hideous claw. "And note similar effects on all the victims, brought on by a sudden paroxysm. Would you concur, gentlemen?"

Roper nodded. "The stomach contents will prove it beyond any doubt," he said in a moribund voice.

Gregson shrugged. "Poison is poison, Holmes. And death is death. It was the champagne what did it, either way. No other explanation."

"And what of the door, Inspector? I assume you noted its condition?"

"Efforts had been made to break it down from the inside, yes, I saw it," said Gregson. "What's your point?"

"That escaping a poisoned champagne flute simply requires that one not drink from it."

"Who can say what kind of panic gripped them, Holmes. Trapped within, poisoned, I suspect fear took hold."

Holmes nodded, but I could tell he was far from satisfied. "Indeed, Inspector. 'A man may fish with the worm that hath eat of a king, and eat of the fish that hath fed of that worm.'"

Gregson frowned.

"Upper or lower class, Inspector," said Holmes, "we are all but food for the worms in the end."

"A cheery thought."

"To go with our cheery surroundings," Holmes replied, and then turned sharply to me. "Watson, I have seen all I need to here, and the inspector clearly has matters in hand." He made a show of checking his pocket watch, and I felt again a sting at the loss of my own timepiece. "I have another matter to attend to."

"Eyes and ears?" I inquired, knowingly.

"Quite so, Watson," answered Holmes, delighting in Gregson's confusion as he took his leave. "I shall be at the Running Horse when you have concluded your business here."

CHAPTER SIX

RENDEZVOUS AT THE RUNNING HORSE

I met Holmes in the Running Horse public house later that afternoon, having spent a good few hours in the Scotland Yard morgue. As predicted, each of the victims presented with almost identical symptoms, suggesting that they had been poisoned.

Holmes was not alone when I found him sitting in a leather-backed chair, warming himself by an open fire. He had a scruffy-looking urchin with him, a grimy little blighter if ever I did see one, who could not have been much over eight years of age.

Ever since I have known him, Holmes has always possessed a willingness to indulge the common folk. He has a seeming affinity for their condition that I have always believed extends beyond their mere usefulness to his work or even a desire to understand the vagaries of the criminal mind—for many such individuals as Holmes has in his loose employ could be considered such—but rather has a more altruistic motivation at its heart. Whatever the case, or his intent, I have never pressed Holmes on it, but have had cause to meet several of his informants during the years of our friendship. I have trusted not one of them.

"Watson!" said Holmes, his sudden excitement at my appearance causing several of the patrons to turn and look upon the newcomer in their midst. I doffed my bowler uneasily and that seemed to satisfy the curious amongst them who soon returned to their ale and muttered conversation.

"May I introduce Hobbers," said Holmes with a flourish.

As I sat down in the facing chair, the urchin grinned broadly to reveal several missing teeth and those teeth he did still possess were ill kept. He doffed his ragged cap at some mimicked attempt at gentlemanly behaviour, revealing a scraggy red mop of hair underneath as greasy as a pan of kippers.

"Pleased to meet you, sir," he said to me, extending a hand that looked like it hadn't seen soap or water for a good long while, much like the rest of him. I declined to shake his hand, favouring the young scrapper with a friendly nod instead, which he seemed satisfied with.

"Hobbers here is a most observant young man," Holmes went on.

"Most obsivant," Hobbers parroted, badly.

Having been bitten already, I kept my hand upon my wallet but did so surreptitiously so as not to offend the lad.

"Tell Dr Watson what you saw, Hobbers," invited Holmes. The urchin began to regale us with a tale of how he occasionally went "dipping" around the streets of Mayfair, and that he kept his "lamps" open for any "swells" that came here or there. He most vehemently protested he was no "lurk" or "shivering jemmy", and that he had no desire to get "nibbed", but had keen eyes and knew that "Mister Ohmes" rewarded useful titbits with some "chink" should the information prove useful.

"And what, or rather whom, did you see, Hobbers?" asked Holmes, prompting the boy.

"A right swell," Hobbers said, "a fella what lives in Mayfair, the one who Mister Ohmes 'ere is looking for. I 'eard about 'im from Ned, who got a tip from Sharp, who spoke to Whipper, who once polished this fella's shoes, and 'eard 'im say where he lived."

Holmes laid out a handkerchief that the urchin had daubed on, though I suspect it was from memory rather than an actual ability to read or write, much the pity. I also noted, belatedly, that the handkerchief was in fact my own.

"Holmes, is that—" I began.

"Yes, yes, Watson, but look here…"

Scribed in the urchin's crude hand were the letters "D.G.", rudimentarily marked but discernible none the less.

"It was on his gate, Mr Ohmes," said Hobbers.

"Our D.G. of Mayfair resides in Berkeley Square," said Holmes. "The hour is a little late to go calling, but first thing tomorrow we should pay him a visit, Watson, don't you think?"

"The chap really is quite the 'swell' isn't he?"

"We shall find out," said Holmes, rising smartly from his chair. "Hobbers," he said to the urchin, "you have provided good service and shall be rewarded."

I saw Holmes toss the boy a few farthings, which he snatched out of the air and secreted away in short order.

"Shall I keep my eyes open for 'im, Mr Ohmes?"

"Please do."

Hobbers then bowed and was on his way.

"Perhaps he can find my pocket watch as well," I muttered, my wallet clenched firmly in my hand until Hobbers had taken his leave.

"I hope so, Watson," Holmes replied. "And at least you have your handkerchief," he added, offering the soiled garment to me at the end of his cane.

"I think not, Holmes."

Holmes frowned. "Really, Watson. At times, you are quite contradictory. Up in arms about an old pocket watch but content to leave a fine handkerchief to any fellow who happens along."

The next morning, we arrived at the Mayfair address. It was a most impressive townhouse, finely appointed and opulent in every way. Whoever this "D.G." was he was clearly well off, so much so that his initials were inscribed on the wrought-iron gate to his property just as Holmes's urchin had described.

A short flight of stone steps led up from the street to a broad black door with a gilded knocker the size of a man's clenched fist. The house had at least three floors, as far as I could tell based on the number of windows, and was a good deal wider than our own humble lodgings at 221B.

"Somewhat affluent," I said to Holmes. "It would appear this D.G. has done rather well for himself in… well, whatever business he is in."

"Let us find out then, shall we?" he replied. "I wonder if anyone is home…"

Upon reaching the top step, I gave the gilded doorknocker a good hard rap, fully expecting a housemaid or butler to open the door within moments. When the door remained closed, I began to wonder if we had in fact missed our quarry and even began to entertain the idea that he had somehow gotten wind of our interest and made himself scarce, taking his servants with him. Either that, or the street urchin Holmes had put his faith in had let us down.

"Confound it, Holmes. Have we missed him?"

Holmes suddenly leapt back down the steps and back onto the street where he stood staring at one of the upper-floor windows until he returned triumphant.

"I believe we are in luck, Watson," he told me and proceeded to turn the doorknob. Unsurprisingly, the door was locked.

"Do you hear that, Watson?" asked Holmes, pressing his ear to the brass keyhole.

Hearing nothing, I shrugged. Holmes then beckoned for me to take his place, which I did and heard what sounded like a struggle coming from within.

"A commotion, Holmes?"

"Undoubtedly," said Holmes, producing a set of lock-picking tools from his jacket pocket. "Stand aside please, Watson, this won't take a moment."

True to his word, Holmes picked the lock in short order and we entered.

Upon crossing the threshold, we found ourselves in a long and opulent hallway. Against one wall was a large oak bookcase with a finely upholstered chair on either side and a small pedestal table on only the left side. A silver-plated samovar sat upon the pedestal, empty and apparently decorative. A velvet carpet, deep crimson in colour, ran underfoot and led to a broad stairway and half landing.

Holmes exchanged a brief glance with me. "A shadow, Watson. Seen cast against an interior wall, the angle of which would have been impossible to make out whilst standing directly under the eaves. Someone is at home."

We had made our way up the stairs and advanced a few steps beyond the first landing when I again caught the sound of the commotion I had heard at the door, coming from farther up the stairs. I heard a deep grunt, then several loud and heavy exhalations of breath. Then a heavy thud, as of booted feet moving quickly on the floor above.

"A burglar, Holmes!" I hissed, confirming my suspicions, and proceeded to run full pelt up the stairs.

Arriving at the main second-floor landing, it was immediately apparent that the sounds of a scuffle were emanating from a door to my immediate left. Without delay, I threw open the door and burst into a long gallery but instead of a thief intent on stealing valuables I found a man in his shirtsleeves, staring at me with a mix of anger and confusion.

"D.G. we presume," said Holmes, calmly walking in after me, having not exerted himself one jot.

"You knew, didn't you, Holmes?" I said.

"I suspected," said my companion, looking at the other man. "The rapid movement, the breathing, it had a pattern that suggested hard exercise rather than larceny."

Bowing and doffing my hat, I apologised to the man. "We... I thought you were being burglarised, sir."

The man smiled. "And here I thought the two of you were the trespassers. I do hope you didn't break my door down. It was expensive."

Holmes brandished the lock picks before returning them to his pocket.

"Well that's something, I suppose," said the man. "Most enterprising."

His attire was that of a pugilist, a fact further supported by the punching bag he had come to blows with and the gloves tied to either fist, which he now proceeded to remove. Trapping the gloves under one arm, he walked over to us with his right hand extended in greeting.

"Damian Graves," he said. "Pleased to meet you. I think. It's not every day two gentlemen break into your house, claiming it's for your own benefit. I have yet to form the proper reaction."

He smiled again, warmly, with just a glint of good humour in his blue eyes.

"D.G." said I, and shook his hand.

"I believe that's me, sir," he replied.

"No, I meant—"

Mercifully, Holmes stepped in before I made an even greater fool of myself. "This is Dr Watson, and I—"

"Sherlock Holmes," said Graves, his smile broadening.

Holmes replied with a short nod.

"I thought I recognised you," said Graves, and threw aside his gloves. "Who in London would not?"

He was muscular but lithe, not unlike a dancer, of average height, and the gallery was entirely given over to paraphernalia and equipment devoted to physical improvement and fitness. I noted a large sparring mat as well as the punching bag, several sizes of barbells and dumbbells, fencing attire and a rack containing a number of foils and sabres. Most curious, however, were the contraptions and apparatus designed for both traction and extension, consisting of various weights, pulleys and cords. Damian Graves clearly placed a good deal of stock in staying in his prime.

"Do you mind," he said, stooping to retrieve a skipping rope. "I am in the middle of my fitness regime and would hate to break it. I assume you are here on some business?" He began to vigorously whirl and jump the rope.

I confess, I found his manner a little disconcerting. We had entered his residence without permission or invitation but here the man was casually skipping and making conversation as if it were all perfectly normal.

"Of the gravest kind, sir," I said, donning my hat when it became obvious that civility was not amongst this man's better qualities.

"Grave…" He laughed. "How appropriate. Speak then, sirs. I know you both by reputation if not history, so I assume this matter is of a criminal nature?"

"How well do you know the Grayson Gallery of Wellington Street?" asked Holmes.

"Extremely well," Graves answered between breaths, the rope whipping past in a blur. "I have an exhibition there."

"Are you a patron of the arts then, sir?" I asked, taking note of the paintings hanging on the wall. Most of the pieces were portraits of Graves himself, I realised with further disdain for the man. There were also several small pedestals and glass cabinets within which I saw various items of obscure and ancient provenance. I noticed an old sextant made from brass, an ornate spyglass, several vintage coins and a few vases and sculptures.

"I have many interests, Dr Watson," said Graves. "Art is one of them. History another."

"I see," I replied, still not knowing what to make of the man.

Graves stopped skipping and set down his rope. Reaching for a towel to mop his brow, he asked, "Where are my manners? I should show you my collection. It is quite extensive; I think you'll find it interesting."

Confident fellow, I thought to myself.

"Are you not concerned," I said, as Graves ventured over to the nearest cabinet, "having these valuables so close to hand in such an environment? A stray flick of the rope, a trip… one mistake, it could be rather costly, couldn't it?"

"It teaches me to be careful, Doctor. Besides," he said, somewhat haughtily, "I do not make mistakes. Here," he said, and gestured to a silver coin that appeared to be extremely ancient. "A denarius coin," said Graves proudly. "That's the likeness of Julius Caesar on the face. It dates back to 49BC." He paused, doubtless waiting for our admiration, which, to my utmost surprise, Holmes provided.

"My word, that is indeed impressive," he said. "Antiques of this variety have always piqued my interest."

Incredulity at my companion's bizarre demeanour rendered me quite speechless. Graves, on the other hand, had no trouble whatsoever.

"Then you will find this piece most intriguing, I think," he said, skilfully manoeuvring Holmes to a second cabinet. "A pair of Chinese guardian lions made of marble and white granite, from the eighth century. These are but trinkets, however…" He made his way over to a blank section of wall, and pushed upon it. To my surprise it gave, revealing that it was actually the door to a modestly sized hidden room.

"*This*," said Graves, his smile both self-satisfied and irksome, "is my *true* collection."

Within the room were exhibited around forty or fifty antique swords. I am no expert in such things but I recognised a Scottish claymore, a sword from the English Civil War and a huge medieval blade, which looked like it could have dated back to the Crusades. Despite my dislike of the man, I could not help but stand agog at such a display of wealth and history.

"Remarkable…" I said.

"Each has a story, which I would be happy to relate," offered Graves, warming to his role as host.

"All of them fascinating, I am sure," said Holmes. He was examining one of the paintings that hung on the walls in the "armoury". "But we shall have to refuse, I am afraid. Perhaps another time," he added, turning his attention back to our host. "Are these works by Ivor Lazarus? He had several pieces in the exhibition."

"Ah, yes, the exhibition," said Graves, as if reluctant to change the subject. "They are indeed, as are a great many throughout the house. I keep these ones here on account of the grim subject matter not being to everyone's tastes."

"Quite," said Holmes. The paintings were similar in nature

to that of the *Undying Man*, which we had seen in the Grayson Gallery, bleak meditations on death and mortality.

"So, as a patron, you know Ivor Lazarus then?" I asked.

"I am familiar, yes." Graves frowned. "What is this regarding, gentlemen?"

"Murder, I'm afraid, Mr Graves," said Holmes, his voice level. "Might I ask, Mr Graves, why you were not in attendance at the exhibition?"

"I never attend an exhibition where my own work is on display," replied Graves. "The Ivor Lazarus you mentioned. I am he. It's a pseudonym I use to assure my anonymity. My art, it can sometimes attract... detractors. My business is more commercial in nature, and I prefer the two not to mix. As I'm sure you can appreciate by now, I deal in antiques of the rarest and most valuable kind. I have had some fortune in this line of work, hence this house. The art is more of a hobby. Does that satisfy your curiosity?"

"In part," said Holmes.

"Tell me, then," said Graves. "What happened? Who was murdered?"

Holmes grew sombre. "Everyone who attended the exhibition, sir. Poisoned."

"All of them?" Graves appeared shocked, his geniality gone. He looked away from my companion for a moment, as if to calculate the loss.

"I am surprised word has not reached you," I said.

"I have heard nothing. I confess, I am not the easiest man to reach, even when in residence."

"Did you know any of the invited guests?" I asked, to which Graves shook his head.

"No, I had no part in the guest list. I always left that to the gallery to arrange." He looked back again. "This is a terrible tragedy."

"Indeed it is, sir," said Holmes.

"Well, thank you for coming here in person to tell me," said Graves, ushering us from the hidden room. "I will contact the gallery at once and see if there is anything I can do. I assume the police are involved?"

"An Inspector Gregson is leading the case."

"Does he have any suspects?"

"He believes the crime was politically motivated."

"How so?"

"A reaction to the decadent rich," I said, at which Graves was finally offended.

"Unless there is anything further…"

"Nothing further," said Holmes, smiling again. "I am so sorry to have disturbed you, Mr Graves. I assure you, the lock on your front door has not been damaged but you might consider getting a better one."

"Then perhaps you have done me a service, Mr Holmes."

"Perhaps… Before I go," he gestured to the rack of foils and more conventional sabres, "I have never seen such a fine array of weaponry, aside from your antique swords, of course. Might I try one out?"

Graves frowned, but acquiesced with a sigh. "Please, do so."

Holmes removed his gloves as he advanced on the rack. Then, carefully selecting a foil, he proceeded to flail about with it. I have seen Holmes fight, most ably, both armed and unarmed. His fencing skills are exemplary, so the ineptitude I witnessed was most uncharacteristic.

"*Chert*," I heard Holmes mutter. I had no clue as to the word's meaning, but felt now was not the time to ask. He tried again, but conspired to trip over his own feet, which sent the foil arcing through the air. Thankfully Mr Graves stepped to catch it expertly before it could do any harm.

Holmes flushed a vivid shade of crimson, and stooped to retrieve his hat, which he had also lost during his antics. "I do apologise, sir. I am usually much more assured with foil and sabre. Perhaps the weight? The lightness took me quite by surprise."

Graves smiled politely, but I saw mockery in his eyes. "They are unique. Certainly not for… *amateurs*."

Clearly embarrassed, Holmes nodded vigorously and made to shake the man's hand by way of a hasty farewell. He was but an arm's length way when he appeared to stumble, and would have fallen head over heels had Graves not reached out to catch him.

"*Spasibo tovarishch*," Holmes said, taking a firm grip of Graves's hand to steady himself.

"*Pozhaluysta*," Graves replied, adding, "Well, at least your Russian is better than your fencing, Mr Holmes. I must say, you are not quite what I expected."

"Nor, Mr Graves," said Holmes, straightening his jacket, "are you. Good day."

Once we were back out on Berkeley Square, I turned to Holmes and said, "Quite the disagreeable gentleman."

"You did not warm to him then, Watson? I would not have guessed."

"I found him particularly odious, Holmes. A most self-important fellow, and arrogant with it. What manner of man commissions his own art exhibition?"

"Not Damian Graves."

"But he just said—"

"His hands, Watson," said Holmes. "Calloused, yes, from use of the blade. Judging by that alone, he must be a consummate swordsman, and one doesn't invest such wealth in antique swords without more than a passing interest in the craft. But an artist?

No, he is not Ivor Lazarus. His hands were not those of a painter. Bereft of any stain or mark, nothing around the fingernails, no thickness of the skin around thumb and forefinger that would suggest hours spent with a brush. And for a man clearly so self-obsessed, he showed little to no interest in his so-called works."

"Ah," said I, smiling at my own ignorance, "hence the chicanery. You wanted to ingratiate yourself with the man."

"A task made all the easier by your obvious distaste for him. His Russian was excellent. His accent was almost as flawless as my own, but not quite up to the standard of a native speaker."

"I did wonder at that. Why did you speak in Russian to him?"

"A silver-plated samovar in the hallway, a bookcase with several volumes written in Cyrillic, one of which pertained to the Alexandrinsky Theatre in Saint Petersburg, all facts to support a theory."

"That Graves spoke Russian."

"Indeed. I merely needed to test it."

"But what does it mean, Holmes?"

"An excellent question, Watson, and one to which you are charged with finding the answer," said Holmes, as he hailed a hansom.

"I beg your pardon, Holmes?"

"To truly know a man, we must know his routines, his haunts, how he chooses to spend his time. I want you to follow him, Watson, when he leaves to go about his business. Note everything he does, everywhere he visits and whom. Be sure to leave nothing out."

"But how shall I know when he is leaving? Am I to wait the rest of the day?"

"Oh, I fully expect him to leave his residence at any moment. Our visit was just the spur. I suggest you find a place to observe without being seen yourself, Watson. Perhaps over there, by that bench. You could get a paper. You wanted to read the news, did you not?"

I sighed, exasperated yet secretly impressed at my companion's quickness of thought.

"And whilst I am covertly following Graves, what will you be doing, Holmes?"

Holmes gave a wolfish grin as he stepped into the hansom. "I have other matters to attend to, Watson. Not least of which I must analyse the evidence taken from the gallery. Don't worry," he added, clearly noting my frown. "Put some of your military training to good effect; I'm sure you'll do admirably."

CHAPTER SEVEN

INSALUBRIOUS PURSUITS

Holmes was right, of course. Though I waited over an hour, during which time I had thoroughly read the article concerning the arrival of the Grand Duke Konstantin, I saw Damian Graves emerge from his residence wearing a smart suit and frock coat.

He stepped into a waiting growler. As soon as it had departed, I got up from the bench from where I had kept my furtive vigil and hailed a cab of my own. As I boarded, I instructed the driver to follow; at the driver's bafflement, I assured him that our quarry was an old friend whom I was planning on surprising once he had arrived at his destination. He seemed little the wiser for this information but acceded to my request to keep the other carriage in sight but removed enough so as not to spoil the surprise. An extra few farthings saw to his complicity, and off we went.

The manner of this careful pursuit was not without peril, for on a few occasions I feared we had lost the other carriage amongst the general morass, but each time we were able to pick up the trail again.

After a relatively short trip, I saw Graves alight at Barclay,

Bevan and Co. of Lombard Street. His cab waited for him, and upon his return carried him to Cunliffe's of Princes Street and finally Threadneedle Street and made for the Bank of England. I had watched him enter all the previous establishments but knew nothing of his business within for fear of raising his suspicions should I have been spotted. I determined, however, that the risk was worth the taking now so I might at least gain some inkling as to my quarry's purpose. Certainly, it was unusual for a man of Graves's status to perform such errands personally and this alone was reason enough for me to take a closer look.

I entered furtively and saw to my relief that Graves had his back to the entrance and to me. Whilst Graves saw to his finances, I watched him from above in the Bank of England's reading room. Again, I did this with all due caution, taking care to stand as far back as possible to obscure my presence should Graves have the occasion to look up. Thankfully, he did not, and so I observed his dealings relatively unimpeded. From what I could tell, his transactions were dealt with swiftly and conducted without incident.

Suddenly there was a commotion. I turned to see smoke billowing between the reading room's bookcases, which prompted a good deal of scrambling of patrons and general panic. Amidst a flurry of clerks and customers, I made my way to the origin of the smoke, and saw that a bank employee was pouring a pail of water onto a small fire in a wastepaper bin.

Realising there was no emergency, I looked around for Graves, and spotted him making his way out of the bank and back onto Threadneedle Street. At the door he collided with an elderly gentleman wearing a monocle, who appeared quite bewildered by all the excitement. Graves made a hurried apology, and the delay allowed me to make my way down the stairs and reach the entrance in time to see him clamber into a new cab and bellow to the driver to take him to Savile Row.

I dutifully followed on foot for about a mile before hailing another cab, the general bustle of the morning traffic enabling me to keep up with the carriage, albeit at a brisk pace. I freely admit, I began to revel a little in the subterfuge and the drama of it all. After Graves had disembarked in Savile Row, I kept a good distance from him so as to avoid alerting him unduly. He lingered at several shop windows, and I took care not to stand opposite in case he caught my reflection in the glass. We did not know each other so well that he would instantly recognise me, but one man observing another has a habit of standing out. From across the street, I saw him visit Huntsman, emerging from this establishment carrying packages. He went on to visit Henry Poole's, and here I decided to follow inside to determine what Graves was buying. Again, this was something of a risk but Poole's was busy that morning and in the event of Graves seeing and recognising me I decided that I would feign surprise and suggest the matter a coincidence.

Poole's is as fine a tailoring establishment as you will find in all of London, and I will freely admit to a pang of envy that Graves could afford such bespoke attire without concern for his purse. Working my way surreptitiously around the tables of fine garments and bolts of cloth, I found a position behind an ornate marble column from where I could observe Graves unimpeded. That was until an obnoxious gentleman began to complain loudly to the poor tailor attempting to fit him for a dinner jacket.

"I tell you, sir," he said, most sternly, "you pricked me. See here!" he said, and showed his thumb to the tailor, who was on one knee attempting to measure the hemline. "Blood! As plain as the pin that pierced my skin, sir."

I averted my gaze, as did the other patrons, leaving the poor tailor to apologise profusely and his customer, who was a large and overweight man, to storm off and find the man's superior.

Evidently, Graves found the whole thing rather amusing, and carried on with his shopping, though I saw little after that and failed to discover what he had purchased. Thwarted, I could only watch him leave Poole's and continue the chase.

After the mild excitement of Savile Row, Graves took an early dinner at St James's Hall on Regent Street, where with what little spare money I had to hand, I ordered fish soup so I could observe the man whilst maintaining my facade. I had picked up the morning paper on my travels and hid behind it as effectively as I could. I kept my distance of course, finding a table where I could remain unnoticed and where Graves had his back to me. I also made a passable attempt at masking my voice. Sherlock Holmes is an expert in such matters and whilst my ability pales in comparison to his, I have picked up a few things here and there. Despite my best efforts, I did manage to attract the attention of a waiter, who had obviously seen me nursing my soup overlong and glared at me over wire-framed spectacles and a thinly cropped moustache.

Mercifully, Graves ate quickly, and I followed him back out onto the street, where he hailed a cab. At this point, I could only assume he had sent the other cab on some other errand or perhaps with instructions to take his purchases from Savile Row back to his house in Mayfair. Graves had climbed aboard and was on his way by the time I had even procured transport, but the streets were busy enough that I was able to see where his cab was headed and keep it in view until it stopped just outside Spitalfields Market. I instructed my driver to keep on a little further, hoping I would still be able to find Graves once I too was on foot.

A minor panic set in at first, as I could find no sign of Graves amongst the busy market and its patrons. I considered trying to find some higher vantage point with which to more easily discern him in the crowd but thought better of it. The attention that would garner would surely reveal my presence.

As luck would have it, I caught sight of him moving through the general ebb and flow. I took pains to get closer for fear of losing him again, but stayed a good few paces back in the hopes of not being spotted. Should Graves turn unexpectedly I felt certain he would see me, but there was no alternative.

I followed him through the market and on into a warren of alleyways. I knew this place as the Old Nichol, an unpleasant sinkhole of dirty tenements, a refuge for the desperate. A part of Bethnal Green and Shoreditch, I could think of fewer places as forbidding.

I pressed on, down muddy avenues, choked by pools of filthy water and refuse. As I walked, I felt the narrow lanes encroach, and through grimy windows I saw hungry eyes watching. A pall saturated the Old Nichol, but it was not the foulness of the air but something less definable, a malaise of the spirit that had infected everything, all the way down to the very brick.

Into this gloom Graves moved swiftly, and though I could not fathom what possible business he could have in this dreary hive, he went about it with purpose. I followed him through foetid alleyways and beneath mildewed terraces. Not once did he pause, or turn. He *knew* this place. He knew it as well as his own luxury residence in Berkeley Square and appeared at home here, in spite of the obvious incongruity of his presence.

I kept my hand on my walking stick, and my instincts alert.

I rounded a corner and emerged in a grubby square, with black brick tenements on all sides that blocked out the light. Of Graves, there was no sign. I turned back the way I had come, but the streets were unfamiliar and though I had tried to take note of every turn I had taken, I realised then that it would be no simple feat to retrace my steps.

When I looked back, Graves stood before me.

"Why, Doctor…?" said Graves, clearly searching his memory for my name.

"Watson," I answered, my fists clenched. I did not know if Graves meant me ill, but I knew little of the man, so resolved to trust my instincts.

"Yes, Dr Watson. A nice evening for a walk, wouldn't you say?"

"Perhaps, if the surroundings were slightly more salubrious."

His manner was curious, almost amused, though I detected more than an undercurrent of annoyance, even anger.

"Which makes your presence here, Doctor, all the more perplexing." Though he took no step towards me, I felt a certain threat in Graves's tone and overall demeanour. "Why are you following me?"

"I caught sight of you in Spitalfields. I had thought you might be amenable to talking further about your antique sword collection, and was about to call out to make myself known when I saw you heading in the direction of Shoreditch… well, my curiosity got the better of me." I had no better answer, a fact that Graves quickly seized upon.

"A flimsy story. You track me down, illegally enter my house and now follow me here," he said. "I have been aware of your presence for some time, Dr Watson. Long before you followed me into Spitalfields, or did you think a newspaper could hide your presence so perfectly? I wondered how far you would go, and here we are. What is it you hope to learn?" He shook his head. "Never mind, it doesn't matter. You are a faithful hound, are you not?"

"I beg your pardon, sir?" I said, mustering my indignation. "How dare you—"

"Oh no, Doctor. *You* are the daring one. To come here, alone, as evening creeps in. Whatever could have possessed you, I wonder?"

I was about ready to roll up my sleeves at the man's impudence, when Graves laughed. "A jest, Doctor, only a jest. You will have no need for that stick you grip so tightly. Is there a blade secreted within the shaft? I imagine so. I have spent a great deal of time studying weapons, particularly swords, even the less noble examples such as the one you carry. I can always tell when a man is armed. But then you are no stranger to combat, are you, Doctor? What was it, the Afghan War?"

Graves was deliberately provoking me, I realised, playing on my own annoyance at being exposed as a sneak, and trying to force me into action I knew I would regret. I determined then I would not give him the satisfaction.

"You were wounded, were you not?" he said. "Your gait, it betrays a slight limp and your look, Doctor... it is colder than most. It suggests you have seen much in your life, much that perhaps disagreed with you. And your thinly veiled excitement at my armoury..." He smiled, smugly. "Only a military man would act thusly."

I was genuinely taken aback for here was Graves, whom I had mistook for a self-absorbed dandy with entirely too much money and too little wit, displaying observational acumen that would not have been out of place coming from Sherlock Holmes. I attempted to rally, but trod cautiously.

"You are not all you claim, are you, Graves?" I said. "Yes, I was following you. I do not believe we had the truth of it back at your residence, sir. An artist?" I scoffed. "Yours are not the hands of an artist. And do not think me fooled by your false bonhomie, either. You have secrets, I think, and not just your hidden cache of swords. And I know you are not a military man, though you entertain the idea as a fancy. I met men like you in the desert, boys playing at being soldiers. They tended not to last long."

Graves smiled, though his eyes remained cold and utterly without emotion.

"Do not follow me again," he said in a menacing tone of voice.

"I do not respond to threats, sir!" I informed him.

Graves retreated into an alleyway, his last words shrouded by shadows.

"Is it not a threat. Goodbye, Dr Watson. I do hope we shall not see each other again."

Another backwards step and Graves was gone, lost to the dark. After a few moments I followed but could find no further sign of him. If he was indeed a rat of this warren then he had scurried off into some place where I could not go.

Regardless of the man's obvious lies, he was right about one thing. The hour grew late and it would be as well for me to leave the Old Nichol before the night fell in earnest.

CHAPTER EIGHT

ON THE SUBJECT OF VERMIN

By the time I reached Baker Street it was dark, and I was grateful to be met at the door by Mrs Hudson. She carried a small oil lamp in her left hand and squinted at me from behind a pair of wire-framed spectacles. I imagined she had fallen asleep and been wakened by me fumbling with my keys.

"I do apologise for the lateness of the hour, Mrs Hudson," I said. "I'm afraid the day quite got away from me."

When the landlady saw my shabby appearance, her eyes widened. "Oh, Dr Watson, you look positively downtrodden. When did you last have a warm meal?" she asked, hurriedly ushering me inside.

"Well I—"

"I should have thought to prepare something to warm up on your return. I must have dropped off whilst reading the paper." Mrs Hudson looked thoughtful. "I had the oddest dreams. Quite morbid, I don't mind telling you." She leaned in towards me. "I was reading an article in an old copy of *The Times* about a suicide somewhere outside the city. A teacher, it said, a lady. Whatever could have possessed her?"

"Well, the rigours of modern life can be trying, I'm afraid, Mrs Hudson. All too often—"

"A small meal before you retire?" asked Mrs Hudson, seemingly able to flit from one subject to the next and barely pausing for breath. Had I the will and the cause, I might have tested her pulse for she appeared quite... *animated,* especially given the lateness of the hour. "I must insist, Doctor. You are practically wasting away!"

Whilst that was hardly the case, I had to confess I was famished, having missed breakfast and lunch on account of Holmes's hurried investigations, and with little more than fish soup to sustain me all day.

"Well, perhaps something modest?" I ventured.

"I think I have some roast pork," she said, staring into the middle distance as she tried to recall the contents of her larder. "Perhaps some soup?"

I frowned. "Not fish."

"Pea and mutton."

I smiled. "Ah, yes. Splendid."

"I shall warm it up on the stove, Doctor. And I can rustle up a little bread and butter for dipping."

I felt my stomach groaning hungrily at the very prospect.

"Thank you, Mrs Hudson," I said, slowly ascending the stairs. "Is Holmes about? He mentioned—"

Here Mrs Hudson's expression grew dark, her concern for me transformed into mild contempt for my companion.

"He is not, and frankly, Doctor, I am glad of it," she said, exasperation writ large upon her face. "Cooped up in there most of the afternoon, he was. Banging and clattering. And there was smoke!" she said, eyes widening. "It came spilling out from under the door." She leaned in close to whisper conspiratorially.

"I swear I saw rats, Dr Watson. Rats! Taken straight off the street. Lord only knows what he wanted with them. I prepared a lunch, which he left untouched, shouting out he didn't care for mutton. Yet when I enquired as to whether there was anything he should want before I went out on an errand, I got no answer but for a horrible stench emanating from the sitting room. I returned to find him gone, though I have no idea where. I dare not enter in his absence, for fear of what I might find."

I glanced up the stairs, trying to imagine what might wait beyond the door to our lodgings.

"Rest assured, Mrs Hudson, I shall see that everything is in order."

I did not completely believe my own words. Despite my medical expertise, his experiments were often baffling and esoteric, branching into scientific matters both enterprising and arcane, so it was with a degree of trepidation that I turned the knob to the door of our lodgings and poked my head inside.

It was dark within and cold. I saw that Holmes had indeed been engaged in some form of experimentation, for upon his chemistry bench next to his desk there stood an array of phials and alembics, though the nature of the tests remained a mystery to me. He also left the window open, which explained the chill in the air, and I shut it immediately.

I moved to his desk, where upon closer inspection I spotted a small microscope, as well as several glass slides. I saw also a small mount of crushed blue powder, which I suspected had been derived from a piece of cupric salt Holmes keeps to aid with chemical detection. Reduced to a sulphate, it had been liberally spread upon several sheaves of parchment paper currently residing beneath a hermetically sealed bell jar. Glass dishes of Holmes's own design contained a number of liquids I could not identify, but I did notice a stoppered bottle labelled "methyl alcohol". A Bunsen burner felt warm to the touch, so I deduced it had been recently used. The specimen of a dissected rat was a grim sight, and its purpose in Holmes's endeavours I could only guess at.

Accepting that I would fail to discover what Holmes had been up to, with my curiosity out of the way and feeling the weight of my own day's activities, I sank down into my chair by the fire to await my evening meal from Mrs Hudson.

I ruminated again on my encounter with Damian Graves. It had been on my mind ever since I had left the Old Nichol. What purpose a man like Graves—whose social status and means were far beyond that of the poor wretches living in such squalor—could have there was beyond my ability to reason, though I sincerely doubted his motives were altruistic. He appeared most incongruous in such a setting and yet seemed utterly in his element. I resolved to inform Holmes later once he had returned.

The pleasant aroma of pea and mutton soup arrested my brief reverie, and it was with some anticipation that I opened the door for Mrs Hudson. However I had managed only a few mouthfuls when I found my eyelids heavy, and slipped into a grateful sleep.

I awoke some time later to complete darkness, and, barring the ticking of the mantel clock, utter quiet. I managed to light the reading lamp by Holmes's chair and consulted the clock, which had advanced almost two hours!

I realised then I must have been more exhausted than I thought. Either that or my meeting with Graves in the Old Nichol had taken something of a toll. As if to confirm this possibility, I recalled with alarming clarity several forbidding dreams of strange assailants, foreign voices and a fleeing girl whom I was powerless to rescue from her shadowy pursuers.

I was about to seek out my journal to take note of this when I saw a note pinned to the floor with the jack-knife Holmes used to pinion his unanswered correspondence. The note was written in the unmistakeable hand of my friend! Evidently, he had returned to 221B and left me to slumber unmolested.

Watson,

Whilst engaged in scientific endeavour (and please do not touch anything on my chemical bench, for I cannot rightly say that it might not cause harm to you in some lesser or greater degree), I determined that much is still to be learned from our original point of enquiry. Therefore, I have decided to visit the Grayson Gallery on Wellington Street at midnight this evening. Please meet me there at your earliest convenience. I shall be waiting.

Yours,
S.H.

P.S. I have not called upon the services of Edmund Garret, for I would prefer to visit the gallery alone, so we shall have to break in. I considered waking you to avail you of this fact but thought you might resist the idea.

After almost dropping the reading lamp, and quelling a tremor of mild panic at the thought of Holmes breaking and entering, I looked to the mantel clock and realised I had to make haste. Midnight was approaching and given the dubious nature of what Holmes was suggesting, I decided to make my way to Wellington Street on foot so as not to draw any further attention than was strictly necessary.

Taking care not to wake Mrs Hudson for a second time, I grabbed my coat, bowler and walking stick, then set out into the night.

CHAPTER NINE

THE FIGURE IN BLACK

I was out of breath when I reached the alleyway where Edmund Garret had first shown Holmes and me into the Grayson Gallery. Having rushed from Baker Street with all haste, I felt the wound in my leg anew, a reminder of how the jezail bullet still affected me all these years later. In turn, this put me in mind of Graves and his observations back in the Old Nichol. My feelings towards the man had swiftly turned from distaste to a profound sense of wariness. He had known I was following him and had chosen that exact moment in the slums to reveal his hand. I considered why he waited as long as he did to spring his trap. I could only assume it was arrogance, or perhaps he took some kind of twisted pleasure from allowing me to get so close? Whatever the case, I knew now that he was certainly not to be underestimated. He might not be a soldier, but there was much that was threatening about Damian Graves.

Repressing a flutter of mild anxiety, I approached the side entrance to the gallery but was startled by a man lurking in the shadows, smoke hanging in the air around him like a shroud.

A smudged circle of light flared as he stirred the embers in the bowl of his pipe.

"Are you quite well, Watson?" asked Holmes, languidly leaning against the wall.

"By the devil, Holmes, you gave me a fright!"

Holmes gave me a thin but knowing smile. "My apologies, Watson. It appears you have had a most trying day. Tell me, what did you learn?"

"Learn?" I asked, mildly irritated.

"You observed Graves, did you not? You followed him and discovered his mores and habits? What did you learn?"

I frowned. "Is this really an appropriate time?"

Holmes consulted his pocket watch. "What time would you prefer, Watson? Though whichever it is, please decide quickly as it is hardly the place for us to tarry."

I sighed, resigned to my companion's playful goading, and regaled Holmes with everything I had witnessed.

Holmes listened intently to my report, silently absorbing every detail and only occasionally interrupting to clarify seemingly irrelevant minutiae.

"A monocle, you say? Over which eye?"

"And how large was this gentleman's girth?"

"Did you happen to catch the name of this moustachioed waiter?" I answered as well as I could, concluding with my unfortunate and disagreeable meeting with Graves in the Old Nichol.

"What would a man of Graves's standing want in such a place, I wonder?" Holmes mused, gazing into the distance as if the answer lurked somewhere in the night.

"My thoughts precisely, Holmes," I said. "Though I do not mind admitting that I found the experience quite disconcerting."

"Indeed," said Holmes, his mood suddenly more serious. "There is much about Graves that we still do not know." He turned to me. "Though you have yet to answer my question, Watson. What did you *learn*?"

I had to confess that, in practical terms, I had learned very little. Up to the point where Graves had confronted me and exposed my ruse, he had acted as a man of his station could reasonably be expected to act.

"He seemed very familiar with the Old Nichol. His association with the slum is incongruous, for certain," I said. "Though presents little further by the way of enquiry." As I mentally retraced my steps, a thought struck. "His dealings at the banks could shed some light but, alas, I did not manage to ascertain what they were."

"Saint Agatha's," said Holmes, and began to fish around in his pocket.

"I'm not sure I follow, Holmes."

"It's a boarding school for girls, in Cambridgeshire."

"What is?"

Holmes frowned at me. "Dear Watson, for an educated man, you are on occasion somewhat slow on the uptake." He presented me with a slip of paper from his pocket, which upon initial inspection I realised was a deposit slip from a bank. Barclay, Bevan and Co. "Graves was making deposits."

"This has today's date…" I began, before realising the truth. "What the deuce, Holmes? You were there, weren't you?"

"We all had our parts to play, Watson."

"The portly gentleman at Poole's," said I, struggling to keep my voice low, "and the waiter at St James's Hall. Both you."

Holmes held up his finger, and turned his head slightly, the teacher wanting more from his pupil.

My eyes narrowed, and I almost gasped at my next

conclusion. "And the elderly fellow at the Bank of England. You started that fire, too?"

Holmes nodded, and for a moment I thought he might take a bow but managed to restrain himself. "Although in that instance there was in fact smoke without fire. A simple concoction of saltpetre and sugar. Did you really believe I would set a blaze in the Bank of England, Watson?"

"Of course not, Holmes, but I… Well that isn't really the point, is it? I should be annoyed but…. How do you do it, Holmes?"

Here, Holmes did indulge in a slight flourish, twirling his right hand like a stage magician before the reveal to a trick. "Ah, Watson, like Maskelyne, the true artist never reveals his secrets. Your role in this little act of theatre was a crucial one, however. Which you performed admirably."

"And yet he spotted me, Holmes."

"As I knew he would. I believe he knew he was being followed from the outset and had but to confirm it. I hypothesised that once he had located his pursuer, he would not look for another. I took no chances of course, but your presence became the perfect distraction for me to conduct my own covert observations of the man, albeit with the necessary costume and manner."

"Well," said I, "you had me quite fooled, Holmes. But why those particular roles?"

"Consider, Watson, the elderly gentleman. A doddering old chap might attract a glance of pity or amusement from some, but would be overlooked in the main for fear of a request for assistance or the regaling of a long and lamentable story from his distant youth. Then the obstreperous and ungainly patron at the tailor's. Who in such a fine and well-regarded establishment would wish to be associated with such a cad? Mad as hops, and with a predilection for extravagance. And finally the waiter. A man as self-important as Graves would not deign to look at the person serving them their beef and potatoes. And so, I had my camouflage and a most effective deception it proved to be. After your encounter with Graves, I followed him farther into the Old Nichol, my guise that of a dishevelled tramp that went beneath all notice."

It was true; even as I brought the memory of that place to mind I could not recall any such individual, skulking or otherwise.

Holmes went on. "Having sent you on your way, Graves walked with the confidence of a man who thought he was unobserved, so it was an elementary matter to shadow his steps until he entered a rather downtrodden estate in the vicinity of Church Row. I didn't follow further, as the street led to a dead end and I deemed the risk too great of being discovered, so there my trail went cold. Alas, though narrowed down to a rough area the precise lodgings or tenement remains a mystery for now."

"And what of this deposit slip, then?" I asked.

"Ah, yes," he said, as if only just remembering it, but I knew this too was just more theatre. "Disguised as the elderly gentleman and with the added misdirection of the smoke, it was easy enough to bump into Graves on his way out and covertly relieve him of said deposit slips. There were several, of course, for Graves is a man with many interests and a degree of indulgence when it comes to his finances, but this one…" and here he brandished the slip with a flourish, "…it got my attention on account of the rather sizeable sum involved." I had to look closely at the slip, but now that I did, my eyes widened. I could only imagine the extent of Graves's wealth, which made his visit to the Old Nichol even more confounding.

"It is far more than is usual for education and board at any school you could mention. Why then the large sum?"

"I cannot begin to fathom, Holmes, but perhaps we should press on?"

Holmes stared back at me intensely for a moment, before snatching up the deposit slip and slipping it back into his pocket. "Quite right, Watson. Quite right," he said. His smile turned to a grin as he gestured to the door, the lock to which he had already picked, and entered. "Come along now, Watson. We have little time to dally."

Reluctantly I followed, silently bemoaning my lot but also impressed at the soundless way Holmes had gained entry to the gallery. Once again, I was reminded that were it not for his commitment to law and order my companion would have made a rather excellent thief.

"What are you playing at, Holmes?" I whispered, and my eyes searching the dark as if expecting the police to emerge at any moment with shackles at the ready.

Fortunately, the shadows kept to themselves and Holmes and I were left unmolested as we quietly crept to the chamber that had housed Damian Graves's exhibition.

"Fear not, Watson," I heard Holmes call to me, his voice echoing slightly. "Tobias Gregson and his cohorts are doubtless sleeping soundly in their beds and shall not trouble us, I think."

A silvery gloaming had settled upon the exhibition hall, cast through the high windows at either end. Moonlight, rarely able to pierce the smoke and fog that often lays heavy over the metropolis, limned the frames of each painting and the benches arrayed down the middle of the room and thus it was surprisingly light, despite the lateness of the hour. Little had altered in our absence, save of course for the macabre spectacle of the dead lying in grim repose.

"What now then, Holmes?" I asked. "Are we to vandalise the exhibition also, and compound our evening of petty crime?"

Somewhat disconcertingly, Holmes chuckled to himself

as he strode into the middle of the room. "What do you see? For we are here to *observe*."

"I see a room much as we left it, although mercifully bereft of any corpses."

"Look at one of the doused gas lamps," said Holmes, his eyes closed as if already composing some theory and awaiting further evidence to confirm it.

I did as asked, and saw a dark, fire-blackened bowl of soot. I remarked as much to Holmes.

"What of the hearth?" he asked.

"It looks recently used. There are even a few logs, well burnt."

"And there," he said, though his eyes remained shut, "the flower arrangement set upon that left pedestal by the entrance, what do you see?"

I first noticed a nearly full bottle of champagne on the right-hand pedestal and then saw the flowers on the left, which, although once beautiful I had no doubt, were now wilted.

"Most assuredly, they are beyond revivification, Holmes."

"Dead, much like the gallery patrons," Holmes concurred. "And yet there is water left in the vase. Stifled, Watson."

"The patrons or the flowers?"

"Both, Watson."

"Garret said the gallery patrons would only feel the cold upon entry to the exhibit. One presumes it was warmed up a short while after that."

"That he did, Watson. The temperature in the room must have been increased significantly."

"To ward off a cold London evening. I confess, I am baffled, Holmes. What are you getting at?"

"Much about this case is baffling, Watson, but a pattern is forming..." his eyes then sprang open as he turned to look me in the eye, "...and I can with absolute certainty tell you this—the

guests were not killed by the champagne, despite what Tobias
Gregson might assume. He has clutched for the obvious, Watson,
the facile, and ignored the salient facts. Roper's report will prove
it beyond doubt, but that is not what interests me."

"If not by the champagne, then how?"

"Precisely, Watson. As I said in the Scotland Yard morgue, I
am in agreement with one aspect of the inspector's theory—that
it *was* poison."

"But how can you be sure it wasn't something in the
champagne? It could easily have been tainted."

"Indeed it could, Watson, but earlier this evening I paid
a visit to Edmund Garret, who was most accommodating in
giving me a list of all the guests, including those he knew to be
teetotal. Several, including Mr Garret's unfortunate colleague,
did not touch a drop, Watson."

"So how were all those people poisoned, Holmes?"

"That is what we are here to find out, Watson," he said,
advancing across the room towards the painting of the Undying
Man, which was as grim in moonlight, if not grimmer, as it was
during the day.

"A little more light, if you please, Doctor," said Holmes.
The ambient light coming in through windows at either end of
the gallery had been sufficient illumination thus far, but further
investigation would require something more direct. I found an oil
lamp and lit it, keeping the flame low so that any passer-by would
not be alerted to our presence, and offered the lamp to Holmes.

"Thank you, Watson."

Holmes then proceeded to examine the grisly portrait of the
Undying Man, which was rendered still more forbidding in the
flickering light of the lamp.

"Hold this for me please, Watson," said Holmes, handing
the lamp back to me. "Keep it close and steady, if you would be

so kind," he added, snapping open his pocketknife.

"Holmes, what are you going to do? You cannot mean to—"

"Have you ever heard of pentimento, Watson?"

"I beg your pardon, Holmes?"

"Pentimento. It is an Italian word that means repentance. It has a certain resonance here, I believe."

"I'm not sure I follow, Holmes."

"Then allow me to demonstrate," he replied, and proceeded to scrape at the painting with the edge of his knife.

"Holmes, I—"

"The light, if you would be so kind, Watson. I need the light."

I steadied the lamp, as Holmes defaced the painting, now realising why he wanted to come to the gallery at night and without Gregson looking over his shoulder.

"Upon our first visit to the scene of the crime, I was able to scratch a small sample of the painting while you and Garret were distracted. Gregson had yet to make his entrance, and so for a few seconds I was unobserved and thus able to covertly collect a modicum of evidence."

"I see, Holmes. You really are quite devious at times."

"I shall take that as a compliment, Watson."

"Please do," said I, watching fascinated as Holmes began to reveal something beneath the top layer of paint. "Good lord, what is that?"

"Pentimento also refers to the alteration of a painting, a change of mind if you will, on the part of the artist. It is the painting *within* the painting, Watson."

"I see," said I, "but what does this have to do with the poor souls who were poisoned?"

"I have a theory, but only a theory," Holmes replied. "For now, I shall keep it close." Then he stood back and I brought the light closer.

"I'll confess, Holmes, I am none the wiser."

There was indeed a second image beneath the first, a fragment of script. A curve, a straight line, almost like a letter, although as to its meaning I had no clue.

Holmes pondered the defaced portrait for a few moments, no doubt fixing every detail of the original in his mind for later consideration. "A portrait of a man, neither dead nor alive, frozen in ice," he said. "Torture and penance, Watson. Wouldn't you say?"

I could only agree, but had no idea as to the significance of it. "What can it all mean, Holmes?"

"Torture and penance, Watson. Though whose remains a mystery."

Our business concluded for the evening, at least as far as the Grayson Gallery was concerned, we left the exhibition hall. We were halfway down the corridor that would lead us back out onto Wellington Street when Holmes froze.

I saw what had disturbed my companion only a moment later, clapping eyes on a shadowy figure, dressed entirely in black. I swiftly realised that he too must have broken into the gallery, although I doubted his motivation was solving a crime.

"Good evening," said Holmes warmly, though I heard his grip tighten around the walking stick in his hand.

CHAPTER TEN

THE THRILL OF THE CHASE

Evidently the figure dressed in black had not expected company. Without a word the interloper turned and bolted back the way they had come.

"You there," I bellowed, throwing aside all caution, "stop at once!"

Though Holmes and I had more than bent the rule of law, I suspected the figure in black had a more nefarious purpose. Alas, my order fell on deaf ears.

"I do not think they are listening, Watson," said Holmes, as we gave chase.

I raced down the corridor ahead of Holmes and out onto Wellington Street. After a brief glance around, I caught sight of my quarry fleeing in the direction of Tavistock Street, a cloak billowing out behind them, and turned smartly to stay on their heels. As any man who has been in the British Army will attest, a rigorous fitness regimen is insisted upon before one can serve one's queen and country. Even in my civilian years, I have managed to maintain a level of physical ability, but the injury to my leg was telling and had begun to ache. I kept the discomfort at bay through gritted teeth, determined to see justice done.

I assumed Holmes had fallen behind, but did not glance over my shoulder to confirm this as all of my concentration was bent towards catching the interloper. Certainly, they were fast and their level of fitness put me instantly in mind of Graves, though the distance and the darkness made it difficult to make anything approaching a definitive identification. I considered that perhaps I was in pursuit of an athlete in peak condition and resolved to mention as much to Holmes, should he put in an appearance.

"Holmes, you had better be just behind me…" I huffed, as I began to feel the strain of the protracted pursuit.

The streets were all but deserted, and I saw no constables— which was just as well—but not a hansom or growler in sight either. A light rain was falling, which left the cobblestones wet underfoot. I almost slipped more than once, cursing my bluchers and their unsuitability for a foot chase through London.

A few yards or so ahead of me, the figure in black took a sharp turn down Tavistock Street, then a side street, splashing through the puddles that had begun to form. I followed, but was falling behind, the treacherous ground underfoot a hindrance, and as I reached the side street I could see no sign of my quarry. The street was narrow, and cluttered with empty wicker baskets and a stack of wooden barrels at the end. Strung overhead, a washing line swayed in the breeze, an old shirt still pegged up and as sodden as the Thames.

I was about to curse my bad fortune, as well as my shoes, but then the stranger miraculously appeared from an alleyway that led off from the side street in which I was standing. They walked backwards, wary and as if recoiling from something I could not see.

The rain had grown heavier since the pursuit began and I could see it glittering on the figure's cloak. I gauged it would be a good deal heavier too as a result, and began to hope that I would bring them to heel. Regardless, I decided to try something.

"Damian Graves," I declared, "halt and go no further!"

The figure turned sharply at the name, pausing only for a moment before it took off again. Holmes then emerged from the alleyway, having doubtless dissuaded our quarry with his presence and having likely taken some oblique route to get ahead of the figure in black.

"Took your time, Watson," he called to me, and I bristled at the gibe. "You've beaten out our prey, though. Good man!"

"I hadn't been aware that was my charge, Holmes," I said.

I hurried over to Holmes, who looked like he was out for a gentle evening's stroll. I found his lack of urgency most perplexing, and he saw as much in my exasperated expression.

"It's alright, Watson," he assured me, as the figure slipped past the stack of barrels and disappeared around a corner ahead of us. "We are about to catch our prey."

I could scarcely breathe, let alone answer, so confirmed with a shallow nod instead.

As we both rounded the corner, the figure in black stopped no more than twenty yards in front of us, facing a brick wall.

"Cornered, I believe is the word," said Holmes. He raised his voice to address the stranger. "You have nowhere left to run, I'm afraid. Now, I would be extremely grateful if you would explain exactly what you were doing at the Grayson Gallery."

The figure in black did not move, not even to acknowledge our presence, though they kept to the shadows so as to be almost invisible.

"It's over, you might as well reveal yourself, Graves," I said, having recovered enough to speak. "There's no escape," I added, taking a firm grip on my stick, though more for support than any thought of self-defence. The frantic pursuit had taken quite a toll and I feared I would be unable to resume the chase. Mercifully, it appeared the chase was over as the figure turned to face us, a hood and thin scarf swathing their face in even deeper shadows.

As I took a step forwards, however, our quarry shrugged the cloak off their shoulders to reveal a slim but athletic frame. Still hooded, they then bowed.

"Watson!" said Holmes, urgently, and lurched forwards into a sprint as the figure in black performed a half pirouette and scaled the wall, springing from window ledge to gutter pipe, demonstrating the kind of agility I have only ever seen in a feline.

I gave chase after Holmes, first snatching up the discarded cloak, but we were both far too slow and much too late. By the time we reached the dead end, the figure in black had climbed onto the roof and was quickly lost from sight.

"Come, Watson!" urged Holmes, who about-faced and hared off back down the alleyway.

Groaning inwardly, I followed. Holmes gained a fair lead on me, only stopping once he had reached the foot of a ladder. My companion had already scaled halfway up the ladder by the time I reached him, and as I began to make my ascent Holmes was at the edge of the roof.

I gained the roof in time to see him loping after a diminishing figure and resolved to pick up my pace so he would not face them alone. Throwing caution aside, I began to run but after only a few steps I slipped on a loose tile. Teetering vertiginously, I watched it fall and smash to pieces on the cobbled street below.

"You'll be the death of me, Holmes," I muttered under my breath. My heart thudding a rapid tattoo, I quickly gathered my wits and kept on after Holmes, the cloak still clutched in my left hand and flapping as I ran.

I saw our quarry approach a gap between two rooftops. It was hard to be sure in the dark, but I guessed it could be no shorter than twenty feet. They gave a quick glance over their shoulder, then leapt. I expected them to fall short and plummet to their death, but instead they reached the other side, clinging to the adjacent rooftop before scrambling on to it. When I saw Holmes backing up to take a run at the jump, a feat I knew was beyond him, I cried out, "Holmes!"

Mercifully, my companion pulled up just short of the edge and glowered into the London night.

I reached him shortly after that, a pronounced limp in my step, and sank to my haunches to try and catch my breath. Surveying the rooftops, I realised the figure in black had gone and was beyond our grasp.

"I thought you were going to jump, Holmes," I gasped between breaths.

"I very nearly did, Watson."

"Then it would have been your death, I fear," I replied. "What do you think, Holmes? An acrobat? A gymnast?"

"The one that got away, Watson."

I nodded. "In any event, an incredible leap… Have you ever seen the like of it, Holmes?"

Holmes said nothing further, his gaze yet to waver. His left hand was clenched in a fist, his right wrapped tightly around his walking stick. Our prey had eluded us, for now. Catching sight of something amongst the rooftop debris, Holmes stooped and retrieved it. From what I could tell, it was a boot heel, though Holmes made no comment and merely secreted it in his jacket pocket.

"I shall be glad to return to Baker Street," I said.

"And so we shall," said Holmes, "but first we must return to the gallery."

"Really, Holmes? For what purpose?"

"To scale the roof, Watson," Holmes replied, already on his way as he called behind him. "We shall make use of that ladder, I think. Very handy."

Too weary to protest, I sighed and followed Holmes off the roof.

The rain had abated to a fine drizzle by the time we returned to the Grayson Gallery. Using the ladder we had carried from Tavistock Street, Holmes climbed up to the gallery roof and I followed, though to what end I did not yet know.

"Would you mind telling me why we are up here?" I asked as I clambered onto slick tiles, careful with my footing. "Or have you found a sudden interest in clambering over rooftops?"

"Take care, Watson," said Holmes, crouched by a chimney, inspecting something in the brickwork. "It is treacherous underfoot."

"I am trying to be, Holmes," I replied, glancing over the edge and trying not to imagine a fall to certain injury and possibly even death.

"Look here, Watson…"

Gingerly, I crawled across the tiles and found Holmes peering into the chimney's cleanout door. It was dark and I could not discern what it was Holmes wanted me to see.

"If we have ruled out ingestion as a means of poisoning," said Holmes, "based on the evidence to hand, then how else might the victims have succumbed?"

For a moment, I had no answer, my thoughts clouded by weariness.

"Inhalation would be the next most logical method," supplied Holmes. "Certainly, it must at least be ruled out. But

I believe I have found further proof of it, that the cyanide that killed the patrons of the Grayson Gallery was released as a gas."

"It sounds most plausible, Holmes, but how does clambering about on a rooftop in the middle of the night prove such a theory?"

"A few scraps of wool and threads from the sack it was carried in, Watson."

"I'm not sure I quite follow."

"If I am correct and the victims of this heinous crime were indeed gassed, what is remarkable about Edmund Garret?"

I frowned at first, but soon caught on. "He's alive, Holmes."

"Indeed, he is."

"If our murderer did indeed effect some kind of gas chamber in which to kill their victims, then poor Garret would have died the moment he opened the door to the exhibit."

"Quite so, Watson. But he did not. And why?"

"Well," I said, "the only explanation would be the gas had somehow been released earlier."

"And hence the sack of wool," said Holmes. "There are scraps of it embedded in the chimney, threads of hessian sacking too."

"The murderer used the cleanout door to access the chimney and block it up?"

"A sack of wool is easy enough to come by and light enough to carry whilst climbing up onto a roof, especially for one as apparently nimble as our murderer."

"It's devilish, Holmes."

"It's calculated, Watson. They must have climbed up here to first block the chimney. Cyanide gas rises, it disperses quickly in air, but the packed wool would have made an adequate seal I think. Then, once the deed was done, the murderer returned to retrieve the sack of wool and unblock the chimney."

"Thus releasing the gas harmlessly into the air."

"Exactly, Watson."

"Fascinating, Holmes, and quite horrid. I wonder though, if that is all, might we return to 221B and get out of this damp and miserable night?"

CHAPTER ELEVEN

A FORBIDDING DISCOVERY

Upon our return to our lodgings, Holmes had not been in the mood for talk and swiftly retired to his chair without a word. There he sat, his chin resting on his fist, brooding. I knew not to disturb him, so I hung up the black cloak—which I still had in my possession—on the coat rack. A casual examination of the garment had revealed nothing remarkable. It was, as far as I could discern, a common enough cloak that had served to mask our mystery figure until such time as they needed to make their escape.

Holmes's irritation had been palpable, but had lessened the closer we came to our lodgings, replaced instead by deep, almost trance-like introspection. Despite being thwarted by the figure in black, the night had yielded much in the way of evidence, and though only Holmes knew the import of it, I for one did not deem our clandestine venture an abject loss.

I considered joining Holmes by the fire laid by Mrs Hudson, the last embers of which were slowly fading, but having dragged my weary body up the seventeen steps that led to our rooms, I thought better of it.

"I think I shall retire," I said, and was about to bid my companion a good night when at last he spoke.

"A moment, Watson. If you would be so kind."

"Of course, Holmes. What is it?"

"A matter I should like to resolve."

My frown served as the only enquiry.

"What do you recall of your altercation with that rough fellow on Regent Street, the one who chased the girl?"

"The thief who stole my pocket watch, you mean," I said, sitting down in my chair to ease my leg, which still ached with the night's exertions.

"That's the fellow."

I thought back, but remembered little else than what I had already imparted. I said as much to Holmes.

"I see," he said. "As you know, Watson, my research into the human mind is extensive. During my studies, I have come across several intriguing theories that could be put to use in the field of deductive reasoning. Tell me, what do you know of hypnotism?"

I frowned, thinking on the question. "Not a great deal. It has ever been the province of stage magicians and petty conjurers."

"Would it surprise you to learn that the British Medical Association has endorsed its scientific validity?"

"I believe I read something of the sort in a journal. What is the relevance?"

Holmes turned to face me. "I have made a study of it and believe, however unorthodox, that it might be of some use to us in this case."

I leaned forward, intrigued. "How so?"

"I should like to hypnotise you, Watson."

"I beg your pardon, Holmes?"

"I would not do so without your permission, and I can

assure you the process is both completely harmless and you will, in time, remember everything that occurs. I believe it will also allow you to remember your encounter on Regent Street with greater clarity."

"You feel there is some clue hidden in my memory?"

"I do, Watson."

I leaned back in my chair again, not entirely at ease with this turn of events, but I trusted Holmes implicitly.

"Very well," I said. "What must be done?"

Holmes smiled and described the precise nature of how he planned to hypnotise me. I shall not elaborate on the technique here for fear that there may be those who would put it to nefarious use. Suffice to say that with a few softly spoken phrases and the metronomic swinging of his pocket watch, Holmes did indeed hypnotise me, the effects of which were momentary but profound.

Once again I was in Regent Street, the crowd flowing around me. I saw Holmes up ahead, driven and purposeful, urging me to follow. Muted shouts came from the gathered throng, but were little more than a susurrus of indistinct voices. What I saw through my mind's eye appeared vague too and feathered at the edges, as if I were looking through a dirty lens.

I saw the young woman, fear and determination written on her face. I wanted to reach for her, to seize the hand that would steal my watch, but I had no will to exert. I merely observed, a prisoner of my own memories. Then came the man and our confrontation played out as it had before. Then I discerned Holmes's voice, not from Regent Street but as if from above. And a brief darkness followed, accompanied by a sensation of rising.

When I woke I was standing by our window.

"Was it a success?" I asked, not knowing then what I had revealed.

Holmes nodded. "Indeed it was, Watson. Indeed it was."

"And so what did you learn?"

"A great many details, mostly superfluous, but one fact that quite caught my interest. About that rough fellow who was after your thief."

"Well then I beg of you, Holmes, avail me of it for I can sit in ignorance no longer."

"A word, innocuous enough. *Sabaka*."

Now my companion had said it aloud, I recalled uttering it myself.

"What does it mean?" I asked.

"It's Russian," said Holmes, his expression pleased yet pensive, "and it means 'dog'. He was insulting you, Watson, but in his native tongue."

"Remarkable, Holmes," I said, impressed. "Do you not think it feels a tad more than just coincidence that all of this was going on at the same time as a Russian grand duke was at large in Regent Street?"

"Indeed," Holmes replied, "but then I have never believed in coincidence, Watson."

"What does it all mean?"

"That, Watson, is the truth we seek. Thank you, old friend, for your indulgence."

"I am pleased I could be of assistance. I fear, however, this is where my usefulness shall end, at least for this evening."

"Then I bid you goodnight, Watson. I think I shall stay up a while and ruminate on the day and night's events."

"As you wish, Holmes," I said. "Goodnight." He had lit his pipe, and the smoke had begun to curl around him viperously as he gave a curt, absent-minded wave. Framed by the lambent glow of the fire, the shadows crawled across his eyes as he stared into the darkened room. I feared he might seek stronger stimulation than tobacco to loosen his thoughts, though I had not seen him use cocaine in several weeks, and the Morocco leather case was not to hand.

With little else for it, I turned in for the night, determined to face whatever the next day brought refreshed and revitalised.

I slept fitfully, my mind plagued by rain-lashed streets and the mysterious figure in black. I can only compare the acrobatic spectacle I had witnessed to the time I saw the high wire and trapeze act of the Barnum & Bailey's Circus at the Olympia. Such dexterity, physical strength and supreme confidence had been a marvel to behold. What I had witnessed in a dreary London night was no less impressive. We must be dealing with a singular individual. This, in itself, would suggest our list of suspects was small, yet we had little more than a chance encounter and whatever Holmes could make of the evidence collected.

I wondered again whether it was Graves beneath the hood. I clearly remembered the figure reacting when I had addressed them as Damian Graves. A connection, certainly, but nothing conclusive.

These thoughts tumbled through my mind, but not for long as fatigue claimed me and I fell into a merciful sleep.

I was rudely awoken by a sharp exclamation of delight that had emanated from the sitting room. Dragging on my dressing gown and slippers, and feeling a profound sense of déjà vu, I emerged bleary-eyed to find Holmes dressed, his shirtsleeves rolled up and at his chemistry bench. I also noticed the Morocco leather case on the arm of Holmes's chair and fought back a scowl.

"I thought we had seen the end of that, Holmes," I said, my tone chastening.

"A necessary evil, Doctor. Surely you would not begrudge me if it brings us closer to a solution?" answered Holmes, his back to me. "In any event, Watson," he added, quite ebullient as he beckoned me over, "your timing is, as ever, impeccable. Observe."

Deciding there was no reasoning with him, I joined Holmes at the chemistry bench. To my mild disgust, I noticed he had another rat, this time alive, imprisoned inside what appeared to be a hermetically sealed bell jar. Around it, Holmes had assembled a bewildering array of complex chemical apparatus, though my eye was drawn to the length of rubber tubing connecting the bell jar to a chemical flask, the base of which was being exposed to a gentle flame.

"What's in the flask, Holmes?" I asked.

"Hydrogen cyanide," said Holmes, as if he'd just commented on the inclement London weather.

"Good lord, Holmes!" I recoiled, instinctively covering my nose and mouth, though had my companion made any miscalculation in securing his apparatus then we would both be dead in moments, irrespective of my efforts.

"It's perfectly safe, Watson," he said, his gaze fixed on the rodent. In less than a minute of being exposed to the fumes, the poor creature collapsed, dead.

"Perfectly horrendous, Holmes. What was it you were burning?"

"Not burning, warming. Do you remember the painting from yesterday evening, how there was another image beneath the one of the so-called Undying Man?"

"Of course."

"In sufficient quantity, ground into a powder and exposed to the appropriate temperature, the flakes I took from the painting give off lethal hydrogen cyanide gas."

"And with the chimney blocked by wool…" I began.

"A gas chamber, much as you described, Watson. This here is but a small amount, though a large enough sample to test on our verminous friend inside the bell jar. A much larger quantity would have been needed to gas an entire room. I suspect all of the Lazarus paintings were poisoned thusly or perhaps the firewood in the hearth was tainted. Whilst a rodent will expire in under a minute, I estimate that a greater concentration of the gas, in a room the size of the exhibition hall and when introduced gradually into the air, would kill a grown man or woman after an hour of exposure."

"So, the poison was in the painting then," I said.

Holmes nodded.

"And the temperature of the room…" I continued, Holmes allowing the indulgence of my deduction, "had been raised to initiate the chemical reaction." I smiled ruefully at the devilishness of it all. "The wilted flowers, the blackened lamps. The fire in the hearth."

Again Holmes nodded, his eyes alight with a fervour that burned away all doubt. "Our artist, whoever they are, for I think we can both agree that Graves is not he or she, mixed a powdered concoction of the poison in with their paint and kept it at a sufficiently low temperature so as to remain inert until the exhibition. The cold would have assisted here. Seemingly innocuous, the murder weapon in plain sight and so grotesque a study as to be gratefully ignored by most."

"It explains the commotion within. It must have been quite the panic. Those poor souls. Quite devious, Holmes."

"And even deadlier, Watson. It also had a message to impart, the exact nature of which eludes me for now, but I have an idea as to where and when it shall be revealed."

"A message?"

"Yes," said Holmes, lighting the shag tobacco in the bowl of his briar pipe.

"For whom?" I asked. "All the patrons were dead."

"Not for the patrons, Watson. Torture and penance, remember. A warning," said Holmes, exhaling a perfectly round smoke ring. He peered through the slowly dissipating circle, as if an answer lay within. "The truth of it is close, Watson," he said, seemingly distracted, "but there is more afoot than we, at this present stage of the investigation, know."

"It's really rather forbidding, when you think about it."

An insistent hammering at the street door arrested any further discussion, but had Holmes sweeping across the room to burst out onto the landing to investigate who had come calling. I heard Mrs Hudson making a remark about my companion's excitable nature, to which Holmes insisted she just answer the door to end the "infernal knocking".

I joined Holmes on the landing, as much out of a need to referee whatever followed as curiosity, so was there to see Mrs Hudson open the door to Inspector Gregson. After bidding the inspector a good morning, Mrs Hudson invited him in. Gregson gave a polite nod, before his gaze swept up the stairs to where Holmes and I were standing.

For a fleeting moment I considered the fact that Gregson might have somehow gotten wind of our visit to the gallery in the dead of night, and had come to arrest us for trespass and vandalism, but it was nothing of the sort.

"Good morning, Mr Holmes, Dr Watson."

Holmes smiled thinly, while I acknowledged Gregson with a nod.

"My apologies for visiting unannounced," he went on, "but a delicate matter has arisen, one suited to your unique talents." He removed his hat as a gesture of humility. "Scotland Yard is in need of your assistance, Mr Holmes."

Holmes blew out a plume of grey smoke, his mood insouciant. "In what matter, Inspector?"

"Yours and the good doctor's presence has been requested," said Gregson, declining to answer the question.

"By whom?" asked Holmes.

"If you would just accompany me, sirs, I should be most grateful," said Gregson.

"Most intriguing," I said, to which Holmes scoffed and disappeared back into our rooms to fetch his hat and coat.

"Come along, Watson," he bellowed from within, "let us not keep the inspector waiting. If his lips were to get any tighter I suspect he might never be able to open them again."

For the second time in as many days, I dressed swiftly and met Holmes downstairs where Gregson had a hansom cab waiting to take us to our destination.

"So, tell me, Inspector," Holmes began, sitting opposite Gregson with me at his side, "what possible business could the grand duke have that requires my immediate attention?"

Gregson leaned forwards in his seat. "I never said it was anything to do with the Grand Duke."

"And yet you don't deny it, either?"

Gregson leaned back.

"You have an aroma, Inspector," said Holmes.

"I beg your pardon, Holmes," said Gregson, offended.

"No, Inspector, not of the unwashed but rather of birch oil and leather. It is quite distinctive." Holmes leaned out of the cab a little. "We are currently headed east and soon north, I think, on to Regent's Park. Given your man's urgency in applying the lash, and since Regent's Park is only a relatively short distance away, I suspect our guest is unaccustomed to being made to wait. Yesterday morning, a certain grand duke visited Regent Street where he procured a gift for his son. The close proximity of Regent Street to the Langham, combined with the fact that it is the most likely abode for a visiting foreign dignitary, would more than strongly suggest that this is where the Grand Duke Konstantin is staying. All of which, considered alongside the fact that the scent of birch oil and leather are synonymous with the Russian nobility, leads me to the conclusion that you have already met with the grand duke and have been sent to request our presence. Did you follow all of that, Inspector?"

Gregson muttered something and looked away out of the window.

"Well done, Holmes," I said, though Holmes waved away any praise.

"A mere trifle, Watson. What is more perplexing is Inspector Gregson's steadfast silence on the matter, as well as his misguided belief it would keep me from the truth, not to mention why the subterfuge in the first place?"

"What reason would the grand duke have to request your presence, though, Holmes? It won't be your first meeting with royalty, but even so, it's intriguing."

"Murder, Watson. It can be nothing other," said Holmes, pausing to regard Gregson, who kept up his stony demeanour.

Holmes went on, "I briefly considered a different scandal, a kidnapping, perhaps a theft, but such matters would have been handled by the grand duke's entourage—I expect he has brought several resourceful men with him across the Baltic. Indeed, the lack of constables at our door, the fact it was only Gregson, here, is evidence of the fact in itself. The deed has already been done, and there is little restitution for it other than to seek justice against the perpetrator. What else could be it be but murder?" Holmes briefly glanced again at Gregson. "The question is, whose?"

CHAPTER TWELVE

A ROYAL ENGAGEMENT

A prestigious establishment, and the largest hotel in all of London, our investigations had taken us to the Langham before, admittedly somewhat tangentially. At the door to the hotel, Holmes noticed two of the grand duke's men. They were wearing tweed suits, no doubt purchased from Savile Row, but from their uncomfortable demeanour—tugging at stiff collars—and the fact their boots looked to be of foreign origin, I hazarded a guess that these men were not residents of London, or even Britain for that matter.

They watched us closely, even Inspector Gregson, who did not so much as favour them with a look, although I believe he must have known who the men were. I saw no officers of the Metropolitan force. It seemed Scotland Yard's presence in this matter was strictly limited to Tobias Gregson.

After several flights of stairs, which saw the ache in my leg flare up anew, we arrived at the grand duke's luxurious accommodations. Much like the lobby of the hotel, the door to the grand duke's suite was guarded by two men, both severe-looking fellows who eyed all three of us closely as we approached.

Gregson took the lead, introducing himself and telling the men he had brought Sherlock Holmes as per the grand duke's request. To this, one of the men nodded and silently entered the suite, closing the door behind him while the other man maintained his steely vigil.

After a few moments, the first man returned, declaring that Holmes and I would be granted an audience but that Gregson must wait outside. I thought for a moment that the inspector might object. Certainly, he looked more than a little perturbed at his exclusion, but from his dignified capitulation in this matter, I got the distinct impression he had already attempted to reason with such men and reached nothing but an impasse. Holmes favoured Gregson with a glance and, I suspect, a quick smile, before we followed the first man into the suite and left the inspector outside.

Decadent would hardly do the rooms justice, for they were luxurious in the extreme and, I would happily wager, the very best the Langham had to offer. They even put Damian Graves's opulent mansion to shame, and I took some cheap but cathartic pleasure in that thought.

After passing through a lavish hallway, we came upon a study where a man sat in a leather chair facing a fine mahogany desk, looking out of a large window onto London below.

"Such a drab and dirty place, your London…" he muttered, his back to us. Grand Duke Konstantin was a broad-shouldered man with light brown hair, well-groomed, and in a pearl-white suit with embroidered gold cuffs. His boots were black, knee-length and polished to a sheen that would have even satisfied my former sergeant major.

"The endless scurrying, here and there," he said, swaying his arms back and forth for emphasis, "like little rats, as your factories fill the air with shadows. Such industry, you British. Your proud empire." He gave a short laugh, as if concluding a private monologue, before turning to us.

"You are very welcome," he said, standing, and I saw he was tall as well as broad-shouldered, his smile wide but his eyes narrow as he got the measure of us. I did not dislike him, but was immediately wary. "Gentlemen, there is no need to be so reserved, you are not at Buckingham Palace," he added, with a laugh intended to disarm us.

We followed our host into a grand sitting room, and he dismissed his man, no doubt to join his colleague and Gregson in the corridor. I imagined the inspector was fairly unhappy about his exclusion from affairs, but the grand duke's sturdy custodians did not look in any mood to disobey orders. Both men had appeared tense, and I wondered then if the grand duke's bracing good humour was intended to mask his own anxiety.

A trio of finely upholstered Chesterfields flanked a broad but low mahogany table in the sitting room. The grand duke smiled warmly and beckoned for us to sit down.

"So, you must be Sherlock Holmes," he said, looking piercingly at my companion. "The inspector tells me you are the greatest detective in all of London, perhaps even England."

Holmes nodded humbly. "I am he, though to the inspector's reported accolade, I could hardly attest."

"Of course, I have heard of you," the grand duke went on, nonchalant. "The name Sherlock Holmes is renowned throughout the world. I insist upon the best, as you can see." He gestured to his surroundings. "They are modest accommodations, but what is it you English say? It will do?"

"It will do nicely," said Holmes.

"I beg your pardon?" asked Grand Duke Konstantin, and I thought I detected a mote of surprise at the interruption. Here, I think, was a man used to speaking and having others listen until he deigned to allow them to comment, if at all.

"The expression you are looking for, it will do *nicely*."

The grand duke gave a smile, but some of the warmth had fled from it. "No, I think my version is better. More accurate."

Holmes gave a shrug as the grand duke's attention fell upon me.

"And this here is clearly Dr Watson. You were a soldier, is that right? Yes," he said, nodding and without waiting for me to answer, again taking his measure, "you have the look of a fighting man."

"I did indeed serve," I told him, "with the 5th Northumberland Fusiliers, until I was attached to the 66th Berkshire Regiment of Foot."

The grand duke leaned back in the Chesterfield, apparently impressed. Though I knew the Russians had interests in the Afghan War, our host, to his credit, made no mention of the fact, nor did it appear to colour his gregarious demeanour in any way. "You were an officer?"

"Army physician. I was wounded at the Battle of Maiwand." I instinctively rubbed at the old wound in my leg.

Despite the grim memories of conflict, I found it strangely fraternal to be discussing such matters with the grand duke. Holmes knew much about a great deal, but he had no experience of battle, nor did he possess a great deal of empathy.

"A doctor," said the grand duke, nodding as if he somehow approved of my history, "yes, I can see that. You will have seen much blood, I expect."

"More than enough to last a lifetime."

"I too was a soldier. I killed… many men. Many Turks," he said, quite matter-of-factly, without relish as far as I could discern. It was his duty to his country, and so he did it. He waved away the memory, as if it were an unpleasant fug of smoke. "But listen to me, discussing such grim matters."

"As I understand it," said Holmes, who had been listening patiently, "it is a grim matter that has brought us to your door, Your Royal Highness?"

The grand duke's face briefly darkened before a young boy came bounding into the sitting room from one of the adjoining rooms. His attire was also white, though less ornate than his father's, for this could be none other than the grand duke's son.

He eagerly leapt upon his father, whose face brightened at once. Grand Duke Konstantin caught his son with aplomb, making a show of how heavy he was, and how big he had grown in the short time since he had last seen him. After indulging the boy, the grand duke calmed him down and spoke a little to him in Russian before pointing to the pewter figure the lad had clutched in his hand.

It appeared father asked son about the nature of the soldier, his regiment and colours, eliciting a cry of laughter from the boy. Once they were done, the grand duke appeared to remember he had guests and gestured to Holmes and me.

"Sergei, come and meet the renowned detective Sherlock Holmes and his friend, Dr Watson." The boy turned and gave a shallow bow.

"Please to meet you," he said, in halting English.

"And you, Your Royal Highness," I replied, shaking the boy's hand as it was offered and doffing my hat.

Holmes gave a forced but polite smile, and said to the grand duke, "He is the very image of his father."

The grand duke beamed at the boy. "Indeed he is," he said, not taking his eyes off his son. "Sergei is my heir and one day he too will be *velikiy kniaz.*"

He said the word in Russian, presumably so the boy would

understand, who saluted crisply in the manner I am sure he imagined the soldier in his hand would have done had he been flesh and blood.

"Such precious innocence…" the grand duke said softly as he cradled his son's chin, and once more I saw the faint impression of anxiety in the tightness of his lips and the shallow frown that began to form on his brow. However, it faded as quickly as it had formed, the grand duke clapping a hand on the boy's shoulder as he said, "Off you go then, son, to your duty."

He smiled as the boy saluted again, his father saluting back, before Sergei marched off and we were left alone.

As soon as the grand duke was sure his son was out of earshot, he picked up the threads of our earlier conversation.

"Grim matters, yes…" he said dolefully, and looked off into the distance, his mind briefly elsewhere, but when he met Holmes's gaze again his eyes were stern and purposeful.

"My visit to your country was intended to be for pleasure," he said, "but regardless, I always take Grigori wherever I go. He is my…" he struggled with the correct word for a moment, "manservant, and attends to a great manner of things for Sergei and me. He comes from good family, Andropov, who have served my family for generations. Grigori and I, we fought together, side by side. He has saved my life," said the grand duke, his eyes narrowed, "many times. This is a bond not easily broken, a debt not easily repaid. But more than this, he is my comrade, my friend. I am sure you gentlemen can understand such a relationship, yes?"

I nodded, though briefly considered that the grand duke considered me Holmes's assistant, rather than his friend and colleague.

"Yesterday I decided to take my son to Hamleys. He had heard of it, of course, and would not let me rest until he had seen it for himself." He leaned in, as if about to impart some earnest secret. "Sergei is *everything* to me. There is nothing I would not do for him, Mr Holmes, nothing. In this regard, I always keep Grigori close by, to keep us safe, but mainly to look after my son. So it was, the first time I realised that something was wrong was when we returned to our carriage and Grigori was not there. This was most unusual for Grigori. He is a… watchdog, so for him to abandon his post, there must have been a good reason.

"The day wore on, and still there was no sign of him. I began to become worried for my friend, for I had received no word."

"Did you contact the police?" I asked.

The grand duke leaned back, and shook his head. "I prefer to deal with matters in my own way."

"But you have contacted Scotland Yard now," I said. "One of its inspectors is waiting outside."

Here, Grand Duke Konstantin nodded. "I did, yes. Your… *Gregson*." His mouth struggled to form the hard consonants. "In truth, I did so in order to reach you, Mr Holmes. I knew you by reputation, but not where I might find you. I considered that your police, your Scotland Yard, would know. This inspector, now you are here, is of no use."

Holmes gave a faint smile. "Indeed, sir, but what *use* would you put me to? I have yet to hear of a crime in need of investigation. Your man, he has not returned, I presume?"

The grand duke paled a little. "I am afraid he is dead. Found earlier this morning. I have yet to see the body—I have no wish to see him thus, and I will not leave Sergei alone until this murderer is apprehended—but it has been described to me. It is none other than Grigori. He has not been touched, not by the man I sent to confirm his identity, and not, I understand, by any of your policemen, either. Such things matter, do they not?"

Holmes nodded, and I thought I detected his attitude

softening towards the grand duke.

"You must understand," the Russian went on. "I must know who did this."

"And should you find them, sir, the one who killed your man, what will you do?" asked Holmes.

"That should be of no concern to you. I merely wish to see justice done."

"There are many interpretations of justice."

The grand duke gave a curt smile, rising from his seat, and I got the impression our meeting with him was nearing its end, as was our host's patience.

"I did not summon you to debate the law, Mr Holmes," he said. "I am in need of your skills as a detective. I beseech you, find who killed Grigori."

Holmes stood, as did I.

"Tell me, sir," said my companion, "what brings you to London?"

"A gala performance is to be staged in my honour, a ballet at your Royal Opera House. But I fail to see how this has any bearing on Grigori's murder."

"Possibly nothing," said Holmes, "possibly everything. One can never know, but no detail is ever wasted."

Grand Duke Konstantin frowned. "So, you will take this case of mine? You will find Grigori's murderer?"

"I will not," answered Holmes, brazenly, and I admit I was taken aback by his boldness.

"You refuse me?"

"Regrettably, I must do. I am presently engaged in another case and cannot divert my attention from it. This meeting has already taken me away from my investigations for too long." To my astonishment, Holmes then gave a curt bow, tipping his hat, and turned to leave. "Come along, Watson."

I had begun to follow when the grand duke got over his apparent shock and cried out, "Is it money? I can make you a wealthy man."

"I am perfectly comfortable already, thank you," Holmes replied, and again I marvelled at his sheer nerve.

We had reached the door when the grand duke made his final gambit.

"This displeases me greatly. I had heard you were a great man, committed to justice and the law. You have principles, and I respect that, but I am in need of your help, Mr Holmes. Would you at least consent to see the body and share any thoughts you might have? As I said, it has not been interfered with. Would you at least do me this favour? I should not like to beg, but I will."

Holmes paused at the door, then turned. "Very well, sir, but this and no more."

Gregson had already gone by the time we emerged from the lavish suite. The two guards eyed us as suspiciously as before. Holmes gave them a polite tip of the hat, to which they seemed unsure how to respond, and we continued on.

On the way down to the Langham's lobby, I asked, "Had you always intended to accede to the grand duke's request, Holmes?"

"Of course, my dear Watson," he said, as light as the day, "I merely wanted him to ask politely rather than assume I was his servant to command."

I shook my head, and gave a rueful smile.

We found Gregson waiting for us below, looking less than impressed at his treatment. "You going to see the body then, Holmes?" he asked.

"I am."

"Very well, then," answered Gregson, seemingly pleased to

be leaving the Langham and self-entitled foreign dignitaries.

In truth, so was I.

"Where was the grand duke's man found?" I asked.

Gregson glanced at me over his shoulder. "A most unlikely place for a royal manservant," he replied. "The Old Nichol."

CHAPTER THIRTEEN

THE FACELESS MAN

It could not be mere coincidence that I had followed Damian Graves to this very same part of London, but a day ago. Holmes had yet to remark upon the significance of the location, and had maintained a pensive silence throughout the journey from the Langham to the Old Nichol, but I could tell his interest had been piqued. There was more here than simple murder.

I briefly considered whether or not we should mention the fact to the inspector, but knew that Holmes had his methods and would do so when he deemed fit. In truth, there was little to report, save that Graves had come here the same day, a fact that hardly pointed to murder and would appear wholly coincidental. Indeed, any attempt to implicate Graves in nefarious matters, if unsubstantiated by evidence, would only serve to make him aware of Holmes's interest and thus make any future efforts to discover his deeds more difficult.

So it was that I came to the Old Nichol with a great many questions still unanswered.

The four-wheeler that had swiftly conveyed us from the

Langham came to a halt a fair distance from where the body had been found, awaiting our return in one of the marginally more salubrious parts of the district, meaning we had to make the rest of the journey on foot. Even in these invisible outskirts, I felt the oppressive presence of the Old Nichol again, wretched in all its squalor.

We left a fairly broad street, descending down narrow stone steps beneath a looming arch that felt like the gates to some underworld labyrinth, as ugly tenements of black brick rose up on either side of us and the stench of the unwashed and the fetid filled the nostrils. It might have been my imagination, but the air felt colder, the weather appreciably bleaker the deeper we went. A vile keening struck up and for a moment I thought we had strayed upon some poor soul being murdered in the shadows, until I realised it was the wind whipping between houses that crowded and choked the streets.

Though it was my second visit in as many days, the effect of the Old Nichol had not lessened with familiarity.

"To live in such a place..." I muttered. Holmes heard me, though that was not my intent.

"And yet there are those at this nadir of society who still value the law."

Holmes was no socialist, but he had a keen affinity for the downtrodden, his Baker Street Irregulars a perfect case in point. It was at times like these that I was reminded that a compassionate man still resided behind his cage of logic.

According to Gregson, the local constabulary had been alerted earlier that morning. One of the poor denizens of Columbia Road had thought the dead man an inveterate drunk, a ubiquitous sight in these parts for sure, but one they wanted waking and moving on. I considered my earlier assumptions about these people when I had come to the Old

Nichol before, about their wretchedness and perfidy, and found them unworthy.

As we walked, Gregson took out his notebook and read aloud from it. "Woman by the name of Molly Bugle found the body," he said. "Has a domicile on Columbia Road. The constable who she spoke to is waiting for us at the scene."

"Has she been interviewed yet, Inspector?" asked Holmes, his eyes fixed ahead as he kept up a brisk pace.

"Next thing on my list, Holmes," replied Gregson, tapping the notebook with his pencil for emphasis.

"If it is agreeable, I should like to be present. Rest assured," added Holmes, "I shall not interfere in your questioning, but merely listen and observe."

Gregson gave a grunt of assent. Then he pointed. "Here it is."

The body of Grigori Andropov was lying face down in the gutter, the limbs tangled up in the refuse of a narrow dead-end alleyway. A pair of constables, one of whom had made the initial response and both here by Gregson's charge, watched over the body to ensure it wasn't interfered with prior to it being taken back to Scotland Yard for further examination.

"Has anyone touched the body?" asked Holmes, ignoring the constables as he moved a little closer. Although the grand duke had assured us no such tampering had occurred, it was only prudent to check with the officers at the scene.

Gregson shook his head, before giving a sharp nod to his two cohorts to step back and afford Holmes some room, which they obligingly did. "Save to ascertain whether or not he was simply inebriated or more permanently impaired."

Holmes gave a nod, only half-listening as he took in the state of the man. "Well, Inspector, he most assuredly *is* dead, so in that at least you have not erred."

Gregson bit back a retort, his eyes wide and annoyed as

he looked to me. I had no reply, so merely smiled by way of mute apology.

The dead man was shabbily dressed, certainly not the attire of a royal manservant, and I immediately wondered whether he had been redressed for some reason. His hands and nails were clean, making him quite out of place here in the Old Nichol. Other than that, there was little else to distinguish him from the common dregs that washed up in this most impoverished part of London.

"How was he killed, Inspector?" I asked, unable at first glance to detect any obvious means of death.

"We hoped you might be able to help with that, Dr Watson," Gregson admitted.

"The manner of his limbs and the fact he is lying face down in the dirty street would suggest he was killed where he stood and fell into this position immediately afterwards," said Holmes. "However he met his end, he did so swiftly and violently, though we will know more once he is turned over. Watson, would you mind?"

"Of course, Holmes," I said, knowing that my companion would want to observe everything as the body was moved in case a crucial piece of evidence was disturbed during the process. It was a grim task, but nothing I was unacquainted with.

"Inspector, if I could prevail upon the assistance of one of your constables?" I ventured.

Never a man afraid to get his hands dirty, Gregson stepped in himself. With his help, I managed to turn the body over and found to my dismay that the victim's face had been badly disfigured through the action of a sharp blade or perhaps a broken bottle, for there were many lying about.

"Lord, someone has made a good mess of him," said Gregson, standing back to regard the body.

I had seldom seen a grimmer sight on civilian streets, save perhaps for an imitation found in one of London's gruesome waxwork emporiums. Here was true horror rendered in flesh, and all the more ghastly for that.

Gregson had taken off his hat, and ran a hand through his hair. "Have you ever seen the like?" he said with scarcely breath enough to whisper.

"It is a bad end, indeed," I said.

"How did he come to such an end, though?" said Gregson, donning his hat again. "A mugging, perhaps? This is hardly Mayfair."

"Nor is it the butcher's block," I replied, unconvinced by the inspector's hypothesis.

At Gregson's order, one of the constables checked the dead man's pockets, but found no wallet.

"Whoever attacked him has emptied his pockets," I said. "If this was a mugging, it was a brutal one."

"I think not, Watson," said Holmes. "Rather it was intended to appear as if he had been mugged. Observe," he added, pointing with his walking stick, "his boots. Not footwear one would find at Lobb's."

Holmes referred to the corpse's leather boots, in a military style that covered both foot and foreleg. I realised with sudden excitement that I had seen very similar attire worn by the Life Guards who had accompanied the grand duke in Regent Street.

"Curious though," added Holmes. "Any mugger worthy of the name, especially in the Old Nichol, would strip anything of value. To leave his boots is more than incongruous."

"As incongruous as why the man would be in this part of London in the first place," I said.

"Perhaps they tried but couldn't remove them?"

"An intriguing thought, Inspector," said Holmes. "Watson," he added, gesturing to the dead man's feet, "If you wouldn't mind."

I leaned down again to give the left boot a tug, and it came off easily enough.

"Perhaps they were worried about being seen?" suggested Gregson.

"Given where the body now lies," said Holmes, "the attacker would have had ample time to take whatever they wanted without fear of discovery."

"Unless all they wanted was his life," added Gregson.

"Quite, Inspector. No, this was no mugging. I believe the boots were an oversight. I presume this is how you identified the man as Grigori Andropov?"

Gregson nodded, puffed up with no small amount of pride. "I suspected it was him, given that the Russians were looking for one of their own. One of the grand duke's men confirmed it, but has since been and gone."

"Not entirely unintelligent, Inspector, to draw conclusions about a man's identity based purely on his footwear."

"We're not all dullards, you know, Holmes. We have solved crimes in London without your assistance."

"Perish the thought, Inspector. I am sure the people of London will sleep safer in their beds for knowing it."

Gregson scowled, but deigned not to take the bait. "Duke Konstantin has said he will make a formal identification when we get back to the Yard, but I wanted you to see the body where it lay, Mr Holmes."

Holmes knelt down by the body for a closer look. "If the wounds to the face were intended to obscure Mr Andropov's identity, then why not remove his boots? And consider the nature of the wounds themselves. I count more than twenty separate cuts, the length of each varying but deep enough that they were delivered with some force. It was anger that drove the killer to wound this man thusly."

Holmes leaned in close to sniff the dead man's fingertips.

"So, they could have known each other then?" asked Gregson, my companion's eccentric behaviour familiar to him by now.

"It is possible," said Holmes, seemingly satisfied with the olfactory analysis.

"Or perhaps the killer was not of his right mind?" Gregson ventured further.

"Again, possible, though not determinable from the evidence here. And consider also the location of the crime." He gestured to the alleyway. "Dark and hidden away from prying eyes. Whoever did this took efforts to ensure they were not observed. An imbalanced mind, in the way that you suggest, Inspector, is not capable of such malice aforethought.

"Consider also the manner in which we found him. No skin or hair under his nails, or any evidence that he put up struggle; there are no defensive wounds on his arms. It suggests he was surprised by his attacker, though if lured into this alley, it would also imply he followed them and was not expecting foul play." Holmes gestured towards the gutter. "See here." It was so dark in the shallow recess that I could scarcely make out what my companion was indicating to until he rolled it into plain sight with his stick. It was a cosh.

"Not the weapon of our attacker, I think," Holmes asserted, "but rather our victim."

"The grand duke's man came here to do harm to his murderer, then," said Gregson.

"It's possible, but Mr Andropov was charged with the grand duke's protection, which is reason enough for him to be armed. All we can know for certain at this point is that the murder weapon was not the cosh."

"Granted, Holmes. But why did he end up *here*?" asked

Gregson, gesturing to the nearby houses. "Do you think whoever he was after lives in one of these lodgings?"

As with much of the Old Nichol, the streets were overlooked by lurching tenements. In some, I saw faces crowded at grimy glass or gawping out of open doorways. None were bold enough to challenge us. With glum acceptance, I realised that death and even murder were an all too common sight in these parts and supposed the only novelty was the appearance of Sherlock Holmes and myself at the scene.

"Unless the victim was redressed, and we can assume this wasn't the case given he is still wearing his boots, and that his shabby attire is not in keeping with a royal manservant's garb, then he procured these clothes in order to blend in. This would suggest he did not wish to be recognised and that his intended quarry knew him. Whatever Mr Andropov was doing here in the Old Nichol, he needed to remain unobserved. He had to improvise. Somewhere in this run-down, notorious part of London, I suspect we will find a suspiciously well-frocked, if not well-heeled, tramp or vagabond. He was looking for someone, and I believe he found them. In wanting to see them before they saw him, he required a measure of anonymity. Nothing that would stand up to detailed inspection but just enough that a casual glance would see his presence dismissed."

"As I understand it," said Gregson, flicking through his notebook, "the grand duke had no word from his man for several hours, not since earlier that day. He could have been following someone or waiting for them?"

"The only thing we can know for certain at this stage, Inspector, is that he was killed sometime after midnight. The presence of rigor mortis in the neck, jaw, eyelids and extremities confirms it. Would you agree, Watson?"

I nodded.

"Which confirms he followed his murderer most of the day," said Gregson.

"I believe so, Inspector."

"He was a tenacious fellow then," Gregson remarked.

"Either that or he found them and waited for an opportune moment to challenge them," said Holmes. "Whomever Grigori Andropov was after led him to Columbia Road and this very alleyway. Perhaps they were then successful in evading capture, thus enabling them to, in turn, trap our man here and kill him."

"And how did he die then, Holmes? I can see no obvious wounding beyond that on his face."

I wondered if poison could have again been the cause, for I was starting to suspect some connection between this dead Russian manservant and the events at the gallery.

"The wounds to his face occurred after death. See how there is little blood." Holmes opened up the man's clothing. Hidden beneath a tatty-looking jacket, there was a faint dark stain on his shirt, little more than a needle prick, over his chest.

"One quick thrust to the heart with something very sharp, very deadly," said Holmes. "Killed instantly. What do you make of this, Doctor?" he asked, and shuffled aside so I could get a better view.

I examined the small wound in the man's chest. "I'd say this was done with an extremely thin blade, a stiletto or a very thin sword…" I was instantly put in mind of Graves, and his penchant for blades, including his collection of fencing foils and sabres.

"Can't say many Londoners are running around with swords, Doctor," offered Gregson.

I could think of at least one.

"Nonsense, Inspector," said Holmes. "Many an English gentleman furnishes his evening wardrobe with a walking stick, and many of those harbour a few feet of steel."

"I can't arrest every fine fellow of London with a sword-stick, Holmes."

"And nor should you, else I expect our own dear doctor here would find himself in gaol."

I smiled politely at the inspector, who did me the service of not playing along with my companion's jest.

"No," Holmes declared, "we must look a little closer…"

As Holmes inspected the wound again, I noticed something had been carved in the flesh.

"Good heavens, Holmes. What is that?"

"Our murderer's mark," Holmes replied. "Do you recognise it, Watson?"

I did, but would not say in Gregson's presence, for it would reveal the fact we had visited the Grayson Gallery under cover of darkness.

"I cannot say I do, Holmes."

It was the same kind of curved script we had seen daubed beneath the painting of the Undying Man. Not exact, but in the same written style. It could not have been a coincidence.

"What does it mean, Holmes?" asked the inspector, craning his neck for a better look.

Holmes stood, and dusted off his coat. "It means there is a great deal more to Mr Andropov's death than a simple mugging."

Gregson frowned, evidently hoping my companion's observations would prove more conclusive. He then gestured to one of the constables to arrange transportation for the body.

"We'll get him back to the Yard and see what Roper can find. Perhaps the grand duke will have some ideas, also."

"Very good, Inspector," said Holmes, "and in the meantime, perhaps we should speak with your eyewitness?"

Gregson regarded the body for a moment or two, looking quite disgruntled at the loose end. Deciding that this was not about to happen in the immediate future, he turned and gestured for us to follow him.

"This way."

Molly Bugle lived in one of the downtrodden and dilapidated tenements on Columbia Road, which ran across the alleyway in which lay the body of Grigori Andropov. An upper floor lodging, Miss Bugle's domicile looked to offer a good view of the mouth of the alleyway, but I doubted it went as far as the dead end where Grigori Andropov had met his death.

We entered through a black brick arch that led to a communal hallway. It was abjectly dark within, despite the morning sun, which appeared unable or unwilling to penetrate the gloom. A stench pervaded, foul enough to make even the Scotland Yard morgue seem fragrant by comparison.

A rickety wooden stairwell led to the upper floors, dark with mildew and betraying obvious signs of rot. After Gregson gave the railing a good shake, he pronounced it safe and we advanced to the first landing.

"To live amongst filth and detritus like this…" I said in a low murmur, in case any of the residents were listening.

After another flight of stairs, the wood creaking ominously with every step, we reached the domicile of Mrs Molly Bugle. She opened her door on the first knock, having evidently been expecting us, and ushered us in.

The room was small and became quite crowded with the inspector, Holmes, Mrs Bugle and myself in attendance, but it was clean and well tended. A second, even smaller room, not much larger than a cupboard, led off from the first and within its shadowy recess I saw several pale little faces regarding us with fearful eyes.

"Don't mind them," said Mrs Bugle, "we don't 'ave many

visitors, and certainly not fine gentlemen like yourselves." She smiled, but I could see the weariness in her grey eyes and the ravaging of years that I had no doubt made her look older than she actually was.

She wore a dark-blue cotton dress, frayed around the edges, her nails were cut almost to the quick and I saw a reddening at the fingertips that was indicative of vigorous scrubbing. Molly Bugle might lead an impoverished life, but she was clean and her children, for I could assume nothing other, were well behaved.

"Mrs Bugle," Gregson began, removing his hat out of respect, "I understand you spoke briefly to one of my constables about the man you noticed in the alleyway?"

She nodded. "I thought he must've been to tickle his innards, him being tight as a boiled owl on neck oil, or so it seemed to me, Officer."

I exchanged a covert glance with Holmes, who, noting my confusion, mouthed "drunk" by way of explanation.

"And when did you see him, madam?" asked Gregson, writing feverishly in his notebook.

"It was on my way home," she said. "I had just done my shift in Budden's Laundry, and I swear my fingers were red-raw and my back as stiff as a board. Weary I was, sir," she added, with a furtive look at Holmes and me. Briefly, I considered introducing us both but thought that it would only prolong our stay. "I remember, I had stopped on account of my feet hurting like the devil," she gestured out of the window to the street below, "there on the corner. At any rate, I saw your man go into the alley, and he didn't look right on his feet to me, but he weren't the first to go in there, and that's what I found odd."

"You saw someone else?"

She nodded again. "I ain't no blower, Officer, but I did see another go into that alley before your man, but I didn't see them leave. I didn't see neither of them leave, and I waited a while, on account of it being odd."

Gregson exchanged a brief look with Holmes but my companion's attention was fixed squarely on Molly Bugle and her intriguing testimony.

"And can you describe this other man, Mrs Bugle?"

"It were hard to tell much about him… I mean, I didn't see his face on account of the fact he wore a long coat or some such." She frowned, as if searching for the memory. "No, not a coat. It was a cloak."

Holmes, who had just begun making a discreet visual inspection of Mrs Bugle's home, turned, his interest suddenly piqued.

"Did it have a hood, by any chance?" he asked, somewhat languidly.

"Why yes, it did, sir. He was a short fellow, much shorter than the other one. Anyway, he follows the short fellow in and neither comes out. I waited for a little while, before having a look." She frowned again, trying to remember exact details. "Something about it," she said, "didn't seem right. So, I walked to the end of the alley and when I looked down, there he was all five or seven and not up to dick."

"Who wasn't, madam?" asked Gregson.

"I beg your pardon, Officer?"

"*Feeling well*, which fellow?"

"Oh, the larger man. He did not look well. I dared not disturb him, for I had no wish to cop a mouse should he be violent. Of the shorter fellow, though, the one he followed in, I saw no sign."

"Are you absolutely sure, Mrs Bugle?"

"I swear it, Officer. Two went in, none came out. I mean, I suppose he could have hid, what with it being dark…" she said. "I went to find an officer straight after that, not wishing to have some lushington all but on my doorstep. What else can I tell you, sir? I'm sure I don't know."

"You've been very helpful, Mrs Bugle," Gregson replied, giving her a smile. "We'll bother you no further—"

"I have only one more question," said Holmes, now looking through the window at the street below. He looked to Gregson. "If you would allow me, Inspector?"

"Would it matter if I objected, Holmes?"

"Not in the slightest, Inspector, but I thought it good manners to at least seek permission."

Gregson shrugged and gestured for Holmes to do whatever he pleased.

"Madam," he said, his penetrating stare now upon Molly Bugle, "might I ask *how* the shorter man walked?"

She screwed up her face, apparently perplexed at my companion's enquiry. "Not sure I follow, sir."

Holmes took a step from the window until he was only a stride from Mrs Bugle. "His manner, how would you describe it?"

"It was light, not like most of the oafs you see around here, but not like no Mary Ann or whatnot. He almost… well, glided, I suppose. Like a dancer."

Or a swordsman, I thought.

"No one walks like that who lives here, sir," Mrs Bugle went on. "They have heavy feet, weary feet. This chap, and the other who was with him, they didn't belong, not in the Old Nichol."

"I think you are right, Mrs Bugle," said Holmes, and gently clasped her hands in his, a most uncharacteristic gesture for my companion, "and we thank you for your good service."

Holmes let her go and, as Gregson was taking his leave, I noticed he had left something in the lady's hands. I could not swear to it, for Molly Bugle squirrelled it away in the pocket of her dress as quick as grease, but I thought I caught the shine of a few farthings.

"Madam," I said, nodding my farewell, silently proud of my friend's quiet compassion.

Once we were back out onto the street, Gregson remarked to Holmes, "What was all that about then, with all that talk of hoods and how a fellow might have carried himself?"

"Data, Inspector," Holmes replied, with an air of nonchalance, "merely data. In order to solve a mystery, especially one as violent as murder, one must amass as much data as one can." He nodded to Gregson's notebook. "Knowledge is the needle by which we might unstitch a conundrum and lay its secrets bare."

"So why is it I think it's you who is harbouring secrets, Holmes," Gregson replied, narrowing his eyes.

"Not secrets, Inspector," Holmes reassured him, "but nascent deductions, far too inchoate to reveal at this stage in proceedings. Rest assured, I shall inform Scotland Yard of any developments, but for now, Watson and I have other business."

"We do?" I asked, genuinely surprised.

"We do," said Holmes. "No need to accompany us, Inspector, I'm sure we can manage without a police escort. Come along, Watson."

"Is that it then, Holmes?" said Gregson, a little put out and clearly hoping my companion would furnish him with some insight he could use to solve the murder and thus earn a self-aggrandising headline in *The Times*.

"I am afraid so, Inspector, though I should be grateful if upon seeing the grand duke again you would ask him a question for me?"

"I'm certain I don't follow, Holmes, but yes I can do that."

"Ask him if he knows a man called Reginald Dunbar."

Gregson frowned. "You were just with him, Holmes. Why didn't you ask him then?"

"Then it was not pertinent, whereas now it might be, depending on his answer."

"I still don't follow, Holmes."

"It is of small importance, I think, Inspector," said Holmes, waving away Gregson's concerns as if wafting smoke. "I imagine you will be wanting to get the body to the Scotland Yard morgue. If there is room, of course," he added.

CHAPTER FOURTEEN

A HURRIED DEPARTURE

We left the Old Nichol and picked up a cab on Threadneedle Street. It was only once we were aboard the hansom and on our way back to Baker Street that I let down my guard.

"Though it shames me to admit it, I find a great deal of ill-feeling towards that place."

"There is a great deal of ill done within it, Watson, but don't judge too harshly those whose lot has left them in such low circumstances. There is murder and perniciousness aplenty in Mayfair as well as The Mount."

"Justly spoken, Holmes," I said, and felt my own social conscience lacking in comparison to my companion's. "But surely you can agree it is a grim and villainous place?"

"No more so than the bastions of Whitehall, where the mechanisms of justice find themselves ill-equipped to account for the slithering manoeuvrings of the arch politick, and behind every smiling facade there lurks the potential for deceit of the most deplorable stripe."

"Holmes, you surely cannot believe that," I said, then

lowered my voice. "Why, you would taint your own brother with the tarred brush."

"Not entirely, though Mycroft has his secrets, and I have yet to meet a servant of Whitehall that did not have a serpent's smile. Men with power have much to lose, and will often do much to hold on to it should it be threatened. Let us consider Mr Graves, shall we?"

"A rich man, but not a politician."

"Indeed not, though his motivations might be such."

I considered the fact that Graves might have some political affiliation but could find no hook upon which to tether my thoughts. Instead, I considered the facts at hand and what was very likely the return of our mysterious adversary from the Grayson Gallery.

"The cloak and hood, Holmes," I said.

"Yes, Watson," he replied, and the faintest trace of irritation returned, I suspect at the memory of our thwarted pursuit the previous night. "I believe it was our figure in black."

"Evidently they have a penchant for mystery, and a wardrobe with a ready supply of cloaks."

"And, it would seem," said Holmes, "for murder."

I gazed out of the cab's window for a moment, watching the streets flit by, my mind going back over everything we had seen and heard over the last few days.

"A single thrust to the heart," I said. "A difficult blow to land with precision, but made with skill. Can we be certain that Damian Graves is not somehow involved in all of this? I take it we are to pay him another visit?"

"Almost certainly, Watson," Holmes replied, though looked preoccupied, "but he is not our murderer if that is what you are suggesting."

I turned to Holmes, dumbfounded. "You dismiss him out of

hand, Holmes? He is both a consummate swordsman and was seen acting suspiciously in the vicinity of the Old Nichol."

"Hardly proof, Watson. But consider all the salient facts."

"Such as?"

"The physique of the figure in black does not match that of Graves."

"How can you be sure, though, Holmes? It was dark, and the man was wearing a cloak."

"Many things are possible, Watson, but the description given to us by our witness suggested a short individual. How would you reconcile this information with what we know of Damian Graves?"

He was deliberately leading me to see if I could respond to the intellectual challenge. I smiled. "I have no wish to impugn the testimony of our witness, but that is surely fallible to a degree also. Furthermore, testimony is not fact."

Holmes smiled. "Indeed, indeed, memories in my experience can often be made to fit the assumed facts. Molly Bugle may have been mistaken. As you say, it was dark and she already admitted she was fatigued. Perhaps also she invented details in order to become a part of the grim romance of a murder investigation; such things are not uncommon. Here, though, Watson, is where I can say beyond all doubt that the figure in black was not Damian Graves."

"You have my full attention, Holmes," I replied.

"During both our encounter in the vicinity of Tavistock Street, and again off Columbia Road, our quarry effected an escape by means both remarkable and highly athletic. A gymnast, perhaps? You suggested as much yourself, Watson. Certainly, Graves's exercise regimen extended to such activities and more besides, judging by the paraphernalia he had arrayed at his home. At both scenes, though, I noted marks on the wall:

hand and boot prints. Such a dextrous feat would require the full extension of the body to achieve, and a mental reckoning of the distance between the extremities places our figure in black somewhere between five feet five inches and five feet seven inches, if one then subtracts the three inches of boot heel intended to suggest they were taller." Here, I was reminded of what was recovered on the rooftops of Tavistock Street in the late evening rain—a boot heel, broken off during a pursuit.

"A further attempt to obscure their identity, Holmes."

"Indeed, Watson. Though we cannot say for certain whether or not the figure in black Molly Bugle saw was in fact short or the same individual we encountered at the gallery that night, the apparent reduction in height would coincide with the discovery of the broken heel, rendering their boots unusable."

"To what end though, Holmes?"

"I believe, Watson, they were trying to obscure the fact that they are not a man at all."

"A woman, Holmes!" I cried, for such wanton murder and larceny seemed beyond the fairer sex. "But to have killed a man thusly…?"

"Is it so difficult to believe? It is hardly some mild-mannered ingénue we are dealing with, Watson, but a murderess both skilled and determined. Do you recall our visit to the house of Damian Graves?"

"Of course, Holmes. A fine establishment, crassly flaunted, in my opinion."

"And what do you remember of the fencing apparatus?"

I paused to bring a picture of the room to mind. "It was in great abundance, Holmes. How a man would have need of so many sabres and foils is beyond me, but it tallies with his love of excess in all other matters."

"How indeed, Watson. The blade I held—"

"The one you threw across the room, you mean."

Holmes smiled. "Just the one. A little theatre for our host. It was very light, far too light for a man such as Graves. I have made studies of weapons, edged, blunt, projectile and ballistic—I have even penned several monographs on the subject, for it is pertinent to my work—and I can assert that the weapon I used was not meant for a man of Graves's size. Considering his obvious expertise concerning swords, I do not believe it was purchased in error, either."

"Holmes, what on earth could Graves want with a too-light sabre?"

"I do not believe it was *his* blade, Watson, but rather intended for another."

"The figure in black? This murderess that eludes us?"

"None other, Watson."

"So, they are in league." I clenched a fist, triumphant. "By the devil, I knew he was rotten!"

"Knowing and proving are two different matters. I have a theory, but—" Holmes paused, leaving his thought incomplete. "Ah, Baker Street at last," he said, as the hansom pulled up to 221B.

I followed Holmes as he exited our cab, before opening the street door and swiftly advancing up the stairs to our lodgings. My companion seemed gripped by a sudden fervour and urgency, and by the time I had caught up to him, he had the cloak in hand undergoing inspection.

"There is time only for a cursory examination," Holmes explained, "but this should more than suffice."

"Are we in a rush, Holmes? I was not aware we had an appointment."

"Indeed we are, Watson, and indeed we do. Here!" he said, brandishing the garment as if it might suddenly burst into flames or spring to life. "What do you see?"

I frowned, but stated the obvious anyway. "It is a black cloak," I said, before gauging the length by eye. "I'd say around five foot four inches in length."

"It's five foot six and a half inches, Watson, but very good. So, the length is consistent with our figure in black, as is the hue. But what of the infinitesimal and the invisible?" he asked, as he put his angular nose to the garment and breathed in deeply. "Lavender and rose hips, faint but detectable."

Holmes's olfactory ability was as highly developed as his other four senses, and it never failed to amaze me how he could discern precise aromas.

"Not a man's scent," I said.

"Commonly, no," said Holmes, "but there are two other items of note. Firstly," and he held up a thin, fair hair, far too long to belong to Graves.

"Found at the collar?" I guessed.

"Precisely, Watson. Secondly, there are very faint deposits of a fine powder also around the neck."

"Meaning what, though, Holmes?"

"Meaning beyond doubt that our figure in black is indeed female, highly athletic and almost certainly known to Damian Graves. He put a finger to his tongue. "Chalk, for grip," he said, "transferred from the hands to the neck when the wearer adjusted the collar." I remembered then that the figure wore no gloves. "And something else." Holmes frowned. He then swiftly checked the time on his pocket watch before barrelling past me and into my bedroom, where he began to fling about my clothes.

"Are you possessed, Holmes?" I asked, bemused, as I approached the threshold. "What on earth are you doing? Are you feeling entirely well?"

"Perfectly well, Doctor, as I am sure a man of your profession will immediately attest."

"Then what on earth has gotten into you?"

"Time, as ever, is of the essence, dear Watson."

"Time for what, Holmes?" I asked, looking on aghast as my companion flung garment after garment into the air.

"Quickly now," Holmes replied, as he heaved a modestly sized suitcase from the top of my wardrobe and proceeded to throw it behind him. "Or we shall miss our train."

I ducked, the suitcase only narrowly missing my head and landing none the worse for wear in our sitting room.

"Our train? Holmes!" I cried. "Have you lost your senses? What is the meaning of all this?"

"You will need some warm clothes, Watson, and probably a scarf or two," he replied, ejecting said items in my vague direction. "Some stout boots…"

These I managed to catch, before I decided enough was enough. Striding into my bedroom, I had every intention of accosting Holmes in the midst of his casual vandalism when he turned and quite caught me off guard.

"A trip, Watson," he said, his eyes glittering and eager. "We are bound for the country."

"We are?"

Holmes nodded. "How well do you know Cambridgeshire?"

"I cannot say well, but—"

Holmes clapped his hands on my shoulders in a comradely fashion. "Fear not, Doctor, for we shall be acquainted with it soon enough."

"And where might *your* case be?"

Holmes raised a finger, bidding me to indulge him a moment as he took a second glance at his watch. "Already packed and waiting downstairs. Anticipating this little adventure, I planned ahead."

He then swept from my room, scooping up an array of garments as he went, and began to stuff them in my suitcase.

"I have telegraphed ahead, so we are expected. We will need a cab to take us to the station."

I watched agog, quite wrong-footed by unfolding events. "Once more, Holmes, if you would. You have me at a loss."

He turned and looked over his shoulder at me, paused in the act of shoving an extra scarf into my suitcase. "Our answers lie at Saint Agatha's, Watson."

"The boarding school? The one Graves has been sending money to?" I remembered it from the deposit slips Holmes had lifted from Graves's pocket.

"The very place," said Holmes. "As soon as I discovered Mr Graves's association with the school I made sure to contact them."

"And what do you propose we do when we get there?" I asked, starting to gather up my belongings from where Holmes had thrown them so casually.

"All in good time, Watson. For now, I shall have Mrs Hudson find us a cab." He then scurried out of the door, pausing only to snatch up his hat and stick. As his hurried footsteps resounded on the stairs, he called out. "Come along now, Watson. We haven't got all day!"

I sighed, quickly grabbing what I could, and followed my friend.

CHAPTER FIFTEEN

LEAVING THE METROPOLIS

At Holmes's request, Mrs Hudson had secured the services of a clarence, so both our belongings and ourselves could be easily accommodated.

After paying the driver in advance, Holmes said little more as we drove through the streets of London. During my mental solitude, I was able to reconsider all the facts of the case thus far. It appeared likely now that Damian Graves, although not the murderer, was involved in the ghastly killings at the Grayson Gallery, or at the very least, knew the person responsible. His relationship to this individual, a woman it seemed, was still unknown, as was how the earlier deaths related to the demise of the grand duke's manservant, Grigori Andropov, the only connecting factor being the strange markings found both on the painting of the Undying Man at the gallery and the manservant's flesh.

As I mulled what we knew over and over, I paid scarce attention to our journey but in seemingly short order we reached Charing Cross station and boarded a train bound for Cambridgeshire.

We sat in companionable silence, Holmes and I, and as he read a newspaper he had brought along for the ride, I became content to look from my window as urban austerity gave way to the entirely more bucolic vistas of the countryside.

I have often considered the air and openness of the English countryside something of a panacea in all matters medicinal, and after an hour I began to feel the unease of the last few days slowly leave me. Deciding it had been quiet for long enough, I remarked as much to Holmes.

"It calms the humours, don't you think?"

"I see nothing calming about it, Watson."

I frowned. "Surely you can appreciate the lure of nature and the rural idyll?"

Holmes paused in reading his copy of *The Times*, and conceded to lower it so he could stare at me over the fold in the paper. "There is nothing so far from idyllic as the countryside, Watson. Where you see an arboreal paradise, I see only isolation and the propensity for secrets. How many ills have we seen go unremarked and unpunished in a pastoral town or village?"

I conceded there had been more than one occasion, but nonetheless my enthusiasm remained undimmed. The same could not be said of Holmes.

"No, I do not have the romantic notions you speak of, Watson. I much prefer the city. For all its vice and perfidy, London is protected by the law, its agencies of justice close at hand. Out here," Holmes gestured to the verdant pastures passing by our carriage window, "there are gulfs of the unknown and the untamed."

"A cheery thought, Holmes," I said, my mind turning towards our business once more. "So, what do you hope to find at Saint Agatha's? Some further knowledge of Graves's involvement with the school, perhaps?"

"The beginning of a thread, Watson," he said, neatly folding his newspaper and passing it to me.

"What am I looking for, Holmes?" I asked, quickly leafing through the newspaper but finding nothing particularly pertinent. The grand duke's visit was, of course, assiduously reported on, but nothing further caught my attention.

"Page two," said Holmes, lighting up his pipe as he absently stared out of the window, "a death at the school."

I found the article and as I read, I was reminded of the piece remarked upon by Mrs Hudson. Were they one and the same?

"A teacher at Saint Agatha's was found several weeks ago hanging by the neck. Her body has yet to be claimed by her kin and still resides in the morgue," I said, relating the story, but not word for word. "An apparent suicide. Ghastly," I added, "though what has this to do with our current case, Holmes?"

"I'm not sure yet, Watson, but the Graves connection to the school cannot be overlooked."

"You mentioned you have sent a telegram to the school?"

"Indeed, Watson, to the headmistress, whose brisk reply suggested they would be accommodating with our enquiries."

"About Graves or the suicide, Holmes?"

"Both."

"You think they are connected?"

"I don't believe in coincidence."

"Do you think it's foul play?"

"I take great care not to make any assumptions without first determining facts, Watson, but I should like very much to see where it was that the unfortunate schoolmistress took her own life and learn more of Graves's association with the place. Anything further will depend entirely upon my findings."

I returned the newspaper, which Holmes folded and put away. "What do you know of Saint Agatha's?" he asked.

"Very little," I confessed. "Only what I've just read. It is a girls' school, is it not?"

"It is."

Holmes held my gaze and I latched onto the implication at once. "You don't think…?"

"It is not beyond possibility, but merely a theory until proven or otherwise."

I stroked my moustache at the idea of our murderess having been, or possibly still being, a pupil or teacher at Saint Agatha's.

"What do they teach at this school?" I asked.

"Reading, writing, arithmetic," Holmes replied. "And the usual feminine accomplishments of painting and music."

"It doesn't stretch to gymnastics then, at least not the calibre of which we saw in Tavistock Street?"

"Improbable," said Holmes.

"And jumping across buildings in the dead of night?"

"Almost certainly not."

"What about fencing?"

Holmes smiled, "Well, I believe they also learn needlework."

I laughed, despite the grimness of the case in which we were embroiled. The rest of the journey passed without further talk of murder or mysterious figures in black. Instead, we discussed literature, the current state of the theatre in London and other matters entirely more salubrious. All the while though I could see the cogs of Holmes's mind working, and knew that even as he engaged in what he would consider trivial conversation his hindbrain would be analysing, theorising and considering facts. I knew not what we would find at Saint Agatha's, but everything I had learned suggested the existence of something lurking just beneath the surface.

* * *

It was late by the time we reached our destination, my back and legs stiff from the long journey, first by train and then by carriage from the station. We passed through a black wrought-iron gate, which provided the only access through the high wall that encircled the grounds of the school. Both showed signs of dilapidation, and I wondered if Saint Agatha's was in some need of revivification. What I took to be a groundskeeper, given the man's rustic and hardy attire, admitted us through the rusting gate, having evidently stayed at his post beyond his usual hours given the lateness of our arrival, but nodding politely as our carriage drove past, before shutting the gates behind us.

A broad and winding road led to the school itself, which sat in well-tended grounds. The road itself was uneven at first, making our carriage's wheels rattle, but efforts were clearly being made to rectify the problem for our passage grew smoother once beyond the outer reaches of the grounds.

Even with night drawing in, I could discern the school itself, a large building with a set of wide steps leading up to the main entrance. There were also several smaller buildings surrounding it, and a modest-sized chapel. Most of the windows were dark, but there was a light burning in the east wing of the main building and over the entrance. I fancied I saw several small faces pressed up against windowpanes, no doubt pupils in their dormitories, but the shadows were fleeting and as we got closer I lost sight of them.

As our carriage reached the main entrance and Holmes and I alighted, the door opened and a stern-looking woman stepped out.

"Dr Watson, I presume?" she asked, approaching me with a hand extended.

I doffed my hat and shook her hand. She had a tough, formal way about her that brooked no challenge and I immediately saw how well suited she would be to her chosen profession. "Indeed, I am. Good evening."

"And this must be…" she began.

"Sherlock Holmes," said my companion. "Good evening."

"Miss Marion Blanchard," she said. "I am the headmistress here at Saint Agatha's."

Although clearly formidable, she was not what I had imagined. Far from an old spinster, she appeared quite vibrant, if a little severe for one so young. Her hair was dark and tied up tightly in a bun at the back of her head. She had a long neck and pleasant features, with large brown eyes that scarcely blinked. I found her gaze to be quite intense, and considered the fact she would be familiar with staring down recalcitrant pupils and not two London gentlemen. Yes, she was young for her position, but I also detected strength in her character.

"I imagine you gentlemen are fatigued from your journey," said Miss Blanchard. "I have made arrangements with our groundskeeper, Mr Derrick, for you to take a room in his lodgings for the night. Our cook has prepared a light supper. It's not much, but I hope to your liking."

I thanked Miss Blanchard, and expressed my appreciation at her thoughtfulness, and that any meal, however small, would be welcome.

Miss Blanchard nodded. "Very well then," she said, turning on her heel and leading us across the grounds in what I assumed was the direction of the groundskeeper's lodgings.

"Might I enquire, Miss Blanchard," Holmes ventured, "when we might see where your colleague tragically met her end? I had hoped to do so this evening."

Miss Blanchard paused, long enough to suggest that although prepared for the subject Holmes had raised, the mere mention of it still brought her considerable discomfort. She turned, her composure intact, but with an air of resignation.

"I am afraid that is out of the question, Mr Holmes. The pupils are in their dormitories and I have no wish to see them disturbed any more than they have been already, since this dreadful business."

"Of course."

"I can have someone call for you first thing in the morning and I will show you what it is you wish to see," she said, and I noted the language she used, that she had failed to mention the name of the teacher who had died or even make a reference to where the ghastly event took place, never mind the event itself.

No further words were exchanged until we reached the edge of the field where the groundskeeper waited to take us the rest of the way, at which point Miss Blanchard issued a short "goodnight" before returning to the school.

Our host was the same man who had opened the entrance gate for us. He had a pale green shirt, a thick woollen jacket over the top of it, rugged-looking brown wool trousers and wore a simple flat cap. Stray wisps of greyish hair peeked out of the edges like strands of cotton wool. His boots were stout, made of leather and went halfway up his calf. A stick was clenched in his right hand, which was gnarled with age, much like the man himself.

"Don't mind her," said the groundskeeper, Derrick, as he led us towards a small but homely-looking cottage. "She's been here all of her life has Miss Blanchard, since she were a pupil herself."

"As have you, sir?" I guessed.

"Aye," said Derrick, "though I didn't do my learning here," he added, moving with the leisurely gait that some men of advancing years adopt. I found I liked the man instantly, with his easy manner and cheerful demeanour, and was a little envious of the rural haven he had made for himself.

"My father was groundskeeper here before me, and his father before him. I have seen them all come and go," he said with the ready ease of someone used to relating the history of his life and family.

"Did you know the deceased?" asked Holmes. *The Times* had been scant on detail, with no name given for the dead woman. Perhaps it was no longer considered newsworthy.

A sigh escaped Mr Derrick's lips, and I sensed a weariness in him that had risen like a shadow to eclipse his bright mood. "A terrible, terrible business," he said, lightly shaking his head. "Mrs Sidley, yes, I knew her."

"Mrs?" I asked. "She was a married woman?"

"Used to be, as I understand it. I heard her husband died of consumption."

"A wretched illness," I replied.

"How would you describe Mrs Sidley? Her manner and disposition?" asked Holmes.

"I confess, I never warmed to her," admitted Derrick, and I found the simple absence of any attempt to dissemble refreshing. "But she dedicated her life to her pupils, even if her methods were somewhat stricter than most."

"How so, Mr Derrick?" I asked.

"Oh you know, she applied the cane a little too easily, I felt. There wasn't one girl she didn't bring to tears at some point or other, but it wasn't my place to judge. All of them were afraid of her. She wore these shoes, you see," he said, and gestured to his own rugged boots, "they had metal tips on the toes and on the heel. She made this… *clacking* sound as she walked; that's how folks knew she was coming, I suppose. I used to hear it when I was in the field, *clack, clack, clack*, all the way from the schoolyard as she stalked back and forth. Quite the racket, it was. How the girls would scurry when they heard that sound. I can't say whether she liked the idea of that, because her face was always set like a storm, and she was quick to punish the pupils."

"Did you ever see her do so?" I asked.

Derrick shook his head. "I saw the aftermath once, but it was no business of mine. I know what's good for me, Doctor. I keep to my duties and that's that."

"And what are your duties specifically?" Holmes asked.

"I tend to the grounds and to the rose garden by the chapel. I mind the gate too. Miss Blanchard tells me when she's expecting folk and I make sure to let them in."

"The work on the road; we noticed it was a tad derelict near the gate but got smoother as we approached the school," said I. "Was that also you, sir?"

"Oh no," said Derrick, dismissing the notion with a wave of his hand. "Labourers were brought in to tend to that." He sighed, somewhat wistfully. "This old school… she is in need of some tending too, but it's beyond me to set right."

"You mentioned that Mrs Sidley's punishment of the girls was swift," said Holmes, returning to the previous topic, "but that you never saw the act itself?"

"I heard them shouting sometimes, wailing really," Derrick explained.

"During a reprimand?" I asked.

Derrick nodded, staring into the distance, and I reckoned he was revisiting the recollections.

"And in your opinion, Mr Derrick, did this corporal punishment ever get out of hand? Judging by what you heard," asked Holmes, clearly intrigued. "I have no wish to besmirch the reputation of a dead woman, but you said yourself that Mrs Sidley was strict. Not an unusual trait amongst the teaching profession, and you must have seen many teachers come and go, so I can only conclude that you believed Mrs Sidley to be singular in her application of the cane."

Mr Derrick paused before answering. His pace slowed a little as if the incident he had been asked to dredge from the sea of his memory was somehow weighing him down. He licked his lips, the words of his imminent confession having left them dry.

"I remember one occasion when it was really bad… You must understand," he said, "most of the pupils knew what Mrs Sidley was like. She was widowed young, before she came to the school, and had a hardness about her. The pupils respected her, I think, or at least they feared her. The day was sure to come, however, when one of them didn't. I only saw the girl twice. She had fair hair, a pretty girl, I'd say, though she had the look of someone much older than her years. Very stern she was. I thought it was pride, though I believe Mrs Sidley saw it as insolence. They fought, the two of them. I don't mean one raised hand to the other, though I would wager Mrs Sidley did so on more than one occasion. As I said, most of the girls felt the sting of her cane. No, I mean a battle of wills. I overheard Miss Blanchard discussing the matter with another teacher. She was bright, the girl, by all accounts. I think it surprised them.

"Most of these girls, they come here to be educated away from the towns, and know little of the world. But she was different. I don't think Mrs Sidley liked that, to be challenged. I never saw the girl's parents, and don't believe she had any, or at least I never saw or heard mention of them, so there was no one to go to when she overstepped her bounds. She just showed up one day and that's when I first clapped eyes on her. She was alone, but seemed not to mind it."

"Do you happen to know her name, Mr Derrick?" asked Holmes.

"I can't recall, sir. My memory isn't very good for names."

"She arrived alone?" I said. "Was there no one with her at

all? No guardian?" In a moment of what I hoped was inspiration I described Damian Graves, but Mr Derrick shook his head. "Perhaps you might have seen him in the school, in an office or some such," I pressed.

Again, Mr Derrick shook his head. "My duties don't give much call for me going into the school buildings or talking to the pupils. Miss Blanchard encourages me to keep to myself and that's fine by me." He paused. "That's why I was unprepared when it happened."

I frowned, losing the thread of the groundskeeper's account.

"When you saw the girl again," said Holmes.

"Yes, sir," Derrick confirmed. "About two weeks ago. But let me tell you inside. I think I might need a cup of tea first."

CHAPTER SIXTEEN

THE CONFESSION OF MR DERRICK

The groundskeeper's cottage was homely, and Mr Derrick had made it his own. The wooden furniture was well used and rounded with age, but stout and unyielding in spite of the years. A small stove sat in one corner, and Derrick quickly set about putting to use boiling water for tea, after he had shed his coat and hat at the door. The cottage was warm and comfortable, a low fire flickering in the hearth. A light spread of cold meats and bread had been left on the table, the meal mentioned by Miss Blanchard, I assumed.

Holmes and I accepted the tea when it was offered, though I suspect my companion did so out of courtesy more than any desire to drink it, before Mr Derrick then joined us at the table. I ate heartily, though Holmes didn't touch a morsel, whilst our host only picked at a little bread. He then took a deep draught of the tea before resuming his story.

"I had been out most of the morning cutting the grass, when I returned to find the girl on my doorstep. She was in a frightful state and babbling. I have no idea what she was saying.

I tried to ask her what was wrong, but she kept muttering."

I gave Holmes a furtive look. He was staring intently at Mr Derrick and betrayed nothing of his thoughts.

"How did she appear?" he asked. "Leave out no detail, however small, Mr Derrick."

Derrick rubbed at the stubble on his chin. "She had been crying. There were tear marks down her face, and her hands were red raw. She held them together, between the folds in her skirt," he mimicked this gesture with his own hands, clasping them together, "and when she let them go that's when I saw the blood."

Holmes raised an eyebrow.

"It was hers, sir. There were several long straight cuts down both of her palms, and she winced at the pain of them. I was about to ask what had happened, when I saw she had a sharp stone in one hand. At first I thought she might have cut herself with it, but the wounds on her palms looked too long and not jagged enough for that. It was a cane, I felt sure, what had done it, but it must've been a fearsome beating to make her bleed like that." Derrick took a sip of his tea, and I suspect he wished that it were something stronger.

"And the stone? A keepsake, perhaps an improvised weapon?" asked Holmes.

"She scratched something on my doorstep with it. By the looks of the mess she had made, she'd been doing it for a while and only stopped when she saw me coming back."

"A word, some message or symbol?" I asked.

Derrick shook his head again. "I can't rightly say. Just looked like scratches to me, and I didn't ask what it meant. She was angry, though, that much I could tell. I didn't know what to do. No pupil had ever come to my cottage before. I was about to go and find help, when she sprang to her feet.

"She had a look in her eye, which I don't mind telling you, sirs, well, it gave me pause it did. It was like something changed in her. This look… it wasn't fear or misery, it wasn't even defiance or anger, it was… it's hard to explain." Derrick's face screwed up as he fought for the right words. In the end he settled on a different memory to help make his point.

"My father, God rest his soul, he took me to Cornwall when I was a boy. It was the only trip we ever went on together, and it was to bury my mother who hailed from there. We spent three nights in Falmouth, and every night, just as the fishing boats were coming in to harbour, I would watch the tides. On the last night, us having buried my mother during the day, I went out again. I saw a drifter come in, its nets bulging, and amongst the catch was the biggest fish I had ever seen. My father said it was a basking shark. Its flanks shimmered like wet silver in the moonlight, but it was the eyes that struck me. Cold, they were, and black. I shivered when I saw those eyes. That's what it reminded me of, the look the girl had, like the eyes of that shark. I don't mind admitting that I shivered again, just like that night in Falmouth, when I saw her eyes."

He took another sip of his tea, and I noticed a slight tremor in his hands. "She went off after that, though I don't know to where."

"Did you speak of the matter to Miss Blanchard?" I asked.

Derrick looked down into his cup. "Miss Blanchard said she would take the matter in hand. I stayed out of it. I didn't see what harm could come of doing that."

"No harm at all," said Holmes, though his tone had an edge to it that I think our kindly groundskeeper missed.

"Best put a few logs on the fire," said Derrick, rising, "I can feel a chill in the air tonight."

The fire crackled as the logs were added, a bright flare briefly illuminating the sitting room and lengthening our shadows before it settled down again.

"I should like to see what the girl scratched on your doorstep, if I may, Mr Derrick?" asked Holmes.

"Of course. I'll retire to my bed, if you don't mind. I've an early start in the morning. I've set up a room for you at the back of the cottage. It's small, but comfortable."

I told Mr Derrick that we didn't mind at all and thanked him for his courtesy, before following Holmes outside. My companion crouched down and took out a box of matches, then lit one and directed its light at Mr Derrick's doorstep, illuminating a series of small grooves in the stone.

"I can barely see anything," I admitted to Holmes, squinting.

Holmes pocketed the matches and pressed his fingers into the grooves.

"Can you make out anything, Holmes?"

My companion did not answer at first. Having evidently seen everything he needed to, he rose to his feet, snuffed out the match and declared, "I believe I can, Watson. The marks bear some resemblance to the script we first saw at the gallery, hidden under the first layer of paint, and again carved into Grigori Andropov's flesh."

"A connection then."

"Indeed."

"But what of it? What now?"

"Now, Watson?" he said, abruptly turning around to face me, "I shall follow Mr Derrick's example and retire for the evening. I urge you to do the same. It has been a long day."

"This girl, Holmes. Do you think she had something to do with what happened to Mrs Sidley?" I asked. "For one so young to be involved in something so heinous… surely not."

"I make no assumptions at this stage, Watson. None.

Certainly, we must discover her identity. Even with that information, several pieces yet remain."

CHAPTER SEVENTEEN

ONE FOR THE NOOSE

The next morning we rose early. I found I could barely sleep during the night, my dreams fraught with the false memories of sharks and their cold, dead eyes staring at me from their deep and silent places.

As wretched as I felt, Holmes's mood bordered on ebullient.

"Do you know, Watson," he said, as we left the cottage and headed towards the school, "I believe your theory about the beneficial effects of the country on the humours could have some basis in fact after all!" He took a deep breath of the clear morning air. The mist was still rising off the fields and shrouded the school in fog, though one utterly unlike what we were both used to seeing in London.

I grumbled, my own humours decidedly out of balance, and trudged after Holmes to the school.

Miss Blanchard was waiting for us at the main entrance, clearly as much a chaperone as a guide, and bid us a good morning before ushering us inside. Holmes said nothing of the conversation with Mr Derrick the previous evening, seemingly content to exchange mild, if slightly awkward, pleasantries with Miss Blanchard on matters ranging from the clement weather to the history of the school.

Much like the road leading up to it, there were signs of disrepair within the school too. As we passed through the various corridors, I saw little of the pupils who, Miss Blanchard informed us, were having their morning lessons. I formed the distinct impression she wished the matter of our visit resolved quickly and quietly, and with every step we took that brought us closer to the place where Mrs Sidley had taken her own life, she grew more agitated.

"I do not know what you hope to find," she said as we reached the door to what I assumed had been Mrs Sidley's office. "Everything has been left as it was, though." She unlocked the door and pushed it open. "Please be respectful of her things, and don't wander the halls."

"I must ask you, Miss Blanchard," said Holmes, as she was about to be on her way, "who found her and in what manner?"

She paled a little in that moment, and before she gave her answer I felt I knew what she would say. "I did, Mr Holmes. Mrs Sidley would sometimes work late into the night. Despite her faults, there was no one who toiled like she did. I think it helped her to forget."

"Her husband?" I asked.

Mrs Blanchard nodded. "I believe so, yes."

"It was evening when you found her then?" asked Holmes.

"No. I went to my bed, with Mrs Sidley still at her desk. She was drinking a strong, bitter tea that kept her alert well into the evening hours. I bid her goodnight and she gave a brusque reply, barely looking up from her cup. I had learned not to take offence at her ways. I found her the next morning." Miss Blanchard was wringing her hands now and I had to fight the urge to go and comfort her, but her gaze held a warning that she would brook no such display of weakness, not here, in her school.

"Tell me, Miss Blanchard," Holmes pressed, and I wanted to reproach him for his apparent callousness in the pursuit of truth, "did she seem to you an unhappy woman?"

Her composure slowly returning, Miss Blanchard paused to consider the question. "I believe she did, yes, Mr Holmes. But I must reaffirm she was a dedicated teacher, whatever might be said of her methods."

"And did she strike you as someone who might take their own life?"

Again, she considered the question, the sheer resolve it took to answer it written plainly on her face. "She wallowed in her misery, Mr Holmes, and that's the honest truth of it. But Mrs Sidley was many things, and a coward was not amongst them."

"I see."

"I do not believe she would do such a thing, certainly not here at the school. No, Mr Holmes, Dr Watson, I do not. Yet, I am confronted with the proof of my own eyes, and it is a sight I shall never forget, though I wish it were otherwise." Miss Blanchard raised her chin a little, perhaps out of pride, perhaps in defiance of her own grief. "If that is all?"

Holmes said it was, and I was relieved at the end of the interrogation, however mild it had been.

"I shall return within the hour," Miss Blanchard informed us. "I trust that will be ample time to conduct your work?"

"Perfectly ample, Miss Blanchard," I said, and we entered the office of the not so dearly departed Mrs Sidley. It was a sparsely appointed office, well ordered but utterly bereft of warmth or comfort. I had seen more inviting cells in Pentonville, such was its bare austerity.

A little paperwork—marking and the like—sat upon the

desk where Mrs Sidley had left it. A chair sat behind it and appeared functional and stout. It looked particularly hard and unyielding and I could imagine Mrs Sidley enduring it, rather than sitting in it, straight-backed, glowering at her pupils, their schoolwork like offerings to appease a cruel deity.

A cabinet stood in one corner of the room, though a cursory examination revealed nothing of interest to my companion. The only meagre light came from a small window behind the desk, shuttered at present, though the catches for the shutters looked seldom used and I assumed the room was usually swathed in shadows.

I noticed a lamp, doused of course, its glass housing cold to the touch. A bookcase flanked the desk, opposite the cabinet, a thin veneer of dust like a funerary veil upon the spines of all the books.

In addition to the papers on Mrs Sidley's desk, there was a cup and saucer. Both were small and without decoration. I stooped over it to peer inside the cup, then sniffed the tea dregs within, which had dried to a dark stain.

"Smells like kippers," I said, screwing up my face.

Holmes licked his finger, then used it to wet the stain and dabbed it experimentally against his tongue.

"A black-leafed variety," he said. "Quite bitter. Lapsang, from the Wuyi region of Fujian."

I glanced at my companion, amazed at the breadth of his knowledge. "I've never heard of it, Holmes."

"It's not difficult to procure, but quite unusual," he explained. "This variety has an incongruous aftertaste. A tincture of *passiflora*, I believe. Passion flower."

"A herbal sedative," I said, familiar with its usage.

"Indeed, Watson."

"An aid to sleep, perhaps?" I suggested.

"Or something less innocent..." countered Holmes. He began to examine the other objects on Mrs Sidley's desk. The only personal items were a picture frame and a small cloth-bound journal. The frame was made from simple brass. Modestly decorative, it held a photograph of a woman I assumed to be Mrs Sidley. She was not exactly how I had pictured her. I expected a towering woman, a gorgon of sorts, but what I saw in the photograph was someone small, young and slight. She could not have been much taller than most of her pupils. Her eyes, though, even in the faded photograph, were piercing and bright. She possessed a fierceness that I think must have made up for her diminutive stature and enhanced her presence far beyond her mere size. She stood ramrod straight—I had known decorated sergeant majors with less regimented posture—her chin raised proudly and her hands clasped in front of her.

Alongside her was a man I took to be her late husband. Much like his wife, he looked austere and serious. He wore a light suit, his hands behind his back. Staring at the faded image, I could not picture either of them smiling, for it would be such an incongruous expression on faces almost chiselled from stone.

As I examined the photograph, Holmes had been leafing through the journal. "What do you make of this, Watson?" he said, handing me the book at an open page.

It was plainly a diary of sorts, comprising notes about the various pupils, the lessons Mrs Sidley intended to impart, attendance and the like. One note in particular caught my eye, and I assumed it was this to which Holmes intended to direct my attention.

The girl continues to be obstinate. Today her insolence grew such that she thought to challenge me in front of the other pupils. I have no doubt she was mouthing obscenities under her breath as I applied the cane.

I shall have order in my own classroom, irrespective of her benefactor's influence. She is a child, admittedly a gifted one, but I will not suffer her blatant disregard for my authority and general disrespect. I am determined to beat this wanton defiance out of her.

This evening I have arranged a special punishment, the scrubbing of the refectory floor, and the washing and cleaning of every dish, cup, knife and fork therein. I estimate it will take her all night, and I intend to supervise every moment of it.

The girl shall come to understand who is in charge. She will learn respect and defer to her betters. To that end, I have asked Mr Derrick to procure several more suitable canes, for I have a strong belief I shall be in need of them before the year is out.

"A battle of wills, it would seem," I said, setting the journal down again. "This benefactor, it can only be Graves surely? His influence, the money he was giving to the school?"

"Quite the contrary, Watson. It could be one of any number of benefactors. There is no outward evidence that this is Graves." Holmes paused, deep in thought. His gaze was on the shuttered window and the weak beams of light it admitted. "What do you see, Watson? Cast your eye upwards."

Following the direction of my companion's gaze, my eyes alighted upon a low beam, one of the several that supported the ceiling.

"Do you notice anything unusual?" Holmes asked.

I squinted. "There is a mark on this one," I replied, indicating the beam directly above the desk where we were standing.

"Indeed. A lightening of the wood, as if from wear and tear, though I think something else made this mark."

"A rope," I said, catching on.

"Friction to be precise. If you would, Watson…" Holmes set himself at one end of the desk and took a firm hold. Understanding my companion's plan, I grabbed the other end, Holmes pulling and I pushing, and between us we managed to move the heavy desk aside.

"Good lord, Holmes," I said, my face hot with effort. "A tad robust."

"Not unlike Mrs Sidley, from every account." Holmes returned to stand beneath the beam and carefully scrutinised it.

After a few additional moments of introspection, he began to cast his gaze about the floor, where, for the first time, I noticed a great many scuffmarks. I remembered what Mr Derrick had said about Mrs Sidley's shoes; the loud clacking heels that presaged her approach and sent her pupils scattering.

Holmes moved in a widening gyre, beginning at a fixed point and spiralling outwards. His attention moved to the desk, then to the chair, then back to the floor. He sank to his knees, producing a small magnifying glass from his jacket pocket at the same time, looking hither and thither with his instrument.

"What is it, Holmes? What have you seen?"

"It is entirely what I *haven't* seen, Watson, that I find most interesting." He sprang back to his feet. "Here," he said, jabbing his finger at the desk, "and here," at the chair.

"I don't follow, Holmes. What am I missing?"

"It is what Mrs Sidley's furniture is missing, Watson. Observe. The floor of this room is marred by umpteen heel marks, a fact that leads me to believe that the deceased was prone to pacing. Not only that, but it was her habit to wear a pair of rather unique shoes, as we already know. Now, consider the beam." He gestured to it. "How high would you say that is, Watson?"

"No less than nine feet," I said, having to gauge by eye.

"Eight feet and nine inches," said Holmes.

"Not an insignificant height," I remarked.

"Indeed not, Watson. Neither desk nor chair has any mark upon it, which strongly suggests that either Mrs Sidley removed her shoes to stand upon one or the other to reach the beam, or that she did not stand upon them at all. I find the former explanation unlikely. For if she were contemplating suicide, I cannot imagine she would have had the presence of mind to remove her shoes, though I am sure Miss Blanchard can corroborate whether she was shod when her body was found. The latter then seems more probable, but insists the question, how did Mrs Sidley hang herself without the elevation of either her desk or her chair?"

I scratched my head. "I cannot say, Holmes."

"The markings on the wooden beam are more prominent here," he said, indicating the left side. "And here, scratched into the floor a little farther to the left of the beam is another mark, this one longer and inconsistent with those left by Mrs Sidley's shoes."

I duly inspected both markings and did, indeed, find them to be distinctive just as Holmes had described, though I sincerely doubt I would have noticed them had Holmes not pointed them out.

"What does it all mean?" I asked.

Holmes smiled grimly. "Much like Miss Blanchard, I do not believe Mrs Sidley took her own life. I believe she was murdered, but was first administered a soporific without her knowledge to make her pliant."

"The *passiflora*," I said.

Holmes nodded. "The strong and fragrant lapsang tea would have masked any unfamiliar scent or flavour. Thus sedated, a noose was then tied about her neck before she was hoisted up over the beam."

"Good lord, Holmes. That's appalling."

"Murder always is, Watson. Here, these scuff marks are from a second individual, almost certainly the murderer, bracing themselves to hoist Mrs Sidley off the ground."

"Not an insignificant feat, even given her small stature," I said.

Holmes nodded. "A strong man could have accomplished such a task easily enough or a small woman, given the use of the beam as a hoist. After ensnaring the unfortunate Mrs Sidley, the herbal tincture robbing her of any resistance, it would have been relatively straightforward for our murderer to have tied off the rope to the leg of the desk."

Holmes crouched down to inspect it.

"Here," he said, allowing me enough room to lean in and see what he had found, "a faint mark in the wood. Evidence of friction, not unlike that which we saw on the beam."

"Well," I said, straightening again, "that desk certainly feels heavy enough to bear the weight of a woman of Mrs Sidley's size."

"I concur, Watson. I imagine she would have awoken before the end, but by then it would have been too late, her struggles in vain. She was, to all intents and purposes, hanged by the neck until dead."

"Ghastly, Holmes. But surely the manner in which Mrs Sidley was discovered would have aroused suspicion of foul play?"

"I can think of but one possible explanation to obscure the fact that the murderer used such a method of lethal elevation, an explanation that a simple visit to the morgue will almost certainly confirm."

"What explanation is that, Holmes?"

"Once certain all life had left Mrs Sidley, I believe the

murderer tied a second noose to the beam and slipped it around the victim's neck. Easy enough for even a competent coroner to miss, but I am certain that Mrs Sidley's neck will bear not one, but two marks of ligature, overlapping but not entirely contiguous with one another. Once the second rope was secured, thus taking the weight of the body, the first, the hoist, could be cut and removed, thus obscuring any obvious suspicion of foul play."

I rubbed my forehead at the sheer fiendishness of it all. "Utterly devilish, Holmes. But how would the murderer be able to reach such a height in order to tie and hang the second rope?"

"First we must rule out the desk as a potential means of elevation. It is approximately two foot six inches in height. Given the height of the beam, in order to reach up high enough to tie a second rope, our murderer would have had to be at least six foot three inches tall. However, by fully extending the arms, one might gain an additional ten inches or so, which leaves our murderer at a minimum height of five foot five inches tall."

"The approximate height of our figure in black," I said.

"Indeed, an individual approximately five foot five inches tall and standing upon the desk, arms fully extended, could reasonably reach a height of around eight foot nine inches."

"High enough to reach the beam," I said.

"Or a little higher if our murderer were, say, five foot seven inches, rather than five foot five. Not impossible, but difficult. Fully extended, standing atop the desk, without shoes to provide additional height as there is no mark to suggest it, it would have been far from easy to tie off a knot."

"Granted, but then what are you suggesting, Holmes?"

"Allow me to explain. Do you remember the figure in black?"

"Vividly, Holmes."

"And do you also recall the manner in which she evaded us on Tavistock Street?"

"Like a spider, the way she scaled that wall."

"A feat far more impressive than climbing up a simple wooden beam," he said, and tapped his foot against a beam that fed up the wall to those bracing the ceiling above. "Indeed, I dare venture even you or I could at least climb part of the way without any training or acrobatic skill whatsoever."

"I do hope you're not expecting a demonstration, Holmes."

"Rest assured I am not, Watson. What would seem inconceivable to any ordinary person would be natural to someone in possession of the acrobatic abilities we witnessed. Furthermore, look here," said Holmes, and gestured to a specific part of the beam with his stick. "A handprint, small and barely visible, the size consistent with that of a female."

And now Holmes had pointed it out, I did see it.

"Good heavens! Is it the same killer, or at least one who possesses the same uncanny ability? But what of the second rope?"

Holmes arched an eyebrow. "How do you remove the murder weapon from the scene of the crime without anyone seeing you do it?"

I considered the question, but could find no plausible answer and told Holmes as much.

Holmes stamped down hard on one of the floorboards and the edge sprang up by half an inch.

"When I paced the room earlier, this board gave more than one might expect…" He crouched down on one knee, his pocketknife already in hand, and proceeded to prise the board loose with the blade. It came up surprisingly easily, revealing a small compartment beneath. As soon as I saw what was inside, I had the answer to Holmes's question.

"You do not remove the murder weapon at all," I said, and saw a rope, easily long enough to hang poor Mrs Sidley, and a thick nail about which the murderer had tied it off.

"A gymnasium rope, Watson," said Holmes, "easy enough to explain in a school. I fully expect a second such rope was found tied around Mrs Sidley's neck when she was discovered by Miss Blanchard."

The possibility that someone at the school could be responsible for such an act was almost too awful to contemplate. That the act in itself had been premeditated and calculated to such a degree was genuinely disturbing and again my thoughts turned to the lithe figure in black, almost certainly female. The ages of the pupils at Saint Agatha's ranged, according to Miss Blanchard, from ten to sixteen.

The evidence found beneath our feet was certainly damning, but perhaps more surprising was what had been carved on the underside of the floorboard, only now revealed as Holmes turned it over to examine it.

"What is it, Holmes? Some form of cursive script…"

"We have seen it several times before, Watson, though, admittedly, its meaning escaped me on each occasion. First, at the Grayson Gallery, the symbol described in pentimento, and then upon Grigori Andropov's flesh."

"Thus connecting the poisoning at the gallery to the demise of Duke Konstantin's poor manservant."

"Quite so. But there has been another occasion before this one when we have seen this very mark, or, at least, the makings of it. On the doorstep of Mr Derrick."

"The fair-haired girl, the one Mrs Sidley had such issue with. Good lord, Holmes, could it really be that this girl conspired to kill all of those gallery patrons, then went on to murder Grigori Andropov, having already done away with Mrs Sidley?"

"Given the evidence at hand, Watson, it is a plausible working theory that the perpetrator of these crimes is one and the same, our figure in black. Whether it is the fair-haired girl described by

Mr Derrick or some agent acting on her behalf cannot be proven beyond all doubt at this stage."

"But why carve this strange script at all? Do you think it could be a message?"

I took a closer look at what had been carved into the floorboard, and was able to see the similarities between it and the other symbols, but could not decipher it.

"It's Cyrillic," said Holmes, doubtless noticing my confusion. "Characters of the alphabet, to be precise, though in this case reversed," said Holmes, darting over to the desk to scoop up the picture frame. He then quickly returned to his previous position and proceeded to angle the frame alongside the carving so the reflection in the glass revealed the true aspect of the characters, albeit faintly.

"Can you decipher it?"

"Of course," said Holmes. "I freely admit, the reversal of the characters and the fragmentary nature of the earlier messages confounded me at first. In fact, it wasn't until I saw what had been scratched into Mr Derrick's doorstep that I realised the provenance of said characters and was able to deduce the fact they were reversed. Here," he added, pointing to what was carved into the floorboard, "it is rendered in full and as such, I can translate it."

"And what does it say, Holmes?" I asked, enrapt, for surely we were now at the cusp of a significant breakthrough in the case.

"Put simply, Watson, it reads: 'The legacy of your deeds'."

"I confess, Holmes, I am none the wiser for knowing it, but if the letters are Cyrillic then that would suggest a Russian connection. Such a girl would be notable, though, surely? Considering the grand duke's visit to London and the death of his manservant by what is very likely the same hand, surely it cannot be coincidence?"

"As you well know, Watson, I do not believe in coincidence. I have a theory, but am loathe to voice it until in possession of further facts." He got to his feet. "There is nothing further to learn here, though I believe Miss Blanchard might avail us of some useful evidence."

"Oh yes, Holmes?"

"Yes, Watson. I should very much like to see the school records to discover the identity of the fair-haired girl and determine if she is indeed our murderess, the figure in black."

CHAPTER EIGHTEEN

THE HISTORY OF SAINT AGATHA'S

Miss Blanchard returned exactly on the hour, her mood seemingly unimproved. Our visit and continued presence was clearly taking a toll upon her; the longer we remained the more agitated she became. I could not be certain, but I believed she had been crying and considered that her icy demeanour might be a mask to hide the fact.

"I do hope you found everything you were looking for," she said. "The sooner we can put this sorry mess behind us the better."

"We found a great deal, though I'm afraid I do still have a few unanswered questions," said Holmes, ignoring Miss Blanchard's thinly veiled ire. "Though, perhaps these are not the surroundings?" he added. "Is there a more discreet location that we might use?"

Miss Blanchard paled a little at my companion's suggestion, perhaps wondering what he wished to ask and what we might have discovered. I could detect nothing untoward, but she was clearly disturbed and not for the first time I considered she might harbour suspicions about Mrs Sidley's demise, a notion our recent inquiries had rekindled.

"The chapel will be empty at this time of day," she said. "Will that suffice, Mr Holmes?"

Holmes gave a slight nod. "Lead on, Miss Blanchard. If you please."

The chapel sat in a sheltered spot beside a small copse of birch trees, but still very much within the grounds of the school. We came across Mr Derrick tending a small rose garden, but he lowered his eyes as soon as he noticed us, managing a muttered "good day" before shuffling off.

I felt a pang of guilt at the man's obvious discomfort. Our enquiries had dredged up something that the groundskeeper had fought very hard to forget, but there was a look that Miss Blanchard gave him that suggested something beyond that which Holmes and I had learned thus far. I noticed my companion narrow his eyes and knew then that he believed something was amiss here too. He said nothing of it, however, and followed Miss Blanchard into the dimly lit chapel.

The chapel was empty, and gently echoed the sound of our footsteps. A swathe of candles in tall brass holders provided a little light, and illuminated a statue of the school's namesake in the chancel. A red carpet, worn with age, divided the nave into two equal halves with pews either side.

"I should very much like to see a swift conclusion to all of this," said Miss Blanchard.

"Rest assured," Holmes replied, "this will not take long. I have but a few questions remaining."

"Then shall we get to it?"

"Very well. In what manner did you find Mrs Sidley? Her attire, I mean."

A look of confusion crept across Miss Blanchard's face as she tried to fathom my companion's rationale, but answered that Mrs Sidley was attired precisely as she always had been when at the school.

"What of her shoes, Miss Blanchard?"

Miss Blanchard frowned. "The same ones she always wore. I'm afraid I don't understand your meaning, Mr Holmes."

"And the rope, that which ostensibly she used to hang herself, what can you tell me of it?"

"I did not pay it much heed, Mr Holmes, for my eye was drawn to poor Mrs Sidley's face... Is this absolutely necessary?"

"I am afraid it is," said Holmes, undeterred. "It was a skipping rope, was it not?"

Miss Blanchard pondered a moment, wringing her hands again, but answered, "Yes. Yes, I believe it was. Though, really, I cannot begin to fathom—"

"Please, Miss Blanchard, all shall be revealed in due course. I have only one further question."

"Then ask it and let us be done with this!"

Holmes gave a polite nod, garnering a muttered apology from our anxious host, and I wondered again at what could be amiss for my companion's questions to provoke such an extreme reaction.

"A girl of fair hair, a little taller than Mrs Sidley, one who almost certainly had several notably heated exchanges with her, and of potentially Russian descent. Do you know of such a girl in your school and, if so, her name?"

"I have no knowledge of such a girl," she replied, "although we see a great many at Saint Agatha's, and Mrs Sidley had cause to reprimand a large number who might match that description."

"I see," said Holmes, "and perhaps there are records we might peruse?"

"Yes, of course. But there are no photographs, I'm afraid."

"Might we go there now?"

Miss Blanchard agreed, but did not ask why or what we had found. I think she already knew and was afraid confirmation of the fact would put her suspicions beyond all doubt.

For our part, neither Holmes nor I made any mention of what we had discovered at the crime scene. I was glad of it, for I had no desire to cause Miss Blanchard any further distress, though in the long run that would be unavoidable. For now, at least, we kept our knowledge to ourselves, it being entirely possible that the girl, or perhaps an associate, was still at the school and should be kept ignorant of the fact that the suicide had been revealed as murder.

Nonetheless, Holmes bid me go to the local post office, only a few miles from the school, whilst he began his search of the archives. I did so, glad to be away from Saint Agatha's, which had begun to take on a oppressive, secretive air that I found distasteful. I sent two telegrams, as per Holmes's instructions: one to Scotland Yard for the attention of Inspector Gregson—for there could be no doubt now that this murder was connected to those at the Grayson Gallery and of Grigori Andropov—and to the morgue, requesting the presence of the local police surgeon to conduct a post-mortem examination on Mrs Sidley.

Upon my return to Saint Agatha's I joined Holmes in the school archive room. Situated in the basement, it was hot and stuffy, crammed with bookshelves, boxes and stacked papers. I found no sign of Holmes at first amongst the cubbyholes and shadowy nooks, however, though I daresay one could become lost in such a labyrinth.

As I explored, a cloudy light drew my gaze and lured me, will-o'-the-wisp-like, towards it. Dust motes danced before the lambent glow of a lamp, doubtless disturbed by my friend's activities. I saw no sign of him beyond this, however.

"Holmes?" I ventured, my voice echoing back to me through the morass of papers and files. I guessed the entire history of Saint Agatha's school was kept here, in this dark and forgotten hollow. Some of the stacks rose to a significant height and it was as I traced my eye across them that I first saw the foot of a wheeled wooden ladder and then Holmes's left shoe, followed by the rest of him as he descended. My perception blunted by the close confines of the basement, I had completely missed him in this academical clearing of sorts, where the copious shelves briefly parted around a broad wooden desk that put me in mind of an island amongst a paper sea.

He paid me little attention at first, sitting down at the desk where he had set the lamp and spread out a number of the school's records, which he proceeded to examine.

"I have made progress since your trip to the post office, Watson," he said. "I take it you have sent the telegrams as I requested?"

I confirmed that I had, prompting Holmes to turn to the records again.

"I first separated them according to appropriate year, age and hair colour," he explained. "I then factored in weight and height. We are lucky that the school matron is zealous in her work. I then assessed the provenance of those girls who fit the description of *the* girl, and found mostly English, with a few Scots and one Welsh, leading me to believe that our suspect both lied about her place of origin and could affect a convincing native accent."

"No Russians then?"

"On first glance not, Watson. However, I remain undeterred."

Looking at the pile of records before him, I estimated at least fifty possible suspects. I was about to settle in for the long haul when Holmes cried out and held a sheaf of papers aloft.

"There!" he declared.

I read the name. "Letitia Irwin, from Portsmouth. I am, as of yet, in the dark, Holmes."

"After first narrowing the search by physical characteristics, I realised I would need to use a further filter. I therefore turned my thoughts to Damian Graves, for if our elusive girl is indeed affiliated with him and, furthermore, is operating under an assumed name, then the inspiration for her alter ego might reside in the letters D.G."

"And?" I asked.

"To no avail, Watson," said Holmes. "However, I then considered another alter ego, one already known to us, that of Ivor Lazarus, and the letters I.L."

"But this too drew a blank?"

"Quite so, Watson!" Holmes confirmed. "But then I recalled the cryptic warning on the painting in the Grayson Gallery and then again on the grand duke's manservant, but rendered in full on the upturned floorboard in Mrs Sidley's office."

"'The legacy of your deeds,'" I said, "but I fail to see the revelation, Holmes."

"Not the message itself, Watson, but rather the manner in which it was relayed. In *reverse*. I turned the initials around, I.L. thusly becoming L.I., and found Miss Letitia Irwin."

"But, Holmes, surely there must be dozens of girls with those initials," I said. "They are not uncommon."

Holmes nodded. "Quite so, Watson. But when one considers the age of the girl and her particular aptitudes, the evidence becomes compelling. And there is one final piece of the puzzle." He thrust the file at me, and I scanned the pages.

"Age sixteen. It appears she excelled in languages, science and drill while at the school. Notes pertaining to previous education reference gymnastics, chemistry and art." I looked up at Holmes. "By Jove, I do believe you've got her!"

"It would indeed appear so, Watson, but read on and the final seal of it shall be made plain."

I did so, turning at last to the final page, where rendered in small print was a simple admission: "Ward of D.G."

"Damian Graves," I said. "Her benefactor, and possibly co-conspirator. Do you think she is still here at the school, Holmes?"

"It is almost a certainty she is not. In fact, I believe she has not been in residence at Saint Agatha's for several days, Watson, though I think Miss Blanchard will be able to answer that definitively. As well as a great many other things she has kept to herself."

I frowned, for my companion's tone suggested some wrongdoing on the part of Miss Blanchard, whom I could only see as a dedicated teacher and a victim in all of this.

"Such as, Holmes?"

"The precise nature of Damian Graves's involvement for one thing, Watson, and what he purchased with his sizeable donations for another."

Our final meeting with Miss Blanchard was conducted in her office. To her credit, she attempted no further dissembling and revealed all she had kept hidden as soon as Holmes put the question to her.

"We have had some financial difficulties," she said. "The school, as I'm sure you can see, is in some need of repair and we had not the funds to maintain it."

It took all of my resolve not to comfort her, but Holmes's firm and dispassionate demeanour held me at bay. Miss Blanchard would have to endure her discomfort for whatever part she had played in this grim affair.

"I don't know how Mr Graves found out," she went on, "but he did. He came to us with a most generous offer and all we needed to do was take in an orphan girl, whom he described as his ward. I could tell from her attire and her accent that she was foreign. I requested a birth certificate, some proof of her identity, but Mr Graves gave none. He merely said he wished her to be educated and taken care of, and that he would continue to provide a generous stipend every month while we continued to do so and then for one month afterwards. I had my concerns, of course I did, to take on such a child without any knowledge of her background or character. She had a few paintings with her, and showed great talent as an artist, and I considered she might be a boon to the reputation of the school. The circumstances of her acceptance here were most irregular, and I suspected she was a tad older than Mr Graves had claimed, but we were in dire need."

"Most dire, indeed," murmured Holmes, regarding Miss Blanchard coldly over steepled fingers. "But harbouring this girl and keeping her origins a secret proved difficult, did it not?"

"It did," replied Miss Blanchard. "For the first few months her temperament was genial and courteous. A little wilful at times, perhaps, though that was nothing unusual, and for the most part she was an ardent, if somewhat distant, pupil. She advanced quickly, voraciously in fact, and it was clear her physical aptitudes and those of the sciences outstripped anything we could provide. She became even more adept at English in a few short weeks and had perfected a convincing Cambridgeshire accent. She had, in all respects, become Letitia Irwin."

"And yet, something changed," said Holmes.

Miss Blanchard nodded. "Almost a month ago, Mr Graves paid us a visit. You must understand, this was extremely unusual behaviour from a man we had not seen or heard from, barring his money being transferred to our account, since he had first brought Letitia to our door. He wanted to see the girl, and to speak privately with her. I had little choice but to agree to his request, but the meeting left her extremely agitated, volatile even. Even her paintings, once joyful and uplifting, grew much darker."

"All of which prompted her to leave Saint Agatha's altogether," ventured Holmes.

"Yes, Mr Graves returned a week later and took her and the paintings with him. He said he would continue to provide for the school as we had agreed for one further month, but that we were to keep the unusual nature of Letitia Irwin's stay a secret. I conceded to his terms. That was the day after Mrs Sidley's suicide. I thought she had left because the incident had unsettled her. But I began to wonder… I did not dare believe it, and then I received your telegram and knew something was not right." She looked as if she might break down, and I went to rise from my seat but Holmes kept me at bay with a sharp glare.

"She killed her, didn't she?" Miss Blanchard went on. "Murdered poor Mrs Sidley? She was a bitter woman, but she didn't deserve that."

"There are few who ever do, Miss Blanchard, but you have done the right thing here," said Holmes. "I must inform you that we have sent a telegram to an Inspector Gregson at Scotland Yard, who I imagine will be with you shortly. Please cooperate with him fully, and answer any and all questions he might have for you."

Miss Blanchard nodded, a mild tremor having now affected her that compelled me, in defiance of Holmes's wishes, to at the very least hold her hand in both of mine and reassure her that all would be well, and that justice would be done.

"Surely that is everything, Ho—" I began, only to find

my companion had gone and the door left ajar in his wake. I turned my attention back to the headmistress. "Thank you, Miss Blanchard. I am sure this was quite the ordeal. Rest assured, Inspector Gregson is a good and honest man; he will be reasonable."

"I did not know what else to do, Doctor. I thought no ill would come of it, but I was wrong. More than I know or care to know, I think."

I could only manage a weak smile, for to do otherwise would be to put forward a denial that would make a liar of me. All that remained was to leave Miss Blanchard to her own conscience and the judgement of the inspector.

I found Holmes smoking outside, seemingly deep in thought.

"I hate to intrude upon your musings, Holmes, but feel I should point out that, at times, an adder has the warmer blood," I said, after a few moments.

"I beg your pardon, Watson?" he asked, his attention only partly on me.

"Your treatment of Miss Blanchard. A tad harsh, don't you think?"

Holmes arched an eyebrow. "It was precisely what it needed to be, Watson. I treated her no differently to any other suspect in an investigation."

"Hardly a suspect, Holmes. A victim of circumstance, perhaps."

"Perhaps, but an individual who contrived to conceal the full truth of matters. Her motivations, altruistic or otherwise, are of no consequence, Watson, when the withholding of a salient fact might offer a hitherto unknown clue that could result in a much more heinous perpetrator being brought to justice.

Really," said Holmes, turning to regard me with genuine, if amused bewilderment, "your myopia wherever the fairer sex is concerned is ever a cause of bafflement to me, Watson. You are nigh-on blind to any and all ills they might be responsible for, such is your high—or is it low?—regard for womankind."

"High certainly! And I would not consider that a detriment to my character, Holmes," I said, somewhat offended.

"Oh, Watson!" Holmes declaimed. "Far from it, for it is the very axis around which your good nature revolves. I would have it no other way, though as a consulting detective I must remain circumspect, especially where the matter of murder is concerned. I merely seek facts, Watson, and render no judgements based upon gender, or the apparent character of any individual lest it be pertinent to a case. Low or highborn, male or female, each is equally capable of the same acts of kindness and virtue, or perfidy and sin."

"Just as well that I am here to remind you of your humanity then, Holmes," I said, mollified somewhat.

"Indeed you do, my friend. For there is no better soul amongst man than that of Dr John Watson."

"Very kind of you, Holmes," said I.

"Alas that all of mankind does not share your good and moral nature, but then I fear I would lack an occupation! Time presses on, however..."

"Are we to London then, Holmes?" I asked, recognising in him the desire to be back in the metropolis.

"Indeed we are, Watson. For as much as I have enjoyed this bucolic excursion, there are matters in the city that demand our attention, and I fear there might be little time to address them before our figure in black strikes again."

"Do you think she will, Holmes? If what transpired here at Saint Agatha's was indeed her handiwork, and all facts point to it, then it would appear revenge is her motivation?"

"In the case of Mrs Sidley, I would say it is almost without doubt."

"What then of the Grayson Gallery and Grigori Andropov? Vendettas also?"

"It's possible, but inconclusive," said Holmes. "We must first uncover who Letitia Irwin really is beneath the facade fashioned by Damian Graves."

"Are we going to visit him again?" said I, the eagerness I felt at remonstrating with this man and unearthing the evil for which I felt sure he was responsible evident in both my tone and demeanour.

"Most assuredly, but a visit to Mayfair is not of the most pressing importance, and I doubt it will yield the answers we seek. Not yet, at least. No," said Holmes, determinedly. "First, a short detour to see the deceased Mrs Sidley to confirm my suspicions. Then we shall deal with the matter of the true identity of Letitia Irwin and where she is to be found."

Our visit to the morgue was brief. Upon our arrival we were met by a wizened, greyish man, who went by the name of Brewer. Indeed, his deathly pallor was such that he had much in kind, in both appearance and lack of social engagement, with the corpses in his charge. Mercifully there were few and we were quickly shown the body of Mrs Sidley, which, in spite of decomposition, confirmed all of Holmes's suspicions concerning the use of a second rope to mask the artifice in applying the first.

Brewer said little during my companion's cursory examination, but allowed Holmes to leave a handwritten note to be given to Inspector Gregson upon his arrival that explained our presence at Saint Agatha's, what cause we had in visiting the morgue, and everything Holmes and I had thus far discovered.

"Though they are oft times slow and overly eager to jump to whatever conclusion best suits their narrative, we must not obfuscate the truth from the upholders of the law," Holmes said. "For we are merely the reserves, doing our bit for order and justice. But I will not present notions and suspicions, only facts, Watson. Only facts."

In search of which, we returned forthwith to London.

CHAPTER NINETEEN

A QUESTION OF MOTIVE

We arrived at Baker Street in the evening. Whatever plans Holmes had been concocting on our way back, he seemed disinclined to inform me of them.

As Mrs Hudson prepared a light supper and I gratefully changed out of my travelling clothes, Holmes left our rooms once again on some errand. When I entered our sitting room I heard my companion conversing with someone in the street below.

I looked out of our window to see Holmes consulting with a young street urchin. It wasn't Hobbers this time, but certainly one of Holmes's Irregulars. Upon the conclusion of the child's report, Holmes re-entered 221B, running up the stairs to announce that Gregson had indeed left Scotland Yard bound for Saint Agatha's.

Despite his apparent excitement, I caught more than a note of irritation in my companion's mood and wondered where exactly he had gone.

"I do hope the inspector is lenient with Miss Blanchard, Holmes," I said, tucking in to the supper that Mrs Hudson had prepared.

Holmes eschewed the meal, preferring only coffee and tobacco, as was his wont.

"Really, Holmes, you should eat," I told him, when it appeared I would get no response to my previous remark.

"I need nourishment for my mind, Watson, but... alas! I am thwarted!" He puffed on his pipe, and proceeded to fill our rooms with coiling smoke. Indeed, after a few minutes, I could scarcely see him through the thickening fug.

"Regrettably, I am not as robust as you, Holmes, and first require sustenance of the body."

"Ever the good doctor, eh?" Holmes said.

"Someone has to look to your wellbeing, Holmes," I replied brusquely.

He wafted away my concerns as if they too were smoke, which at least did something to part the veil that had risen up between us.

"My being is perfectly well, Watson, but it would improve greatly as soon as I am given agency towards the furtherance of solving this case! And yet..." Holmes added, agitation turning to mild melancholy, "here I stand."

I abandoned my supper, determined to get to the bottom of my companion's apparent malaise. "What is it that has you so vexed, Holmes? Perhaps I can be of assistance."

"Would that you could, Watson. Would that you could," said Holmes, slumping down in his armchair. "I'm sorry, Watson. My manner is abysmal this evening, but the matter is simple enough."

"Then unburden yourself. What is it that the urchin told you that has affected you so?"

"Very well, Watson. As you know, the eyes and ears of my Baker Street Irregulars are everywhere. No network of spies was ever so observant or covert in my experience. As you already know I tasked Hobbers with keeping an eye on the Berkeley Square residence of Damian Graves, but what you will not be aware of is that I gave the very same duty to another of them, by name of Price. Before we left for Saint Agatha's, I left instructions with Price to keep a regular watch around Church Row and the estate where I saw Graves not a few days ago, after your encounter with him in the Old Nichol. It was my hope that Price could prevail where I had not, and discover where Graves was headed."

"And did he see Graves?" I asked. "Is that what has you in such a twist?"

"Quite the contrary, Watson, and that is the problem. There have been no further sightings of Graves, and no girl matching the description of our figure in black, though admittedly details were scarce."

"You believe this is where the girl is living now?"

"It is a fair supposition. We now know she is no longer a resident at Saint Agatha's, so it is reasonable to assume that she is in the same city as her guardian."

"Could Graves not have been visiting Church Row on some other business?" I suggested.

"It's possible, for there are men of power who prey upon the poor."

"Wretches indeed," said I.

Holmes nodded. "But what other business could he have of such a clandestine nature? Let us consider the facts." He set down his pipe. "Letitia Irwin is an alias created by Graves to keep his ward hidden. Certainly, he is not above bribery in this regard, but has also demonstrated a desire to keep some distance between himself and this mysterious girl. To what end, we have yet to discover. Therefore it is unlikely that she is living at his Mayfair address, but I posit she is likely to be somewhere familiar, somewhere we have seen her or Graves before."

"Our first encounter was in the gallery on Wellington Street," said I, "but that must be over two miles from Columbia Road where Grigori Andropov was murdered."

"It is almost three, Watson, but consider her possible motivations for returning to Wellington Street."

I frowned, trying to recall the precise details of that night. "Her victims were dead, Holmes, so I cannot fathom…"

"I believe she returned to remove any evidence pertaining to her involvement in the crime, for it would have been impossible to do so beforehand. Furthermore, I do not believe there was more than one *intended* victim, but that is for later. Not expecting our presence, and outnumbered, she did the only thing she could in the circumstances and fled."

"And a merry chase it was," said I. " But she could have gone anywhere after she gave us the slip."

"Indeed she could, but what of the second location?"

"Not so much her presence as her grim handiwork."

"Indeed. Andropov was lured into an alley before being stabbed through the heart and then mutilated. Other than the weapons used, how do the murders of the patrons of the Grayson Gallery and that of the grand duke's late manservant differ?"

"Certainly, the gallery murders appeared more artful."

"Ha! Very droll, Watson. But would you say it appeared planned?"

I hadn't intended the pun, but took the compliment with good grace and replied, "Most certainly."

"And what of the alley murder?"

"It evinced a certain low cunning. From Molly Bugle's testimony, it would appear she baited a trap and allowed her prey to spring it."

"Now, what about the death of Mrs Sidley? Was there artistry, however macabre, in that?"

Recent in my memory, I easily brought to mind the two ropes, the second replacing the first in order to give the impression of suicide.

"I'd say there was, Holmes, yes. A great deal of it."

"Given time to plot and plan, to construct her artifice of murder, on each occasion our figure in black has chosen to do just that, but not in the case of Grigori Andropov. In that instance, the reaction was both instinctual and savage. Stabbed to death, then mutilated. Why?"

"Why does any poor soul kill another, Holmes?"

"Why in that *exact* way? A rapier thrust, a quick kill to end a threat. We already know that Mr Andropov was following her. For how long and to what end, we can only suppose."

"But why follow her in the first place? Was she known to him?"

"I have a theory, which I believe will be borne out when we find where our quarry is currently dwelling."

"But if your urchin has seen neither hide nor hair of Graves, how are we to find out where Letitia Irwin is living?"

"Via a combination of facts. First we must narrow the search. Do you recall the boot heel our quarry left behind on the rooftop?"

"How could I not, Holmes. A night of such drama I have rarely experienced."

"During my experiments, I examined a substance adhering to the heel. Colloquially it is known as 'Billysweet', an inferior lime-based material used in the construction of housing, specifically in the Old Nichol slum. In order to accumulate the amount I discovered upon the boot heel, Letitia Irwin must have passed through the area on more than one occasion."

"And you believe this is where she is to be found?"

"I do, indeed."

"I see. Ingenious, Holmes. Although we cannot simply descend upon the Old Nichol and knock on every door."

"Quite right, Watson. Which is why we must wait for the morning and a trip to the Public Record Office."

"A byzantine establishment if ever there was one," said I.

"Yes, but within its halls we will have our answer, a tenancy agreement or some such, for I believe Graves would not risk exposing himself and would have had Miss Irwin seek her own accommodations, albeit with his funding."

"Could she not have fabricated another name?"

"Perhaps, though why add a further lie that complicates the initial deception when one has no reason to do so? One false identity is difficult enough to remember convincingly. In any case, we must exhaust that line of enquiry before contemplating another. We lose nothing by doing so, and if it comes to naught then shall we plan our next move."

"I expect a long and arduous search then, Holmes."

"As do I, so I suggest you get some rest before the morrow."

CHAPTER TWENTY

A MATTER OF PUBLIC RECORD

I rose early the next day and arrived at the breakfast table to find
a delightful repast of poached eggs and bacon, when I found a
note scribbled in the hand of Sherlock Holmes:

Dear Watson,

I have made my way to the Public Record Office, for I suspect,
as you rightly pointed out yesterday evening, that our search
will be both long and laborious due to the chaotic nature of
this establishment. Before you join me, I would be extremely
grateful if you would pay Scotland Yard a visit to find out if
Inspector Gregson made my requested enquiry concerning
the deceased Reginald Dunbar. Should he be yet to return
from Saint Agatha's I feel sure that he will have left a message
for me with one of his constables, for Tobias Gregson can be
relied upon to be both dutiful and a man of his word.

Yours, S.H.

Feeling guilty that as I had slept Sherlock Holmes was already hard at work, I quickly finished my bacon and eggs and went to hail a cab for Scotland Yard.

On the way, I remembered Dunbar as one of the unfortunate patrons of the Grayson Gallery and felt renewed purpose in my desire to assist Holmes in bringing the heinous murderer in black to justice. I did wonder, however, what significance this one victim had for my companion.

As Holmes had predicted, Inspector Gregson was still absent and although his imminent return was expected according to the desk sergeant, he had left a message for Holmes. As it was not in an envelope or even folded so as to conceal its contents, I read it without feeling I had breached the trust of either man.

Holmes,

You were right about the grand duke knowing who Dunbar was, if that's what you were driving at the other day in the Old Nichol. Although, he knew him by a different name, Pavel Zyuganov (I asked the grand duke to spell it for me, in case it should prove pertinent), and only recognised the man from the photograph I showed him that was taken at the morgue. According to the grand duke (and I should add he seemed none too eager to elaborate), Mr Zyuganov had been in service to his family for many years as their lawyer. He left Russia for England after he retired, and evidently changed his name. I would have investigated further when I received your telegram to go to a girls' school, of all places. I am heading there now.

Gregson

I took a hansom from Scotland Yard and was soon at the Public Record Office. I went through the Chancery Lane entrance, passed under the great stone arch that led into a courtyard, then into the PRO proper.

I found myself in a large, angular room filled with wall-to-wall bookcases brimming with copious volumes of legal records. A circular table dominated this first research room, beyond which were several narrower ones, which ran around the edge of the room. A large number of patrons were present: clerks of court, professors, academics and the like, judging from their manner and attire, but as I did not see Sherlock Holmes I pressed on to another room.

It took me several minutes to finally locate my companion, who had spread out a great swathe of papers across one of the side tables, much to the apparent chagrin of his fellow patrons. Absorbed in his research, Holmes paid them no heed and very nearly failed to notice me as I approached.

"Hard at it I see," I said genially.

"It is positively Sisyphean, Watson," replied Holmes, his shirtsleeves rolled up to his elbows and his jacket slung over the back of a nearby chair, his top hat upon the seat. "For though there are records aplenty here, there is precious little in the way of order."

A few of the other patrons looked around at this outburst, to whom I could only politely nod. Holmes appeared neither to care nor notice, and already had his head down amongst a hefty stack of legal papers.

"All the tenancy agreements for Bethnal Green and Shoreditch," he explained, with a wave of the hand. "I believe I have made a dent, though assimilating them from the scattered archives of this place took me almost half the morning! Watson," he added, looking up from his labours to regard me intently,

"I must know the outcome of your visit to Scotland Yard. Was Inspector Gregson returned from the country?"

I replied that he was not, but passed on the note I had been given, which Holmes read silently, his eyes feverishly darting back and forth with such urgency that I wondered what else he had partaken of that morning apart from his usual coffee.

"Ha! It is as I expected," he said at last. He elaborated no further, and I was left wondering again what Dunbar's origins had to do with the case. I chose not to ask, feeling my efforts could be better spent helping my companion sift through the myriad documents he had gathered before him. Removing my jacket and rolling up my own sleeves, I followed Holmes's lead.

"Anything on Church Row, Columbia Road, Bethnal Green Road and whatever lies between, Watson," he said. "She is here, I know it!"

"A shame your urchins could not be put to this task, Holmes," I said.

"I'm afraid the scholars and lawyers of Chancery Lane would be quite ill at ease with the Irregulars, Watson. At any rate, so few of them can read I fear it would only add to the state of confusion."

I could only agree, if young Hobbers was any sort of gauge.

I put myself to the task. As Holmes had spread himself almost across the entirety of one desk, I was forced to take another, though did so less expansively than my companion.

Even with the both of us now poring through the tenancy records of the slum where Holmes had followed Damian Graves, it was the work of several hours before Holmes found what he was looking for.

"This is it!" declared Holmes, brandishing a paper like it was a flag he had claimed upon the field of battle.

"What a relief, Holmes," said I, "for I had begun to think

Graves might have used another alias for the girl after all."

"I had thought he would not," Holmes replied, "and am glad of it, Watson, for another hour or so of this would have driven me to distraction with its mind-numbing monotony." He smiled then, and I saw the spark of victory in his eyes, that true vim that neither meat, drink nor narcotic could ever replace. The case was back on. "We have her, Watson. A small tenement, owned by Graves and rented to Letitia Irwin, our figure in black."

We made our way to Church Row immediately, travelling with all haste from Chancery Lane. Upon arriving at the slum, we were accosted by an urchin whom Holmes introduced to me as Price. Having learnt my lesson from the watch thief on Regent Street, I kept my hand close to my wallet.

"Good eev-ning, Mister Ohmes," Price began in that common Londoner's lilt that all street urchins seem to share. He gave a polite nod in my direction, which I felt bound to at least reciprocate.

"Price," Holmes replied, "you have done your duty in exemplary fashion."

The little street urchin seemed to stand taller at this remark, puffing up his chest like a proud cockerel strutting about the barnyard. Much as I might find the likes of Price and his brood distasteful, I had to admit his service was both loyal and faithful. He doffed his scrappy little cap, and Holmes swiftly popped in several farthings before it was back on Price's scrawny little head.

"Payment as agreed, the usual rate," Holmes told him, at which Price nodded and gave a broad, nearly toothless grin. "But tell me, Price," he asked, "what else have you seen?"

Price then broke into a long and unnecessarily detailed description of almost *every* coming and going that he had borne witness to, which, although colourful and occasionally disturbing, had no connection to our case. At least, I could find none and Holmes's expression said much the same. The last thing he mentioned, however, intrigued Holmes greatly.

"There was a woman who came around," said Price, "but she weren't in no cloak and 'ood. She looked right fine, Mister Ohmes, not like some of the dollies around 'ere. Very pretty she was, sir. I kept my eye on her, I did, but I reckon she must've been lost and ended up in the Old Nichol of all places! Gave me a look and I think she must've had a turn, because she didn't linger after that."

"Very good, very good," said Holmes, after Price had finished his report, then sent him on his way.

"What now then?" I asked.

"I believe Price has done his job. Now we shall set about ours, Watson. Be alert," said Holmes, as we approached the tenements on Church Row, "she might yet be nearby."

I gripped my walking stick a little tighter, silently lamenting the fact I had not thought to bring my revolver. "I have no wish to be impaled, Holmes."

"I should think not. It would quite spoil your jacket, Doctor."

CHAPTER TWENTY-ONE

THE SECRET OF CHURCH ROW

We entered the Church Row tenement just as the sun became lost to the smog of the city and the approach of evening. Holmes led the way, his stick at the ready, and I followed closely behind. According to the tenancy agreement in the Public Record Office, Miss Irwin had rented a south-facing third-floor room.

A shabby hallway led to a stairwell that was rickety and wretched with mildew. I lightly shook the bannister rail to gauge its strength and was instantly put in mind of Columbia Road and the modest home of Molly Bugle. Such conditions can make people desperate, and I had to stifle a pang of anxiety as my companion and I climbed the steps to the third floor.

"Here!" Holmes hissed as we came to the room we had been searching for, that which had been rented to Letitia Irwin, our murderess in black. "Hold this, Watson," he said in a conspiratorial whisper, handing me his walking stick as he sank to his haunches to inspect something by the door.

He first removed a glove, holding it in his other hand as he brought a substance to his nose that I could not immediately identify and inhaled deeply. At a noise from the shadows, I turned sharply, made wary by the dingy confines and the ever present impression of being watched, and was rewarded by a scurrying behind me as our silent audience retreated, unwilling to meet my gaze or challenge.

When I turned back, Holmes was standing up again and appeared a sight more at ease than he had a moment ago. I proffered his stick.

"Thank you, Watson," he said, "but I don't think it will be necessary after all."

"Oh, really," said I, relaxing only a little.

Holmes produced a leather wallet from his jacket pocket and proceeded to remove two thin metal picks with which he would bypass the lock.

"I expect Inspector Gregson would frown upon such extremes, Watson, but we cannot afford to dally further and I am sure there is evidence here connected to the case and the crimes at hand."

It took but a matter of seconds for a dull click to sound and our ingress to be made possible.

"You can be at ease, Watson. Put simply," he said, gently urging the door open with his foot so it swung wide and allowed a good view of the room beyond, "no one is in residence."

Holmes was right; the place was evidently deserted, though we still entered cautiously. It appeared that Letitia Irwin had fled in a hurry, for the dark room was in a frightful mess. I remarked as much to my companion.

"Yes, that much is clear, Watson. Miss Irwin has been put to flight, and thanks to Price, she realised she was being watched and has not returned since that hurried exodus, I think."

"And yet you seem rather pleased with yourself," I said, noting the satisfied smile on Holmes's face.

"Oh, I did not dare believe we would catch our quarry here, Doctor," said Holmes, "and even if we did, I imagine she could have effected a swift escape." He nodded towards the room's only window. The pane was dirty, almost begrimed to the point of opacity, but the latch and frame betrayed signs of wear.

"It looks like she hardly used the door much at all," I said, squinting at the marks on the wooden window frame. In doing so I noted a small scrap of dark cloth, caught by a splinter. "Here," I added, extracting the cloth with my fingers. "It looks like the same material from the cloak we have at 221B," I said.

"Look closer, Watson. What else do you see?" asked Holmes, passing me his lens.

I obliged, examining the scrap of cloth in detail, and though the light was far from good I detected a few faint specks of white. "Chalk?"

"Perhaps," said Holmes, taking both the evidence and his lens and secreting them in his jacket.

"It certainly looks like the same substance we found on the cloak," I said.

Further evidence was revealed as we searched the modestly sized room. A collapsed easel sat in one corner, paint spatters marking the wood, and a vague chemical stink pervaded, as if it had settled into the very floorboards and was reluctant to depart. Holmes sniffed, both the air and the floorboards, as he tried to absorb every scrap of evidence presented by the abandoned room. I noted a bench pushed into one corner with a three-legged stool tucked underneath, and here the chemical aroma was at its most potent.

"Ammonia…" Holmes said, in that absent way that meant I had simply overheard an uttered thought and had not actually been addressed.

There was also a bed and a small wardrobe. Propped up

against one wall behind the bed was a large noticeboard, turned so its blank side faced towards us. Together, Holmes and I eased the bed aside to pull out the board. As we did so Holmes paused, seemingly fixated on a point on the floorboards, but did not remark upon what he had seen.

We hefted the noticeboard between us, turning it to reveal a raft of newspaper articles pinned to it, affixed in what amounted to a manic collage. There were dozens of pieces, some raggedly torn by hand, others meticulously cut out. Several, judging by the obvious voids in the presentation, had been removed. Every scrap of print related to the Grand Duke Konstantin—his visit to London, photographs of his excursions, his suite at the Langham, the crowds on Regent Street. Most prominent was an article about the commissioning of a portrait to be presented to the nobleman that very night before the gala performance at the Royal Opera House. This in itself prompted a trill of alarm in my mind, which only worsened as I read the name of the artist who had been given the honour of painting the grand duke. Ivor Lazarus.

"Good lord, Holmes," I breathed, my voice scarcely more than a whisper, "could she mean to murder the grand duke just as she murdered those poor people in the Grayson Gallery?"

Holmes said nothing. His gaze remained fixed on the clippings, analysing every detail. Beneath the scattered clippings were notes pertaining to chemical formulas, and maps of Bethnal Green, Mayfair and Covent Garden. There were rough pencil sketches of the grand duke from a variety of different angles, and though accurate, sought to portray him in a stern aspect. One rather loose composition depicted two men standing side by side in an alley in the rain.

"Good heavens…" said I.

"Not a bad likeness," said Holmes, first looking sideways at me and then back to the sketch of the two of us on what I took to be Tavistock Street. "Though I do believe she has given you a squint, Watson." He glanced at me again, frowned and then gave a small shake of the head. "I don't see it myself."

"Holmes!" I cried, as a desperate sense of urgency seized me. "We must find Gregson. I only hope he has returned from the country."

"Not yet," replied my companion, and I could barely credit his calmness in the face of this revelation.

"What if she means to murder a foreign dignitary on British soil, Holmes? The scandal alone…"

"Not yet," said Holmes more firmly. He turned from the board and went to the wardrobe, pulling open the doors and delving inside. "Look here, Watson," he said, his head in the shadows of the wardrobe, then reappeared with a silk glove clasped in one hand. "We must learn *everything* before we leave this place. We have no idea who she really is, or what she looks like at this point."

"We at least have her height, weight and colour of hair."

"True, but both her height and weight are fairly average for a woman and she could have dyed her hair or be wearing a wig."

"But we could rally Gregson and his constables, intercept the painting and avert a possible calamity."

"And how then are we to catch her, Watson? In doing as you suggest we may foil one attempt but then if she is not under lock and key what is to prevent her from making another, if indeed that is her intent? No, we must examine all evidence before we determine how to proceed."

"But surely we must act?"

"And act we will, but based on sure and certain facts. Now tell me, do you recognise this article of clothing?"

"The glove?" I frowned, moving closer to examine it. There was something familiar about the garment, but the memory escaped me.

"Consider the incongruity of it, Watson," said Holmes, and gestured to our surroundings. "A rather drab and unremarkable dwelling, wouldn't you say?"

"I would."

"And this," he added, brandishing the glove, "quite out of place, as is the rest of the contents of this wardrobe. I am not an expert on sartorial elegance, Watson, but even my rude knowledge can tell these garments are too refined and expensive for such a place."

"I don't see the significance, Holmes."

"It is simple enough to explain, and serves no greater purpose than Miss Irwin's hooded cloak. It is a disguise, Watson. One I believe that has failed our murderess."

"I see…" I said.

"I fear you do not, Watson, but allow me to assist you. Do you recall the grand duke's manservant? Grigori Andropov?"

"I do, Holmes, his body found on Columbia Road. His face had been mutilated."

"Quite so, Watson. Gregson, displaying a surprising amount of deductive intelligence in identifying the man from his boots, but we met him much earlier. Or, at least, you did."

Dumbfounded, my frown deepened. "Whatever do you mean, Holmes? I had no knowledge of the man before I set eyes upon his corpse."

"Not only that, Watson, but I believe you had already met Letitia Irwin before our encounter on Tavistock Street. I could not be sure until a few moments ago, although I had my suspicions, for what is detective work but the synthesis of theories to corroborating fact, but now I am *certain* of it!"

"Holmes, pray reveal how or I fear I shall become obsessed with this mystery."

"I shall, but first a question."

"Good God, Holmes, you are determined to frustrate me."

"Your pocket watch, you would recognise it I assume?"

"Indeed I would, Holmes. It is very dear to me, and I am most perturbed about its theft."

"And can you describe its appearance precisely?"

I nodded. "It's a silver open-faced pocket watch with a silver chain. The face is white, the numerals black and the metal unadorned. My father's initials are engraved on the back, H.W."

Holmes had his left hand behind his back, his right still holding the glove, but now brought it around to reveal a silver open-faced pocket watch dangling on a silver chain.

"Gracious, Holmes! That's the very one!"

"Discovered amongst the abandoned finery in the wardrobe."

Astounded, I looked again at the silk glove as Holmes returned my watch. "The girl on Regent Street?"

"Yes, Watson. Letitia Irwin is none other than your light-fingered thief. The glove suggests it, for it is the perfect match to the one she wore on Regent Street, but the presence of your stolen watch puts it beyond all doubt."

"And the grand duke's manservant?" I said, only now making the connection. "Her pursuer?"

Holmes nodded.

I gasped in disbelief. "How can you be sure, Holmes? I would not like to bring back the memory, but his face was mutilated beyond recognition."

"It is true that a man's physiognomy can be altered through base and brutal tortures, but other aspects of his physicality; his height, his weight, size of hands and feet—these are much more difficult to obscure. And let us not forget his boots. I only caught a glimpse of him as you remonstrated with him, but my memory captured these details. I think Letitia Irwin meant to obscure his identity."

"To what end, Holmes?"

"To give herself a precious few more hours to flee her lodgings on Church Row. She was discovered on Regent Street that day amongst the crowds, Watson. Grigori Andropov recognised her. Clearly our man was most dogged in his pursuit, and despite your gallant efforts to impede him, later found Letitia Irwin's trail and followed it here. I even believe he succeeded where we could not, at least at first."

"He must have been quite the hunter then."

"As relentless as a Cossack, Watson."

"Still, she must have thought herself rid of him and let down her guard?" I suggested. "She is certainly accomplished with a blade, but perhaps not so artful as Damian Graves at subterfuge?"

"It's possible, but I find it more likely that she allowed him to follow her."

"But how could you know he came here, Holmes? I can see evidence of the girl's panicked flight, but nothing that would suggest Andropov's presence."

Here Sherlock Holmes gave a small smile. "Makhorka," he said.

"What?"

"It is a tobacco, mainly grown in Russia, known for its coarse, strong flavour. This particular strain is unique, with hints of cinnamon and nutmeg in the aroma. It is not uncommon for Muscovites to first grind and then spice their tobacco to a particular recipe, and Grigori Andropov was no exception. His fingertips you see, Watson, carried a potent scent of makhorka as well as the aforementioned spices. I detected the self-same aroma as we reached this apartment."

"Impressive, Holmes, given the overall stench."

"A small matter, Watson. At any account, I found traces of ash just outside the door."

"Grigori Andropov, waiting for the girl to come out."

"Precisely, but she had already left and not the way she entered."

"The window," said I, "judging by those scuff marks and the piece of cloth I found."

Holmes nodded. "We already know his vigil was a long one, and had continued well into the night."

"He was afraid of her slipping through his fingers," said I. "I believe Inspector Gregson described him as 'tenacious.'"

"And that he certainly was," said Holmes, "for he did not leave until he saw his quarry again. Although this time, she was dressed in black after her night-time excursion to the Grayson Gallery, a cloak around her shoulders much like the one she abandoned during her escape."

I suddenly felt grave, and shook my head. "To think, she murdered that man on the same night she escaped us. Had only we been swifter…"

"A fact we cannot change, Watson," said Holmes, and I was thankful for his pragmatism. "Although I wish we had been able to prevent Grigori Andropov's death, there is no doubt in my mind that he met his end that night. The rain and Molly Bugle's testimony make it a certainty, I am afraid, not to mention the state of the corpse."

My brow furrowed as remembered facts came to mind. "Didn't Molly Bugle also mention that the figure she saw wore a hood *and* cloak? It could not have been the same one left behind on Tavistock Street. She must have had a spare and would likely have had to return here to get it. Could she really have done that with Andropov waiting outside?"

"I believe she did, Watson, and used the opportunity to bait the hook."

"Luring her hunter away."

"Yes. I think she returned to her apartment through the window and made certain Andropov would hear her. Surprising for certain, given he would have expected her to come to her door. But see here…" said Holmes, quickly striding to the door, "he hammered at the door, but Letitia Irwin had other plans and fled back through the window. Except she knew Andropov would follow her as soon as he heard her escaping, so she waited for him in the street. Allowing herself to be seen, she then led him to his death." Holmes strode over to a corner of the room. "A small indentation, Watson." He gestured to a mark, which I found difficult to discern until Holmes pointed it out, a rough nick in the floorboard. "Her blade stood here, taken once she decided upon her murderous course."

"Hence the reason she had no sabre when crossing our path."

"Perhaps it is fortunate for us that she did not, Watson."

"And the woman Price mentioned," I realised, "that was Letitia Irwin too. She returned but was dissuaded from entering this building by the presence of your Irregular. No doubt Price was rather obvious in his sentry duty."

"Yes, Watson, I believe Price saw Irwin attempt to return to her abandoned lodgings for some reason."

"To deal with any remaining evidence, perhaps?"

"If she had wanted to do that, she would have done it before," said Holmes. "No, she took great risk by coming back. She had already been discovered once and had to kill a man to keep her identity and presence a secret."

"Then why come back, Holmes?"

"I can think of only one possible explanation," replied Holmes. "In her haste, she forgot something very important."

"Perhaps it was my pocket watch?" I suggested indignantly.

"As fine as your pocket watch is, Watson, I do not think so. No, I believe it was an item of a much more personal nature."

Casting about the room, I could see nothing that matched that description at first. I then glanced over at the bed that we had just pulled away from the wall and the area of floor exposed beneath.

"Another nook, Holmes?" said I with burgeoning realisation. "Something hidden under the floorboards?"

"Given the appropriate encouragement, Watson," said Holmes, "we shall make a detective out of you yet."

I raised my eyebrows at this, and went over to the suspect floorboards. "It is well hidden," said I, noting that the shadows in the room were at their thickest in the spot nearest the bed, but a faint split along the floorboard was visible if one looked hard enough for it. I managed to get the tips of my fingers into the shallow gap—a feat made easier for Miss Irwin, I imagined, for her digits would be slighter—and lifted up the board. The hollow beneath it was small, barely a few inches in length, and not very deep. An object lay within, wrapped in a piece of cloth in order to protect it. Tentatively, I opened the cloth and saw to my surprise a photograph of a man and woman, with whom I assumed was their daughter in front of them.

The edges of the photograph were ragged and the image faded by age and exposure to sunlight, but it still depicted a picturesque winter scene. Snow lay on the ground and clung to the trees in thick, virginal clumps. The family was standing in a communal square of some kind, though not one I recognised. In the background I could make out a statue raised upon a stepped dais but badly obscured by distance and the degradation of the photograph. Farther in the distance was an austere but grand-looking building. The family's attire marked them out as

Russian, with their long thick woollen coats and fur-trimmed hats. The three were smiling, the father with his right hand on his daughter's shoulder, his other hand clasping the mother's.

"A family portrait," I said. "It could only be her, Holmes, surely."

Although the photograph was several years old, the girl with fair hair peeking from beneath her hat looked to be a younger version of the woman we knew as Letitia Irwin. I had not got a particularly good look at her on Regent Street, but I remembered enough to draw a strong comparison.

"A keepsake," Holmes replied, "forgotten in her hurry, but one precious enough to risk returning for it. A plan put to naught by the presence of Price."

"I suppose it is not unusual for a visitor to a foreign land to cling to that which reminds them of their home and family," I said.

"It's Alexandrinsky Square," said Holmes, indicating the photograph, "and that is a statue of Empress Catherine the Great. A trip to the theatre, perhaps," he added, "for that is the Alexandrinsky in the background." He paused. "Given the nature of our case, I thought it prudent to do a little research into Russian culture." He gestured to the photograph. "Turn it over, if you would, Watson."

I did so. On the back of the photograph in faded ink something had been written in Cyrillic, for by now I was familiar enough with the alphabet that I could at least identify it.

"What does it say, Holmes?" I asked, passing him the photograph.

"Saint Petersburg, Laznovich," replied my companion. "There are three names beneath—Arkady, Varvara and Irina."

"Father, mother and daughter?"

"I hardly think they could be anything other, Watson."

"From Letitia Irwin to Ivor Lazarus to Irina Laznovich," said

I, and I confess I felt a surge of relief at finally knowing the name of our murderess.

"To be precise, Watson, Irina Arkadyevna Laznovna, for the name is different for females."

"Fascinating, Holmes; you are indeed the industrious student, but in either case we have her at last."

"Indeed we do, Watson. Now all we must do is stop her," said Holmes, who, despite the victory, still appeared to be rather perturbed.

"Is something wrong, Holmes? Is this not the breakthrough in the case we have been waiting for?"

"It is, Watson, it is."

"And yet, your demeanour is decidedly troubled."

"I am missing something, Watson, some key fact I have overlooked. We have her name, true, but we do not have her method."

"The painting, Holmes, surely," said I. "Damian Graves is Ivor Lazarus's patron and it seems only logical that Ivor Lazarus is Irina Laznovna."

"The method she employed at the gallery required very precise conditions," Holmes replied, pensively. "Replicating such a crime at the Royal Opera House would be much more difficult, if not impossible."

"And the death toll far greater," I said, unable to hide my alarm at the thought.

"There could be some other poisonous agent at work, I suppose, one transferred through touch or mere proximity, but it is imprecise and if she has her victim then why leave such a thing to chance? And then there is the warning to consider…"

"'The legacy of your deeds,'" I said. "You said yourself, Holmes, she means to make the grand duke suffer for some reason, and she has already demonstrated she is willing to commit mass murder to kill one man. The woman is capable of near anything, I would say. Would she not consider using the same method as she employed at the gallery?"

"I believe she would, but it is almost beyond impractical. Do not forget, Watson, she is both a gifted gymnast and swordfighter. Why not simply attack the grand duke at the Langham?"

"It would be incredibly public at the Royal Opera House."

"Yes, and she had made statements before, promises of torture and penance… but for what? I must know, Watson, for it is the very key to the case."

"Let us at least send word to Scotland Yard. I'm sure Inspector Gregson would have returned to London by now."

"And tell him what, Watson? That we believe a painting to somehow be involved in a fiendish plot to assassinate the Grand Duke Konstantin, but that we do not know how or when? The fact remains that if we act now and tip our hand before we have all the facts we will most certainly lose."

"It is not a game, Holmes," I said, my tone admonishing.

"Not it is not, for the stakes are life and death, and a potential calamity that could tarnish British and Russian relations for years to come."

"What then do you suggest?" I asked, exasperated.

"Quite simply, Watson, there is only one person who we must seek out now. It is long overdue that we pay Damian Graves another visit and ask him what he knows of Irina Laznovna. She will not return here now after that first aborted attempt. The fine attire Price saw her wearing, it is much more in keeping with a woman of Mayfair. I can think of no other place she could be at this moment. If she is not at the Berkeley Square residence then I am resolved to find evidence of where she has gone. We must not falter now, Watson. It is imperative that this horror be ended and the perpetrators brought to justice."

CHAPTER TWENTY-TWO

A GRAVE CONFRONTATION

We did not tarry and fairly dashed across the Old Nichol, found a hansom on Threadneedle Street and were swiftly on our way. Holmes indulged a very brief diversion, requesting that the driver slow our carriage on Albemarle Street, just off Piccadilly. Poking his head from the carriage window, Holmes had a terse encounter with another of his young street urchins. I did not recognise the boy, though I confess I find it hard to tell one from another, but it was certainly not Price or Hobbers. No words were exchanged between them, for, even slowed, the carriage was moving too fast for a conversation, but it did give the urchin time to slip Holmes what I took to be a small, dull marble, pale in colour as to be almost white. As soon as my companion had taken possession of the item, the little fellow scurried off into the shadows and we were back at full pelt towards Mayfair.

Sherlock Holmes had a glint in his eye, and turned to me, brandishing the marble.

"It is a simple enough system, for many of the Irregulars cannot read or write."

"I am intrigued, Holmes," said I.

"A bag of marbles, half black, half white. The former indicates a negative response, the latter a positive one. All that remains then is to pose a question that I require the answer to. In this case, the message has come from Hobbers, the question relating to the presence of Damian Graves, who, you remember, I charged Hobbers with the surveillance of."

"I do, Holmes. So what, in this instance, does the message mean?"

Sherlock Holmes gave a broad grin, holding the white marble up to his eye. "Black means our quarry is at large, white that he is in residence."

"I doubt he will be quite so genial this time."

"No, Watson," said Holmes as the carriage fairly raced into Berkeley Square, "I do not think he will."

Night had drawn in and the gala performance at the Royal Opera House was only an hour or so hence; I felt the hourglass had turned against us.

The mansion at Berkeley Square was much as I remembered it. Holmes did not bother to knock and when he tried the knob, to my great surprise, the door opened.

We exchanged a glance, my expression prompting Holmes to say mildly, "It appears we are expected."

He then strode in through the entrance hall and made his way up the stairs, with me close on his heels. We both held our walking sticks at the ready, for who could say what reaction our accusations would provoke in a man like Graves, especially given his thinly veiled threats after he discovered me following him to the Old Nichol.

We found him in his exercise room, dressed in a fine black

woollen suit, his jacket draped on a nearby chair. I saw no top hat, but assumed he had this somewhere to finish off the ensemble. Wherever he was headed, I thought it could not be the gala, or, if it was, then perhaps we had been mistaken about Miss Laznovna's intention to repeat what she had done at the Grayson Gallery on a much larger scale. If he thought anything of this, Sherlock Holmes gave nothing of it away in his expression or manner but maintained his absolute composure.

Graves glanced over as we entered the room, his mood seeming to prove Holmes's theory about us being expected. He was evidently trying to straighten his bow tie but ended up making quite the hash of it.

"I do find the tying of knots confounding without the benefit of a mirror," he said, undoing his previous effort. "Or the assistance of a second pair of hands."

"Have you no servants to assist you, sir?" asked Holmes.

"Regrettably, I have had to dismiss them from my service. I will no longer have need of them. My business demands that I shortly leave the city. I would ask one of you fine gentlemen to assist me, but I suspect you might not be in the generous mood. Tell me," he added, letting his tie hang loose about his neck as he turned towards us, "to what do I owe this visit? Are we to engage in more subterfuge?"

He did not, I noted, react in any way to the fact we both carried a stick, and I believed then he also expected a fight.

"It appears we caught you in the midst of preparing for an evening on the town," said Holmes genially, to which Graves pursed his lips and gave a little shake of the head.

"Oh, come now, Mr Holmes, are you really going to keep playing games? I think you know where I am bound this evening."

"One can only assume you are headed to Bow Street for the gala."

Again, Holmes gave no reaction that might betray what he had learned.

"Right again, Mr Holmes. Your cognitive abilities truly are all they are claimed to be. Most of the well-to-do in London are also for the opera this evening," he went on, his feeble attempt at sarcasm doing him no credit at all. "Scarcely of interest, though, I am sure. I note you have yet to answer my question or explain your presence here in my home." He looked to our weapons, brandished as they were. "Armed. Are you come to arrest me?"

I bristled at this remark, the feigned indignation of the man, who knew precisely what we were about and still had the audacity to try and dissemble.

"Are you expecting to be apprehended, sir?" I snapped, my choler rising with every passing moment.

"Not by you."

"Lavender and rose hip," Holmes replied, before my temper got the better of me.

Graves frowned, diminished in confidence for the first time since we had arrived. "I am afraid you have me at a loss, sir."

"Your dealings are known to us, Graves," said I, stepping in, unable to contain my anger any longer.

"My dealings?" He laughed dismissively. "I have a great many. To which are you referring?"

"A great many," Holmes echoed, "but principally concerning a young woman who goes by the name of Letitia Irwin, but whose true identity is Irina Laznovna."

I saw Graves stiffen at Holmes's mention of the name, and there was an angry curling of his lip.

Holmes went on. "You are her patron, Mr Graves, and, I believe, her accomplice. Lavender and rose hip," he repeated, "a most distinctive scent and one unfamiliar to this manse when first we visited, but now all too prevalent in the air. I have a nose for such things, you might say, and I detected this very same aroma but a few nights ago. It belonged to a murderer and a thief, upon a garment she left in her wake as we chased her across Tavistock Street. Is she here now, Graves? I would advise you to be forthcoming, for it might go better for you in the long run."

"I do not know who you are talking about," Graves replied, though his mood had grown decidedly acerbic, "but I would be obliged if you would leave my home immediately, for it might go better for you in the long run."

"I am afraid we cannot do that, Mr Graves, for there is evidence of a most damning nature connecting you to the young woman who has committed murder and who I believe plans to kill again this very night. Rest assured, the police have been contacted and they will soon be on their way to apprehend your Russian ingénue."

This was a ruse on Holmes's part, for I knew no such communication had been made with Scotland Yard but the pressure it applied on Graves became immediately evident.

"You are both ignorant fools," said Graves, still nonchalant. "She has bested wiser men than the two of you."

And so at last Graves admitted he was part of it.

"Indeed," came Holmes's swift rejoinder, his eyes sparkling, "she led us quite the chase across the London rooftops. Alas, we were caught wanting by the task but I think we have regained the upper hand. Your defence of this young woman is admirable, if misguided. She is a callous murderer and must be brought to justice."

"You can protect her no longer, sir," said I.

"That's where you are mistaken, Dr Watson," Graves replied, backing away from us and towards his rack of swords, "for I would defend her to my dying breath!"

"Holmes, he means to draw a blade!" I cried, lunging after

Graves who sprang back like an antelope and suddenly had a sabre in hand.

I felt a hand on my shoulder as Sherlock Holmes eased me back.

"Steady, Watson," he said. "Graves is an accomplished swordsman and I do believe he means us harm, despite the histrionics."

Holmes had not let his eyes off Graves, and though he appeared relaxed there was an air of readiness about him. "Is that not so, sir?"

Graves stared at us both coldly, his expression predatory as a barn owl regarding a field mouse. "Two men enter my house unannounced, unwanted and under the cover of darkness. Mayfair is a reputable and affluent part of the city. If strangers come into my home, how am I to know they aren't thieves? It is every man's right to defend his property. Fearing a burglar or worse, I arm myself, dousing the lights to take the men by surprise and then kill both before they can raise a hand against me. Imagine my horror and surprise when the interlopers are revealed to be none other than the illustrious Sherlock Holmes and his friend Dr Watson. A tragedy to be sure, but certainly, as far as Scotland Yard is concerned, misadventure."

"You should give the humble inspectors more credit," Holmes replied calmly, his legs slightly apart and his stick held before him. "For I believe they would see through the ruse."

"I have no doubt, but by the time they had put the facts together, Irina and I would be long gone."

"Lay down your weapon, Graves," I warned him, hoping we could avoid any unnecessary violence. My words fell on deaf ears, though, as Graves advanced upon us.

"Stand back, Watson!" Holmes cried, stepping in front of me.

Chagrined at being relegated to spectator and fearful for my friend, I nonetheless obeyed. I knew why Holmes bid me retreat, for it is a misapprehension that two men always fair better in a fight when against just one opponent. In fact, when dealing with a man of Graves's apparent skill with a blade, the opposite is the case. Whereas one man can act with one mind and purpose, two men cannot.

Graves swung at my companion's head with his sabre, but mercifully the blow was parried before it could connect. Holmes riposted with a quick jab that Graves countered expertly but which was designed to put him on the back foot. To my dismay he recovered quickly and aimed a lunge. A swift sideways turn of the body, followed by a circular downwards cut had the sabre slicing air instead of my companion, and so I breathed again. Thwarted, Graves came back with a flurry of strikes that I was hard pressed to follow but which Holmes appeared to be the equal of, though I noted his stick had received several cuts and would not endure much longer.

Heart thundering in my chest, I could only watch as the duel ranged across the gallery in a blistering display of expert footwork, one man briefly taking the upper hand before a clever move saw it go to the other. Every thrust and lunge, every parry and cut, was rewarded by the hard smack of steel striking wood. Slivers of Holmes's walking stick flew into the air, and the odd rash of sparks as Graves's blade met the iron ferrule. I tried to follow the fight as best I could, but it had grown positively frenzied, both combatants evenly matched and unable to overthrow the other. I saw a war of attrition taking hold, however, one I knew my companion could not win.

"Did you teach her, Graves?" Holmes asked, his breath huffing in and out with the effort of fending off the other man.

"She needed little tuition from me," Graves replied, similarly exerted. "Though she was a determined student. Revenge is a powerful motivator."

"And you share in it, do you, Graves?" asked Holmes, favouring avoidance over direct intervention as a series of sweeping cuts came his way. "Has her cause become your cause? Would you willingly condemn yourself so, an accomplice to murder?"

"You are blind, Mr Holmes," said Graves, pausing but a moment to withdraw and get his breath. I could see it was a welcome respite for my companion, his earlier poise usurped by determination in the face of his opponent's skill. "I would do anything for her. Murder if necessary. I would not expect you to understand." Graves returned to an *en garde* position and beckoned to Holmes. "Shall we be done with it then?"

Holmes mirrored the pose. "As you wish."

Concerned for Holmes's welfare, I was about to weigh in despite my earlier qualms, when he said, "Find her, Watson, if she's here, whilst I deal with this blackguard."

The two men engaged once more. The fight saw Graves edged off to the side, and allowed me a more or less clear run to the door. I paused but a moment, worry for Holmes warring with his barked imperative to me.

Having miraculously weathered another barrage, Holmes lashed out at Graves's head, who swept the blow aside only for Holmes to spring forwards and land a swift but certain jab to the chin with his fist. Briefly dazed, Graves recoiled, allowing Holmes to press his advantage. A whipping strike to Graves's left leg saw the stick yield at last, splitting apart as half of it skittered across the floor.

"Immediately, Watson," he said, gasping. "And your stick, if you please."

I tossed my stick to Holmes, who caught it one-handed, and then set off into the house. I made my way down a short hallway with a set of ascending steps at the end. Two doors also led off from it. It was darker here, the lamps turned low, and for a moment my concern for Holmes was outweighed by thoughts for my own safety as I considered that I sought a murderess. Having given my stick to Holmes and with my old service revolver safely under lock and key back at Baker Street, I had only my wits to protect me. I ignored both doors, for there was a clandestine air about the steps as they fell away to an inviting darkness.

I forged on, cautious but possessed of some urgency. At the top of the stairs was another door, shrouded in shadow, lit only by the ambient glow of the lamps in the hallway above. During my career as an army surgeon I had developed a nose for trouble. I suppose it helped to keep me alive in those bloodiest of years. I felt it again now, though, that sense of something around the next corner, behind the closed door.

I found the door unlocked, and taking a steadying breath, I opened it and cast a faint corona of light into the room beyond. Picture frames and canvases were caught in the glow, their edges limned in the hazy lamplight. Shadows lingered here too, preventing me from seeing all the way in, and I called out, "Show yourself. Come out now, for this foul business is done. Come out."

No answer came to my summons. I could smell oil paint, and the acerbity of turpentine. Shadows settled in the corners, muddying my perception of the room's size, deep enough to conceal a person should they crouch down. The many frames, rolled-up canvases and easels also made ready nooks to hide in. I am not ashamed to admit, I paused at the threshold, straining every one of my senses to try and discern if I were alone or if another watched me from the darkness, waiting to strike.

Cautiously, I entered the room and upon finding a window thrust the heavy curtains aside and was able to see more clearly in the moonlight. Irina Laznovna was not here, though her art certainly was, the room evidently her studio. Several paintings confronted me, the moonlight revealing their subjects as well as the mien of our quarry. Heavy, sweeping brushstrokes described a host of nightmarish images, rendered in a frenzy. I am no art expert, but I knew rage when I saw it. A veritable gallery of bleak vistas presented themselves: a carrion crow pecking a morsel from the eyehole of a bleached white skull; a figure in silhouette hung from a skeletal tree, an emaciated family looking on; a mournful house fallen to disrepair, surrounded by a garden of shallow graves; and variations of that same tortured figure we had seen at the Grayson Gallery.

"The Undying Man," I said aloud to myself, scarcely realising I had breathed the words.

Amongst this unremitting horror, just one sliver of light, an unfinished facsimile of the aged photograph we had found at the Church Row lodgings. Rendered larger here, more details became apparent, such as the ballet shoes snug under the young Irina's arm. What a life she must have once had, and I felt a small measure of pity for her then, for whatever set of circumstances had taken her from the family she had recreated from memory to the darkness I saw surrounding it.

In the many years we had known each other, Holmes often imparted his methods of deduction to me, and I resolved to apply his methods, examining the room further. Sketches adorned the walls, more studies of death and despair. A few related to the Laznovich family scene, but the majority were devoted to Grand Duke Konstantin. His every aspect had been captured. In some instances it had been ghoulishly transformed and I considered this doppelgänger might be how Irina saw him. Of *the* portrait, I noted, there was no sign. This meant it was likely already at the Royal Opera House.

I turned sharply, calling out to Holmes as I ran back down the stairs, but came to an abrupt halt on the third step as Graves appeared at the landing. Little more than a shadowed silhouette, the rise and fall of his body spoke of the exertion of the duel.

A chill settled in my blood as I considered the fact I had erred in not going to my companion's aid earlier in spite of his protestations. Ice quickly thawed in the heat of my anger.

"Where is he?" I demanded.

"It's all right, Watson," said Holmes, appearing from behind Graves. He had the sabre in his right hand, pressed gently to the other man's back. "As you can see, I have disarmed our adversary."

Graves grimaced as Holmes prodded him for effect and I felt a sudden rush of satisfaction at his displeasure.

"I am bested, there is no need to further prove the point," Graves said. "I must congratulate you on your fencing, Mr Holmes. I suspected your antics in my house a few days ago when you almost dropped the blade were playacting but I had no idea they hid such a rare talent."

"I shall take that as high praise indeed, sir."

"Holmes," I declared, somewhat incredulous at this exchange, "the man tried to kill you."

"But failed, Watson, so let us not dwell on the matter, for our attention is now needed elsewhere." I saw him peer into the room beyond. "Is Miss Laznovna conspicuous by her absence, Doctor?"

"I have yet to search the entire house, Holmes."

"I will save you the inconvenience," said Graves. "She is not here. And you cannot stop her either."

"He is telling the truth," said Holmes, who stared at Graves, "at least the part regarding her absence."

"Regardless, there is a small studio up here," I said, "and I think she did indeed paint a portrait of the grand duke for there are a great many sketches of him on the walls. It is just as we saw at Church Row. It is missing, though, Holmes."

I dared not consider the fact that Irina Laznovna could be planning something so heinous as what transpired in the Grayson Gallery, and on such a scale. Given Graves's apparent attendance at the gala, it seemed extremely unlikely; he would not put himself at risk of poisoning. Not mass murder this time, but something just as public but tailored specifically for the grand duke.

"A commission arranged by Mr Graves here, I suspect, under the pseudonym of Ivor Lazarus. No doubt, it is already at the Royal Opera House," said Holmes.

Here Graves smiled and my earlier smugness at his defeat evaporated. "As I said, you won't stop her," he said, his false bonhomie having disappeared completely, allowing a darker, truer mood to take over. "She is too clever, too clever by half." He glanced over his shoulder at my companion. "Even for you, the great Sherlock Holmes."

"Then I relish the challenge. Shall we?" replied Holmes, as he ushered Graves up the stairs. "Now, Watson," he added, "show me this studio."

As Holmes examined the small room, I took the sabre and kept my eye on Graves who seemed content to keep his silence.

"Alas, dear Watson," said Holmes, as he moved about the room, paying especial attention to the family portrait, "your walking stick did not survive and you shall require another."

"A small price to pay for continued good health, Holmes."

Holmes paused at this, smiling. "Quite so. I do believe my waistcoat is a little worse for wear, though."

I had not noticed it before but the garment bore several lacerations, although they were mercifully shallow. I turned my indignation on our prisoner. "I am sure Mr Graves can make the appropriate restitution and recompense."

A snort of derision from the man suggested otherwise.

"A second studio?" asked Holmes, as he went about the room in his useful fervent manner. "Did she paint here as well as in the room at Church Row?"

Graves only glared, declining to answer.

"I wonder, at what point did you realise her intentions? And when did you concoct this plan about the portrait?"

Again, Graves said nothing.

"It is over, Graves," I said to him, "you might as well confess your misdeeds."

Holmes turned, his examination concluded. "He saved her, Watson. Is that not right, Mr Graves? He saved her when she fled to this country, and from an abusive gaoler, one he mistakenly put her with, before taking her in. You are indeed altruism personified. I should very much like to hear the full truth of it, though."

Graves looked about to protest. Then his shoulders sagged and I realised he would reveal all.

CHAPTER TWENTY-THREE

THE SINCERE ACCOUNT OF DAMIAN GRAVES

"I am not an unlawful man," Graves began, "though I believe the doctor is predisposed to think ill of me."

I remained impassive at this remark, even though it was true.

"I am vain and profligate," Graves admitted, as though this was any revelation. "I think little of money, for I have never had to. My income comes from numerous family overseas investments that have come to fruition. I am, however, the last of my line and not so driven as my father and his father were. I deal in antiques, more as a hobby than a business, but this you already know. It is a distraction, nothing more, and one I have grown increasingly weary of, though it provides a healthy income.

"I have seldom had cause to strive for anything, but if it is a crime to inherit wealth then one would have to arrest a good deal of London gentlemen. I put it to use at first, charities I favoured, self-improvement both mental and physical. I even travelled for a time, until returning to London unfulfilled and buying this house in Mayfair. I spent frivolously and indulged in a great many vices, but a hollow remained in me. I experienced a profound ennui."

He looked hard at Holmes, and I saw the pain in Graves's eyes but could find no pity for him. Many worse off than this man had managed to rise from the doldrums he had described. I saw it as a flaw in his character that he should be so afflicted by the absence of struggle or hard work. It beggared belief that he should consider his circumstances an impediment to his contentment.

"You said that I saved Irina... I believe it was the opposite." He smiled sadly at some past recollection. "It was almost two years ago, and I had taken to drinking heavily, but I sought not the company of my peers, my fellow feckless and over-privileged, of whom there are many. Instead, I went amongst the dregs of society, bawdy old taphouses and dens of ill repute. I frequented them all, and so fell deeper into despair. When this failed to satisfy me, I took to wandering the streets but kept my wits enough so as I never fell foul of the law.

"I reached my nadir somewhere near Shadwell, though I have no memory of how I got there for I was drunk. It was winter and there was a biting wind in the air. Staggering across the dockyards, half dreaming as I watched the ships gently stir with the tides, I saw a girl, no older than sixteen, huddled in the shadow of a tobacco warehouse. An emaciated thing, she was, her skin pale as chalk under the grime and her eyes wild. I think she might have frozen that night had I not come across her. To this day, I still do not know how I even noticed her, but the sight of her all shrunk up like some pitiable wraith, it cut through the drink and I became quite sober. I wonder, perhaps, if it was providence."

I saw Holmes raise an eyebrow slightly at this, but chose not to comment. Graves remained unaware of my companion's scepticism as he went on.

"I cannot say how long it was since she had eaten, but I knew then that I had to take her from that place, and that in so doing I might find some meaning for my own existence. It took some effort to cajole her from hiding, and I was fearful that if I tried too hard I might arouse the attentions of the lesser men who trawled the wharfs. Thankfully, she was simply too exhausted to resist. I took her back to Mayfair, offering my coat to ward off the bitter cold, which she took. I suspect the cab driver thought me in the company of some dollymop, my generosity ensuring his lips remained sealed.

"I did not leave the house for several weeks after her arrival. During the first few days, she said little and ate furtively, but I learned she spoke good English in spite of her apparent dishevelment. Our conversations, if they could be called such, were brief at first, but by the end of the first week I had gained her trust and she mine."

Graves paused to lick his lips. "If I am to give you the story entire, and since you have me a prisoner in my own home, might I trouble you for some water?" he asked, gesturing to a decanter sitting on a low table in the corner.

I confess my mood towards Graves softened a little at this point, as he seemed to cast off the mantle of idle dilettante. It did not excuse him for his complicity in the crimes, through inaction or otherwise, but I did not regard him with the same contempt as I once had.

I poured a glass of water and, once refreshed, Graves continued.

"She had travelled from Russia several weeks before, sailing across the Baltic and the North Sea until reaching England. Hailing from Pushkin, she told me of how she used to visit Saint Petersburg in the winter with her parents. Irina has many passions, Mr Holmes." I caught a wistful look in Graves's eye at this remark. "She painted, beautiful vistas of Alexandrinsky Square in the snow and the Alexandrinsky Theatre. I have been to Russia, but her descriptions of her native land and her paintings made it seem magical. She has a gift."

"Was it the tale or the teller you found so alluring?" I asked.

"In truth, Doctor, I think it both, though I will freely confess she captivated me with her beauty and her courage in the face of such suffering. And this she painted too, the images entirely darker and less optimistic."

"The Undying Man," said Holmes.

"Amongst the others you see here," said Graves, his mood turning grim. "When I found her that night, she was half starved and still fearful of a man she had left behind, despite the ocean between them."

"The *velikiy kniaz*."

"Your Russian does you credit, Mr Holmes," said Graves with a wry smile.

"I only dabble. Your mastery of the tongue is far more accomplished."

"One of many things Irina has improved in me. She learns quickly, a desire and aptitude for study having been instilled in her by her parents."

"So, to the grand duke then," said Holmes, "I assume he was the man she fled Russia to escape? You found her and took pity. I believe you *love* her, Mr Graves. Even though I consider it an impediment to reason, I am not blind to how it can turn men and women against their better natures."

"At first I saw myself as her guardian, but our feelings blossomed over time and grew deeper."

I frowned, for the notion struck me as unsettling and inappropriate. Holmes barely paused and went on. "Having heard her story, you took her under your wing but knew you could not keep her here forever, for such a situation would invite scandal and attention that even you would not wish upon yourself, and so you found a boarding school in the hope that she would find education and contentment there. You lied about her age. You even paid a generous stipend, knowing the school was in dire straits and likely to acquiesce to your needs, in order to keep her enrolment quiet and hidden under a false identity."

"The young woman known as Letitia Irwin," said I.

"Quite so, Watson," said Holmes, before turning his attention back to Graves. "But you had not reckoned on the harshness of Mrs Sidley, though I believe this was merely an exacerbating factor and not causational. Irina had learned of the grand duke's visit through you, had she not? The man she had fled had come to these shores at last."

Graves nodded. "It was just over a month ago. I found out from an old family friend, and though I knew the pain it would cause, I could not keep it from her and so I visited the school. It stirred something within Irina, a desire for revenge."

"You knew of her plan to kill Mrs Sidley?"

"Irina told me of her cruelty, and it was all she could do to prevent me from taking my anger out on the woman. I suspected then she would do something. She wanted to leave the school but not until she had meted out her revenge. I came for her the day after her tormentor met her end, and we returned to London. I had made arrangements for her to stay at Church Row, at her behest, as you already know. Her work on the paintings began soon after, though I maintained a studio for her here.

"An anger had awoken in her, Mr Holmes, one I felt powerless to abate. She was driven, obsessed. Yet even if I could, I would not have turned her from the course she had set upon."

"You think murder is just then, do you Graves?" I said, my jaw clenched.

He turned his cold blue eyes upon me. "In *his* case, it is just, for there is no fouler man than Grand Duke Konstantin. He will suffer, just as the others have suffered."

"As the thirty-seven innocents suffered at the Grayson Gallery?" I said, fighting to keep my anger in check.

Grayson offered no sign of remorse.

"Torture and penance…" said Holmes, and again I was reminded of the Undying Man. "First the teacher, then a mass murder at the Grayson Gallery, though there was but one intended victim, a man by the name of Reginald Dunbar. But like Irina Laznovna, he sought to escape his Russian heritage, having once been Pavel Zyuganov, a lawyer formerly in the grand duke's employ."

Graves's eyes raised a little at this, though Holmes still sought confirmation. "Is that the case, sir?"

Graves nodded. "Yes, you have the right of it, and for his part in this his fate was well deserved."

"On then to the manservant, Grigori Andropov, who was slain out of necessity. A rare upset in the murderous plan, for he recognised her that day on Regent Street when the grand duke was with his son. He followed her, but his tenacity proved his undoing, waiting for her instead of returning to his master, to make sure that she was the girl he believed her to be. It had been several years after all, and she would likely have changed in appearance. Again, there is a gap in my understanding, but suffice it to say, whatever the connection, Irina Laznovna killed him for it.

"Who is the grand duke to her, Graves? I ask for the full truth of it," Holmes warned, "and I shall have it, sir."

"You will not hear it from me," Graves said. "I won't betray Irina. The rest is hers to tell, though I doubt you'll ever get to hear the story."

"Oh, and why is that?" asked Holmes.

"Because Konstantin will be dead and Irina long gone before you even get close."

"Is that so, sir," I said, my anger flaring anew. "Her poisoned painting will never reach the grand duke."

Graves smiled venomously and despite myself, I felt a sudden chill.

"What poison?"

Quite taken off guard by his remark, I saw the glass and heard Holmes's warning too late. A blur of movement caught my eye, the low light reflecting off the glass I myself had given Graves in good faith as it sped through the air. Then came a sharp, staggering pain in my left temple and a sudden flare of heat. I fell to my knees and dropped the sabre from nerveless fingers. Graves did not reach for it, instead taking to his heels and racing back down the stairs.

I went to follow him, but almost stumbled and would have fallen face first had Holmes not caught me. Holmes dabbed the side of my head with his handkerchief, and it came away bloody.

"Can you stand, Watson?" he asked, and made no effort to hide the concern in his voice.

I gave a weary nod, dazed like a punch-drunk pugilist. "Be careful, Holmes," I said, as my companion helped me lean against the doorway, then hared off after Graves.

"Fear not, Doctor…" he called back to me, already halfway down the stairs.

I watched him disappear, but when I saw he had left the sabre behind I became terrified at the thought of my friend facing Graves alone and unarmed. Mercifully, Holmes returned a few moments later.

"As I suspected," he said, "the impending threat of the law has seen Graves on his way."

"We must get after him, Holmes," I replied, my voice groggy.

"Don't worry, Watson. I have a feeling we have not seen the last of him," said Holmes. He put his arm under mine and we descended together. "Now, I must ask you, Doctor: can you walk unaided and find your way to Scotland Yard? It is beyond time that we alerted the authorities." He quickly checked his pocket watch.

"Of course, Holmes," said I, still a little unsteady but my composure returning with the urgency of our task. "But what of you?"

"There is time enough yet before the gala performance. We might not know precisely what Miss Lasnovna has planned, poisoned painting or not, but we can take no chance. I shall make my way to the Royal Opera House and keep an eye out. It might be wise for you to fetch your revolver from our lodgings, though I dearly hope we do not end up having need of it."

"I shall do so, Holmes. Will you warn the grand duke?"

"I should think not, Watson. If we are to trap our murderess, we must let her plan proceed but only to a point. Besides, we have yet to determine the precise nature of the threat posed and from what we know of Konstantin, he is unlikely to be put off by the mere supposition of danger. No, we must let it play on for a while yet. I am not enamoured with the idea, Watson, but I am certain it is the best course."

As he made to leave, I gripped his arm. "For God's sake, Holmes, do be careful. Graves meant to murder you, I think, and we know *she* has killed before."

"Rest assured, old friend," Holmes replied, "I shall take every precaution. I will not act until you and Inspector Gregson are on the premises. I shall observe, and nothing more."

We left the house as quickly as we had arrived, my senses all the better for being out in the London air. We saw no sign of Graves and with Hobbers having been dismissed some time ago we had no way of knowing where he had gone, though I suspected he would not be far from Irina Laznovna.

"I think he might try and warn the girl, Holmes," I said.

"It's highly probable, Watson, for he has formed quite the attachment to her it would seem. I would not let it concern you, though. The plan is too close to completion for either of them to countenance abandoning it now."

"Which means the threat to the grand duke is as great as ever."

"Only the apprehension of Miss Laznovna can put that to rest, I fear," Holmes replied, peering up and down the street.

"What do you think he meant, Holmes, back in the house when he questioned the poisoned painting?" I asked. "I think it highly unlikely Graves would be attending the gala if there was a risk to his life, but can we rule it out entirely? What if Miss Laznovna has some other use in mind for the painting, one we are ill-prepared to counter?"

Holmes scowled. "Whatever the case, Watson, we must obtain that painting to remove any possible threat. But I curse myself for a fool, and for a fact overlooked. I shall say no more now, for I see two cabs approaching and we would do well to take them, but I dare rule nothing out. Be as swift as you can, Watson," he added, leaping aboard the first hansom as it pulled up, the second only a yard or two behind. "There is little time to lose." My companion gave a theatrical wave from the window of his hansom before the driver cracked the whip and he was on his way.

CHAPTER TWENTY-FOUR

GREGSON RALLIES THE TROOPS

Reaching our lodgings, I did not tarry, fairly running up the stairs much to Mrs Hudson's alarm. I retrieved my service revolver, which I hastily stuffed into my jacket pocket before I was off again.

"Doctor, you're bleeding!" I heard our landlady call after me as I shot out through the door.

"Just a scratch, Mrs Hudson," I replied, not wishing to worry her. "Quite careless, really. Good evening!"

I dashed back to my waiting hansom and willed my head to stop spinning quite so fiercely. I slipped the driver an extra shilling to show the beasts the lash and we hurtled with all haste to Scotland Yard, the violent rattling of the carriage doing much to exacerbate my growing headache. I was pleased to see that Inspector Gregson was back from the country and was discussing some matter with the desk sergeant as I burst in through the main entrance.

"Ah, the elusive Dr John Watson," uttered Gregson upon my arrival, his manner insouciant, "and where might your friend

Sherlock Holmes be? I have a fair bit to discuss with him since he sent me off to Cambridgeshire with barely a word of explanation. What am I to make of it all, I ask—" He hesitated, caught short in his tirade as soon as he noticed my injury. "Good heavens, Doctor, what happened?"

I told him everything I knew, for I saw no need or value in keeping the inspector in the dark any longer. We had reached the end of it, this whole sorry business, and Holmes and I would need every ally if we were to prevail.

Tobias Gregson, whilst often brash and overly bullish, is a good and diligent man. He listened carefully to my account, his face betraying no emotion whatsoever but I could tell he heeded every detail. Occasionally, he would ask a question for the purposes of clarity, but for the most part allowed me to divulge all I knew. If he thought anything of the few legal "irregularities" Holmes and I had been forced to commit, such as keeping much of our investigation from the police as well as breaking and entering, then he made no mention of it, and I was once again reminded of the man's pragmatism and general common sense, qualities that set him above a great many of his contemporaries at Scotland Yard.

When I was done Gregson merely nodded, closed his notebook and summoned a cohort of constables to his side.

"And this man, Graves you say, he is still at large?" he asked as we left Scotland Yard mob-handed.

"Regrettably, he fled our custody."

"After the assault on your person, Doctor?"

"Yes, although Holmes believes he is likely bound for the Royal Opera House."

Gregson nodded, his expression stern, and I realised he felt personally affronted by the injury done to me. After all, I suppose my companion and I were upholders of justice, if only the "reserves" as Holmes would occasionally put it. An attack on one was an attack on all, at least so it appeared judging by Gregson's mood.

He rallied his constables, a general addressing his troops. "We make all haste to Bow Street. Look lively now!"

Two sturdy growlers and a Black Maria awaited us on the corner of Whitehall Place as we left Scotland Yard. The evening had turned grey since I had first arrived, clouds gathering in earnest over the City of London threatening rain, and I wondered if this was an omen. The heavily muscled beasts who would draw our carriages, bright-eyed and dark-maned in the gloom, felt it too, I think, scraping at the ground with their fore hooves, impatient to be away.

As the constables climbed aboard the carriages, Gregson loudly declared the dangerousness of the criminals being sought but that he expected nothing less than their swift apprehension.

"Dr Watson," he said to me, catching my arm before I took my place in one of the carriages, "are you sure you wish to accompany us, given that knock you've taken to your skull? There'd be no shame in it and none here would think any the less of you."

I patted him on the shoulder, genuinely moved by the concern, but shook my head. "I am as well as can be expected, Inspector, and shall see justice done."

"Very well, Doctor," he replied, before bellowing for the remaining men to mount up.

Gregson and I, along with two constables, sat in the first cab with three further officers in the second and two more in the police wagon.

During our journey, I learned his own enquiries had come

to naught, directed, as they were, at poor Edmund Garret. Bereft of other suspects, Gregson had pursued the unfortunate gallery assistant quite doggedly but had achieved nothing but the worsening of the man's tremulous nature. I imagine it had been quite the ordeal for the fellow. Gregson had been nearing the point of exasperation when he had received the telegram from Sherlock Holmes requesting he pay a visit to Saint Agatha's School for Girls, at which point he had learned of the murder of Mrs Sidley, Irina and her association with Graves. It had been up to me to fill in the rest.

Gregson did not mention it, but I suspect he was somewhat relieved at my companion's intervention in what now could prove to be a case of some considerable import. Gregson is not quite so brazen about it as Inspector Athelney Jones, but he is not above taking credit for the genius of Sherlock Holmes, and I believe he saw this as an opportunity to further his career. He was, however, as committed to the law as my companion and I felt confident in his ability to see justice done. He requested descriptions of both Graves and Laznovna, which I provided to the best of my ability. The girl, of course, proved rather difficult and, as Holmes and I had recently discovered, somewhat chameleonic. I briefly wondered at what fact my companion had overlooked, that which he had chastened himself so severely for back at Graves's townhouse, but knew I had not the wit to see it if Holmes had nearly missed it. I settled instead on making Gregson aware of the painting commissioned by the Royal Opera House for the grand duke and of its potentially hazardous nature. At this, he frowned, scratching at his fair hair.

"How can a man be so threatened by a portrait, though, Doctor?"

I divulged the discovery by Holmes of the hydrogen cyanide on the painting at the Grayson Gallery.

Gregson raised his eyebrows at this. "Truly horrifying, Doctor, but I cannot see how such a travesty could happen again."

I did not know either, but as Holmes had said, we could take no chances. Anything could go awry, and I did not believe Irina Laznovna would leave anything to chance where the grand duke's demise was concerned. I said none of this to Gregson, however, and merely reiterated that Holmes had instructed the painting found and carefully dealt with to remove any and all doubt, to which Gregson grudgingly conceded.

My head throbbed viciously as the carriage rattled along, and I thought I might have erred in coming along with the inspector after all, but as the Royal Opera House came into sight, the pain abated, dulled by a sense of righteous purpose.

"Find the painting, lads," urged Gregson as we disembarked onto the street. "No man is to lay a finger on it, or even breathe near it. You find it, you find me and nothing in between." He took care to send a man to every exit, their instructions to detain anyone matching the descriptions I had given or indeed any suspicious character seeking egress. "Now, be quick about it!"

We caught more than one nervous look from passers-by as Gregson led us across the street in a determined mood but by the time we reached the main entrance to the Royal Opera House, many of the guests for the gala performance had arrived and a veritable sea of bodies stood between us and the theatre proper. Nonetheless, we forged a way inside into the grand foyer, thronged with dapper-looking gentlemen and ladies in fine ball gowns. Rich carpets clad the main stairs in red velvet, leading off to the dress circle and upper balconies. Ornate columns of marble ran all the way to a vaulted ceiling decorated with classical frescoes. As I had done a few nights before, I marvelled at the ostentation, but my return to the opera house brought to mind Holmes's conviction about coincidence and I briefly wondered what it might portend.

Gregson saw none of the elegance, the man like a fierce bull who used his size to great effect as he fought through the crowds. Bellowing himself hoarse for the guests to stand aside, he found voice enough to send a pair of constables to either wing of the house. I scanned the crowd, but could find neither Graves nor Holmes and so followed in the inspector's wake, who was leading a charge for the second landing. As I passed one of the marble columns, I felt a light tap upon my shoulder. I turned, my heart in my throat, and saw to my surprise Sherlock Holmes leaning against the column quite nonchalantly.

"Good lord, Holmes," I exclaimed, a hand upon my chest. "You gave me quite the fright. What is the meaning of this lurking about? I assumed you would meet us at the main entrance at Bow Street. Have you seen anything of Graves? Is he here?"

"Oh, I have no doubt he is here, Watson, though I have yet to set eyes on him in this crowd. I suspect he is not far, but any attempt to apprehend him would steer us off the correct course." Holmes gave a wry smile. "I see the inspector is making his presence felt."

Gregson had barged his way to the uppermost landing, a pair of constables in tow, and was proceeding to wrestle through the crowds who seemed to be taking umbrage at his indelicate methods.

"Should we not be joining him, Holmes?" I asked.

"If you wish to swim against the tide, then by all means," he replied, "but I have found a more direct ingress."

At which point Holmes drew back a curtain to show me the entrance to the back of the theatre.

"With all this commotion, we can slip in unnoticed. No time to waste, Watson."

With that Holmes set off at pace, swiftly weaving through the corridors and secluded nooks back of house. After passing down several tightly confined passageways, in which I endeavoured not to trip in the half darkness and injure myself, we emerged backstage in the left wing. A dark velvet curtain hid us from sight of the audience, but I was afforded an excellent view down the crossover all the way to the right wing. Scaffolds rose up to the vaults and culminated in a warren of beams and narrow catwalks.

A dizzying array of stagehands and performers scurried about like agitated wasps, and the impression was one of abject chaos as the grand spectacle of the ballet began to prepare for its opening act. I saw none of the corps de ballet and assumed they were confined to their dressing rooms for the moment. It was much as I remembered it from several nights previous, when I had sought a cultural diversion for my companion and found a murderous one in its stead, the death of poor Miss Evangeline. I only hoped this evening's performance would end without tragedy.

Amongst this whirlwind of frantic activity, Holmes and I moved about unnoticed. I was, as of yet, completely in the dark as to our purpose for being backstage, however, and took the opportunity to put the question to my companion as he hovered by a rack of weapons that had been consigned to a corner, of no use to this particular evening's entertainment.

"Whilst I am thrilled at having the opportunity to visit the opera house, you still haven't told me what's going on. Holmes, should we not be with Gregson and his men, scouring the place for the painting? You cannot think it is backstage?"

"It is not the painting that concerns me, Watson, and besides I am sure the inspector has that matter well in hand. No, we have an entirely different task altogether," said Holmes.

"Then pray tell me, Holmes, or I fear I shall expire out of sheer exasperation!"

"*Tut, tut*, Watson," said Holmes, looking askance at me, "you really are quite melodramatic at times. Perhaps, you should also take the stage as part of the evening's festivities? I can think of several roles that would suit you well, but—wait!" He stopped short to face the house, though the thick velvet curtains sealed off the gathering crowds, and listened intently.

"The grand duke is here! We have little time left to lose!"

Holmes was right, though it took me longer to discern the distant announcement of the arrival of foreign royalty.

"I have erred, Watson," said Holmes, as he rummaged about amidst a rack of coats and hats, flinging garments into the air when he could not find what he was looking for.

"Holmes," said I, looking out to see if anyone had noticed his performance, but the frenzy of the night was such that he rather blended in, "what are you doing?"

"It was rosin powder, Watson," he replied, emerging from the clothing rack having traded his top hat for a cloth cap and his suit jacket for a grubby-looking overcoat. He slipped on a pair of rugged brown overalls over his trousers and was thusly transformed. I marvel at how easily my companion adopts his disguises, not only in the mere addition or substitution of attire, but the way in which he affects a manner utterly at odds with his true character. Holmes had even conspired to dirty his face from some source unknown and suddenly wore the same grim, determined expression as all the other stagehands. He then proceeded to role up his sleeves.

"Very impressive, Holmes," said I, as remarkably a passing props man hefted a spooled length of rope to my companion followed by instructions where it should be put away. Holmes gave a grizzled reply that would have made any veteran rigger believe he was kin. Bemused, I could only watch as the man departed to the rest of his duties, shouting to anyone who would listen that the curtain would be up imminently.

"You had best be on your way, Watson," said Holmes, throwing me his discarded garments, "and find somewhere safe to stow those would you? I should hate to lose either, though especially the hat."

"I bought you that hat, Holmes!" I exclaimed, mildly perturbed at its rough treatment.

"Hence my attachment to it, dear Doctor," he replied, and as he headed over to one of the scaffolds before proceeding to shimmy up a ladder, he added, "One of us should warn Inspector Gregson, whilst the other watches back of stage, and since I am already in character…"

"Warn him about what, though, Holmes?" said I, with my companion halfway up the ladder.

"She is here, Watson, amongst the corps de ballet. Find Gregson and then be poised front of stage in case she bolts."

"A ballerina?" I asked. "Since when, Holmes?"

"Since the very start, Watson. She has been under our nose since the very start."

"So she fences, paints *and* dances. Quite the renaissance woman."

"The dust found at the gallery, on the edge of the cloak, in her lodgings at Church Row… rosin powder," said Holmes, steadily disappearing into the rafters with all the dexterity of a chimpanzee. In the vaults, his vantage would be unparalleled.

"I am still none the wiser, Holmes," I called to the shadows above.

"We have been duped, Watson, but there is nothing more for it now than to be ready for when she strikes. Find Gregson and have his men surround the stage," said Holmes, his voice echoing in the darkness before he vanished from my sight.

CHAPTER TWENTY-FIVE

THE STAGE IS SET...

With nothing further to be learned or gained by staring up into the rafters, and left to guess how Holmes might identify Miss Laznovna amongst an entire troupe of dancers, I made my way from the wings and into the front of house. With little hope of finding a path through the labyrinth of corridors we had passed through on our way to the backstage, and furthermore not wishing to emerge somewhere behind Gregson in the sprawling clamour of the theatre foyer, I instead did my best to sneak across the stage. I earned a few jeers and whistles for my temerity from some ninnyhammers in the stalls, but staunchly ignored every one. Urgency compelled me to act in spite of any and all other considerations that night.

Hurrying across the stage apron, under the proscenium arch and nimbly avoiding a painful fall into the gaping orchestra pit—earning several disapproving glances from the assembled musicians—I gratefully alighted in the stalls. By now the lights had dimmed and the orchestra had finished tuning up.

I saw the grand duke had taken his seat in the royal box,

accompanied by his son, a grim-looking Life Guard at either flank. In his finest regal attire, a dark red brocade suit, he looked relaxed if perhaps a tad bored. His son, Sergei, was evidently excited as he leant over the edge of the box for a closer look at the stage. A host of other, lesser dignitaries were also in attendance, some of whom made gestures of acknowledgement and greeting up to Konstantin who favoured them with a thin, humourless smile.

I glanced across the rest of the audience, but shrouded in shadows as they now were, and in such numbers, I caught no sign of Graves. According to Holmes, Irina Laznovna was here, a part of the performance in fact. Surely her suitor would be close by. Scurrying up the nearest aisle, I promptly found a constable who thought at first to question me but upon recognising my face and hearing the inspector's name directed me to where Gregson was to be found.

Somewhere halfway up the lower slips, I met the inspector who seemed bemused at my sudden appearance.

"I thought we had lost you, Doctor," he whispered, causing the glaring disapproval of the theatre patrons within earshot who had come for the ballet and not Tobias Gregson's whispered mutterings. "Have you found Holmes, Graves, anyone?"

I quickly explained that Holmes was backstage, up in the vaults and keeping an eye out for Miss Laznovna who was somewhere amongst the ballet dancers.

"She's a part of the performance?" Gregson replied, somewhat loudly, earning himself more glares.

"A ballet dancer, yes," I said. "Holmes seems to think it has always been thus. What of the painting though, Inspector? Have you found it?"

"I have, indeed," he answered, somewhat proudly. "It is under guard in the ticket office."

"And there appeared nothing untoward about it?"

"Not that I could tell. No one died as a result of its acquisition, at least. Anyway, I thought Holmes wanted to see it? Why is he clambering about above the stage?"

"I think he believes the painting to be a ruse, Inspector. Perhaps a way to divert our attention from where the true threat will come."

"The girl."

I nodded.

Gregson looked to the stage where the first act had just begun. The orchestra had struck up a waltz, and the performers danced around the imaginary setting of a magnificent park, a painted palace providing a splendid backdrop to the scene and not so different to a winter photograph taken at Alexandrinsky Square.

Gregson grabbed a nearby constable, reaffirming his instructions for officers to watch every exit. He then looked back at me. "We had best get ourselves down there, Doctor, and wait for Holmes's signal. I won't lie, if it's as dire as you say, I have half a mind to arrest the lot of them on suspicion."

"In front of such an audience?" I asked, gesturing to the crowd.

Gregson gave a slight shrug, then a scowl as if weighing up his next course of action. "Perhaps not. We shall wait for your companion, Doctor. I promise you this, though, she won't slip by. The only way she's leaving here is in irons."

As his constables fanned out across the auditorium, Gregson and I made our way to the bottom of the lower slips, not far from where Holmes and I had been sitting only a few nights ago. There we crouched, there being no spare seats. Mercifully, those who had come to watch the ballet were trying to ignore us. Some cast a wayward glance at the odd passing constable, but the diligent officers of the law kept mainly to the shadows.

I could not see Holmes, secreted somewhere above the
stage, but knew he would be watching intently. I kept my gaze
on the dancers, but found it almost impossible to tell one from
the other in their vibrant costumes and gaudy painted faces. Like
a dupe in a game of three-card Monte, I could not pick her out. I
don't doubt this was all to Miss Laznovna's design, for she had all
but turned herself invisible in plain sight of over two thousand
patrons. But as the ballet went on, I only prayed that Sherlock
Holmes would be equal to the task and succeed where I had
fallen short.

What Gregson thought of the performance, I do not know,
nor did I care to ask, but I saw his eyes dart back and forth for
some inkling, however small and seemingly insignificant, of foul
play that would give our murderess away. Alas, there was none,
our only reward stiff backs and aching legs. At least my dizziness
had abated somewhat, though it still threatened every time I had
cause to look into the vertiginous depths of the stalls below. I
saw a constable mustered down below, trying his very best to be
inconspicuous. Surely, with so many of us arrayed against her,
Miss Laznovna could not succeed?

Before I knew it, the first act had concluded and the second
came quickly on its heels. During a very brief orchestral interlude
in which the scenery was being changed behind the curtain,
Gregson turned and whispered, "Are you certain of Holmes's plan?
I have never known him to be wrong, but if there is something
else amiss then I would have you tell me without delay."

I knew of nothing further and explained as much to Gregson.
"I promise you, Inspector. He was certain of it. We must wait a
while longer."

Despite my urging for patience, my nerves felt taut. To
reassure myself all was still well, I glanced up at the royal box
and saw the grand duke's son sitting forwards in his seat, quite

enchanted by the drama unfolding on the stage below.

As the second act continued, I tried to employ some of Holmes's methods. If nothing else, I reasoned, it might calm my mind. I put together what we knew of the victims and their fates and ordered it thusly—a Russian lawyer, slain ignominiously and painfully by poisoning; a teacher, again killed in agonising fashion but made to look like suicide, her reputation besmirched into the bargain; a manservant, stabbed and mutilated. Every death had been carefully orchestrated to inflict the utmost pain and indignity on its intended victim. How then to hurt a man such as Grand Duke Konstantin?

A thought took hold in that moment, so terrible that it set my heart to racing. I gripped the forward balustrade for fear I might fall, prompting a sudden interrogative from Gregson.

"Doctor, are you all right? Is it your head?"

I could scarcely find the breath to answer, "I have to reach the grand duke." I rose unsteadily to my feet, half staggering at first but rushing up the aisle and leaving a befuddled Tobias Gregson in my wake. "Stay at your post, Inspector. Laznovna might yet come this way."

Ignoring the displeasure of the patrons, whom I had already disturbed more than once that evening, I made all haste to the royal box. I felt I had little hope of reaching the grand duke, but given the revelation I had experienced I had no choice but to try.

In my panic, I caught brief glimpses of the stage, the second act now well underway as Prince Siegfried had arrived by a moonlit lake with crossbow in hand. I took three steps in one urgent bound, nearly tripping over in my reckless desire to reach the grand duke. All the while, the scene played out as Prince Siegfried took aim at the flock of swans surrounding him. I reached the landing, bypassing an usher then one of Gregson's constables as I gained the stairway to the royal box. In the scene,

Prince Siegfried had set down his crossbow as a magnificent transformation took place, the orchestra enhancing its majesty with a stirring crescendo, and the Swan Queen became the maiden Odette. I had witnessed the same miraculous piece of stagecraft only a few nights before, and then it had been interrupted by a vile tragedy. History could surely not repeat so cruel a deed but as I reached halfway, an usher impeded my path, whom I began to remonstrate with, and the grand duke stirred in his seat at the sudden commotion below. His son leaned further over the edge of the royal box to get a better look at the kerfuffle, and I heard a voice below.

"Arkady Laznovich and Varvara Laznovna!"

I halted at once, our argument suspended as the usher and I looked to the stage. Perhaps accustomed to such uncouth behaviour, the performers carried on without remark, save one seen only by Sherlock Holmes, just visible in the rafters above, who declared, "She is here, Watson! Irina Laznovna is here!"

There could be no mistaking her reaction as she made a sudden impromptu misstep at the memory those bellowed names evoked. Now estranged from her flock, she turned her mistake into a pirouette and then stooped to retrieve the crossbow in the very same elegant movement. A once nameless, unassuming swan hefted the deadly weapon with practised ease, while the other players looked on aghast.

In desperation, I shouted to the royal box. "It's Sergei! Duke Konstantin, look to your son!"

I heard the sharp twang as the bolt was loosed and a great cry rose up from the audience. Never have I seen a man act so quickly and selflessly, for Konstantin all but leapt from his seat and threw himself in front of his son. The bolt struck, but only struck the grand duke's shoulder. At once the two Life Guards seized their wards, pulling them away to the back of the royal box.

"Inspector," I cried, drawing my revolver, but Gregson had already taken to his feet, bellowing at his constables to close in on the stage where a stagehand, a nondescript rigger of little note to most who saw him, nimbly descended a rope.

"The trapdoor," shouted Holmes upon reaching the stage, rapidly divesting himself of his cloth cap so Gregson could see him for who he was, "do not let her reach the trapdoor."

Thwarted, Irina muttered a curse in her native Russian before casting aside the crossbow and hurrying to the middle of the stage where I now realised a trapdoor must be. None stood in her path, too afraid or too dumbfounded to intercede. I knew I could not reach her, so instead I took aim.

I had no wish to kill her and whilst I am not an expert marksman, I felt competent enough to be sure of only winging the girl. Heedless of the terrified gasps at the revolver that had suddenly appeared in my hand, inured to the unfolding chaos slowly gripping the house, I prepared to shoot.

"Stop her, Watson!" Holmes's cry rang loudly in my ears, cutting through the rest of the fog.

To my shame, I could not, for a dreadful vertigo came upon me and not one but three murderous swans swam across my vision. I wavered, the pistol almost falling from my grasp, and knew I could not shoot.

Irina reached the trapdoor and disappeared under the stage. Uproar swept through the house as swift as wildfire, nigh on swallowing Gregson and his constables. People left their seats, some out of fear, others fascination, all to the detriment of the upholders of the law. All except for Sherlock Holmes, who plunged down the trap and was gone.

I quickly realised any path I might take to what amounted to the bedlam below would be fraught with impediment and so, gathering my wits, I headed back to the nearest exit. I barrelled down the stairs, ignoring the pain in my leg and the throbbing in my skull, and found my way outside. Snow lay thick on the ground and was still falling heavily, all of Bow Street blanketed in white.

I met Holmes again as I dashed around to where the stage door met Hart Street, having reasoned this is where she would make her exit.

"Watson!" he cried, and as I looked ahead I saw why. One of Gregson's constables lay upon the ground, having evidently tried and failed to prevent Miss Laznovna's escape. Mercifully, he lived, and stirred dolefully as I ran past, denying every instinct within me to stop and help. Holmes loped a short distance ahead, dishevelled in his rigger's garb but as determined as the devil.

A chorus of whistles shed apart the night as Gregson and his men emerged in force, having battled through the anxious mob. Although a considerable way behind us, it reassured me greatly to know that we were not alone.

"How on earth could she have armed herself?" I said, upon catching up to my companion who had wisely slowed down so he would not face her alone.

"All too easily, I'm afraid, Watson," Holmes replied. "Simple enough to smuggle a bolt and with the bow already taut, it is but a matter of loading it. I believe she rather depended on the fact, Watson, something I plan to put to her in short order."

"I could not have fired, Holmes," I added with no small amount of remorse, for had I been the equal of the task she would likely now be in hand. "Had I done so, I fear I might have killed someone."

"You did the right thing, Watson, have no qualms about that. Besides, she has not eluded us yet—look!"

Following Holmes's outstretched finger, I saw her, almost obscured by the falling snow. A passing gentleman had gotten in her way, it would appear, some pompous laggard who had unknowingly given us a few precious seconds to close the distance. Even so, she did not tarry, putting the fellow firmly on his back and then turning to glance behind, dismayed at our persistence. She ran on, but her ballet shoes were ill-suited to the conditions and she slipped several times, eroding her already tenuous lead over us.

"We have her, Holmes," I said, gasping as my breath turned the air to fog. "We have her."

Alas, my optimism proved ill-fated, for as we drew close to running her down somewhere in the vicinity of the Strand, a hansom barrelled out of a side street ahead of us and came to a halt in front of our quarry. The cab door flung open and with a pang of unfettered revulsion and contempt I recognised Damian Graves pulling the girl inside. He must have been watching the Royal Opera House keenly to know where she would be. Either that, or they had planned this escape, just as they planned everything else. A swift, shouted order to the driver and they were off, the horses put firmly to the lash.

"Damn and blast it, Holmes!" I bellowed, the falling snow melting against my hot skin. "He has beaten us again."

Sherlock Holmes watched the carriage as it careened down the street, but then turned and said, "Not so, Watson. For Tobias Gregson has the bit between his teeth!"

A police growler rattled over to us, an angry-looking Gregson beckoning us inside. "Come now, gents. Don't tarry."

Holmes and I quickly climbed aboard, the carriage taking off before I had chance to shut the door, setting it to flapping wildly until Gregson leaned over to slam it shut.

"Drive like the very hounds of hell are at them!" shouted the inspector to the driver. "You lose them and you'll feel my wrath, Constable." An almost savage gleam had entered Gregson's eye, and I recognised in him the same feral urgency of Holmes when he has a scent of the hunt. Yet my companion seemed sanguine.

"Inspector," he said, genially, "for once, your timing is impeccable." He leaned out of the cab window, his face at once plastered by snow whipped up in the passing air. "I see them Inspector, coming up on Fleet Street. Come now, my good man," bellowed Holmes to the driver, "keep at it, but be ready to turn sharply!"

I leaned out of the opposite window and saw the distinctive gilt edging of Graves's hansom as it sped across Fleet Street.

"He's going to kill someone at this rate," I cried, as a couple out for an evening stroll nearly came to a rough end under the hansom's wheels, the driver barely steering aside in time.

On the chase went, Gregson's constable every bit the tenacious bloodhound. For although Graves's hansom was swifter and less encumbered, it was not as robust as the growler and as we turned onto Farringdon Street towards Blackfriars I saw the right wheel of the smaller carriage begin to buckle under the strain.

"There! He is coming unstuck!" I shouted to Holmes, though I had no idea if he could see or hear me.

We followed. An endless, rattling crescendo filled the carriage, the ragged breaths of our steeds a tortured refrain. The pace became relentless, and I clung to the window frame.

The air thickened with snow, almost blindingly so, as the hansom diminished to a vague silhouette. I withdrew to the relative safety of the cab and found Holmes had done the same.

"How much longer can this be endured?" I asked, and got my answer as a terrifically loud crack resounded from up ahead, followed a moment later by an equine shriek. As Holmes and I peered from the windows, I saw Graves's hansom coming to a shuddering halt. The axle to the right wheel had snapped in half, the sheared edged tearing into the ground, splinters as big as knives flying in all directions as the wheel itself shattered, spokes and all, and the cab pitched violently to the side. It struggled on for a yard or two, driven by momentum and two galloping steeds, before the traces broke. Abruptly loosed, the horses fled, and the driver was flung from his perch.

Upon seeing the calamity up ahead, our daring constable pulled hard on the reins in a desperate bid to avoid the same fate. As we slowed, I saw Graves clambering from the wreckage. He stole a baleful glance at us, before helping Irina from the broken hansom. Then they ran.

Gregson bellowed, "Stop this carriage, Constable!"

Our growler slewed to an abrupt halt, and all three of us leapt out. The figures of Graves and Irina were partly obscured by billowing snow but visible enough to discern their awkward movements, and I reasoned they could be injured. A second police growler pulled up behind ours, the constables on board no doubt prepared to see to the stricken driver.

Ahead, the dark expanse of the Thames beckoned. A few ships still plied its waters in spite of both the lateness of the hour and the inhospitable weather. Other than by boat, the only means of crossing it at this precise point was via Blackfriars Bridge, which stretched before us.

Evidently enacting some hitherto agreed plan, Graves and Laznovna headed straight for the bridge. About a quarter of the way across, I saw Graves stop and bid his love go on without him. They were but indistinct figures in the storm, but his meaning translated clearly enough. The briefest moment of hesitation passed, enough to show her reservation but not so much to put her in jeopardy, before the girl went on. Graves then climbed atop the balustrade and drew out a pistol. I can only assume he had armed himself between escaping us at Berkeley Square and arriving at the theatre. He brandished the weapon with meaning and I had no reason to believe he would not shoot.

The three of us came to a halt, not more than twenty feet away, Holmes holding up a hand in warning as soon as he saw Graves draw a weapon. Evidently, Gregson had also seen the threat and had the same thought as me, for we drew almost as one.

"Hold!" shouted the inspector. "Hold in the name of the law, and put up your arms! Put up your arms, I am warning you!"

"You won't have her," said Graves, his voice raised against the storm but calm in spite of it.

There was a moment of stillness, the usual hubbub of the city muted beneath squalls of snow and all too briefly a peaceful end to this entire affair seemed possible. I dared to hope. It was not to be. Through the blizzard, I thought I saw Graves smile before he raised his weapon… Shots rang out across the night, one from my service revolver and the other Gregson's police-issue pistol.

Graves fell, blood spattering the white snow as he plunged off Blackfriars Bridge and into the dark waters of the Thames. Pistols still smoking in the cold air, Gregson and I raced after Holmes who had run to the edge of the bridge and was peering intently at the water.

A barge passed under the bridge, and Holmes bellowed down to its captain. "You there! Shine a light, sir. Over there, over there." His frantic gestures were met with compliance as the sailor swept his lamp back and forth over the patch of river Holmes had indicated.

"Anything?" he cried, hurrying back and forth along the length of the balustrade to try and get a better vantage. "Can you see him?"

"Nothing," said I.

"At least one of us struck him true," offered Gregson, pointing to the fading patch of red against the falling snow.

If Graves had survived the bullet and the fall, there was no sign.

"And *his* bullet?" asked Holmes, casting a quick glance in the direction the girl had fled.

Gregson was first to the pistol which Graves had dropped before he fell. He looked up at us, his expression confused.

"Not even fired."

Holmes made no comment. Instead, he ran another ten yards up the bridge before stopping to call out.

"Irina Laznovna!"

CHAPTER TWENTY-SIX

THE FATE OF ARKADY LAZNOVICH

She turned, having already slowed at the sound of gunshots. The urgency of the chase left her, anguish in her eyes, not panic. And grief. She had loved him then, and him her if he was willing to die so she might escape.

By now the constables had made their way to the bridge, but Gregson waved them back as he realised the delicate nature of the unfolding situation.

"Did you kill him?" she asked me as I came to Holmes's side, Gregson a few feet behind. His pistol was still drawn though I had returned mine to my jacket pocket. Whatever threat she might have posed had somehow diminished following Graves's apparent death. And now I truly looked upon her for the first time, I saw not a spectre of death, the figure in black; I saw a young woman and all the pain she carried.

I recognised her too, and realised this was the reason Holmes had berated himself back at the mansion on Berkeley Square. She had been there, at the theatre that first night, and had watched from the ring of onlookers as I pronounced Miss

Evangeline dead. She had been waiting in the wings to take the poor dead girl's place so that she might get close enough to the grand duke to enact her murderous plan.

"I don't know," I told her. "Though I say truthfully, it was not my desire to see him dead."

She returned my gaze, icy and impassive, a winter queen inured to the flurrying snow whipping around her, but her eyes betrayed her pain. She strayed a step towards the balustrade, and my heart began to thump.

"It's over," Holmes said, and I thanked God for his timely intervention. "Come now and let justice be done."

"Justice?" she said defiantly. "Konstantin's death would not have been justice."

"Is that why you tried to kill his son?" I asked.

"Yes. The grand duke needed to suffer, and I would have gladly damned myself further to do it."

"He is just a child," said I, finding it difficult to reconcile such a heinous act with the girl standing before us.

"And so was she, Watson," said Holmes, edging towards Irina almost imperceptibly, "isn't that right?" he added, addressing the question to her.

Irina nodded, her small sad smile failing to reach her eyes.

"I would ask you, tell us," said Holmes. "Tell us your story, so we might at least understand. There is no sense in dissembling now. Be heard," he gestured to Gregson, "with an officer of the law present to bear witness, as well as my friend and I."

Holmes edged forwards a half step, and I knew he had seen the same danger as I. "Damian Graves kept your confidence. In that and his attempt to slow us down, he served you until the end. He said it was your story to tell," Holmes added, "and so, pray, tell it."

She cast a furtive glance to the balustrade then back to

us. Holmes held her gaze as a man would stare down a wolf. Mercifully, and to the benefit of my thundering heart, she relented, no doubt realising she had nothing left to lose.

"I loved my parents. They were teachers, and rather than send me away to school, they saw personally to my education. Though strict, my lessons began at an early age and I learned much. We lived in Pushkin; it was where I spent my childhood, and I have never been happier."

"We saw a photograph of you and your family, and a painting of the same image," said I.

Irina smiled. "Yes, Alexandrinsky Square in Saint Petersburg. I begged my father to take me to the Alexandrinsky, so that I could watch the dancers. My mother danced, and performed gymnastics when she was younger. I loved to dance, and paint, though this I learned from my father." Her expression darkened. "I once loved a great many things, for my mother and father instilled in me not only a desire to learn but also a passion for the arts. I considered myself very lucky indeed. It was not to last.

"A bet, a foolish, stupid bet. That is how it began. My father… I am not ashamed to admit, he had vices. No different to many men, he liked to gamble. He played cards, Vint. He said it kept his mind sharp. It did. He was a very intelligent man, my father, and an excellent fencer. He taught me how to fence and like everything I put my mind to, I became good at it. This, and more besides, Damian and I had in common.

"It happened one night during a stay in Saint Petersburg. My mother and I had gone to the ballet while my father went in search of a game. He found one, a tavern somewhere in the city. To this day, I do not know which one. I was too young to understand, but I knew it bothered my mother whenever he went out like that. He had been winning lately, though we were not a particularly wealthy family. A teacher of chemistry is not so well paid as some. Always, my father wanted more, so he could give us the life he felt we were worthy of. It did not matter to us, but it mattered to him. As young as I was then, I realised that much.

"The evening went ahead as planned, my mother taking me to the ballet. I can still remember it… such a wonderful night. We spent a good deal of our money to procure the tickets. The performance, the elegance of the ballerinas… it captivated me. My mother told me I would one day share such a stage, that I would be every bit as accomplished as those dancers. Better even."

"Hence your appointment at the Royal Opera House," said Holmes.

"Yes. Damian made the introductions. His money opens a great many doors."

"And Miss Evangeline?" said I, leaving the implication of a question.

Irina glanced down at her ballet shoes, slowly disappearing under the falling snow. "A necessary evil. Though she was a cruel, spoilt girl who toyed with men's affections as a child would play with a doll. A little push was all it took…" Her hand strayed to the balustrade, fingertips lightly brushing the railings.

"We know about Miss Evangeline," said Holmes, arresting her attention, "and the young stagehand who arranged for her fatal misadventure. A tragedy, one amongst many, but, please, do continue your story. It is no small matter to allow the truth to be known, for there is no one else to tell it."

She looked back to the balustrade. "There is little time for it, sir."

"Which makes the telling of it all the more important. Pray, miss, do go on."

"Very well. After the ballet, my mother and I went back to our hotel, my father yet absent, though this was not unusual. He did not return until several hours later. I had gone to bed, but woke as soon as I heard my father's voice. He spoke very low, very quiet, and though I could not make out the words, I knew something was wrong.

"A little scared, I opened my eyes and saw my father sitting in the room's only chair, his head in his hands, my mother standing by the window. She had been crying. They told me to go back to bed, my father's efforts to reassure failing despite the best of intent. They spoke no further that night, worried, I think, that I would overhear. I learned later that he had lost a large sum of money, more than we could afford. He had found a high stakes game, one that involved men who were a great deal more affluent and powerful than he. Pride got the better of him, though, and he would not be cowed by men who thought themselves his superior. He played, and he lost, to none other than Grand Duke Konstantin, who was visiting the city. My father maintained he had been cheated, but could not prove it and dared not raise a quarrel with a *velikiy kniaz*.

"We stayed a day longer in Saint Petersburg, as my mother and father tried to think what they could do. I wish dearly we had not. We had money enough to return to Pushkin but little else. Shame would not allow my father to go home under such circumstances, and as he left in search of another game, another bet to try and recoup whatever he could, my mother found where the grand duke was staying and went to confront him. Beg him, if necessary. With little choice, she took me with her, and gave me strict instructions to stay close and be quiet at all times.

"He was not at his hotel when we called, so we waited outside most of the day. I remember it was cold, and my mother and I shivered. Evening began to draw in and at last we saw the grand duke returning. Managing to get past his manservant, my mother begged Konstantin to show us mercy. He did not know who she was at first, but deigned to listen. I hoped, though I did not understand everything that was happening, that he would take pity on us. I did not realise he meant to ridicule her. Instead of heeding her plight, he laughed. He said my father was a fool and had acted above his station, that he *deserved* what had been done to him. She pleaded, and said she would do anything to make amends on my father's behalf. He looked at her then, the grand duke, and I felt suddenly afraid, though I could not say why. Seizing my mother's wrist, he asked what she would be willing to do and I saw something hungry in his eyes, something wild. My mother recoiled, but he held her, and would not let go. I started to cry. In the end he warned her to stay away, that if he saw her or my father again it would go badly for us.

"We returned to our own hotel in silence and found my father already there. He had been drinking, frittering away what little we had. When he saw my mother he flew into a rage and demanded she tell him what had happened. Though she did not want to, for fear of what my father would do, she could not lie but begged him to let the matter be done. Drunk and ashamed, my father left in a fit of anger. I was afraid for him. I wanted him to stay, to be safe. I said I would go and fetch *pirozhki* and *sbiten'* for my mother and myself from the street vendors outside our hotel, but I lied. I went after my father instead. I wanted to call out, but I was afraid, so I followed him into the night.

"I was angry too and wanted him to come back. I hoped if he saw me that he would, but a terrible purpose drove him and he knew the city, whereas I did not. I lost sight of him at one point, until I heard the rattle of sabres that I knew so well. I ran towards the sound, my heart beating fiercely, wanting desperately to shout out…"

Here Irina paused, and I believe the memory was almost too painful for her to relate but she found the resolve to go on, her anger renewed by remembrance.

"I saw him kill my father. The grand duke stabbed him in the heart. I almost cried out, but held my hands to my mouth, too afraid to move or breathe as I watched from the shadows. The grand duke and his man, they did not see me. No one ever knew I was watching. I slipped away, leaving my father dead in the street, for I dared not approach him or reveal myself.

"When I returned to the hotel, my mother was angry. I said nothing, still afraid, hoping it had been some terrible dream. The next day when my father failed to return, I knew it was not.

"I told my mother what I had seen, but I could not prove it. We were nothing, less than nothing, and the grand duke was a very powerful man. In the end, the police said he had been attacked in the street. Mugged. There was nothing we could do.

"We left Saint Petersburg, almost penniless and my father's death unsolved, the grand duke exculpated. His lawyer, Zyuganov, saw to this. No charges were laid, the matter of my father's death ignored and forgotten by everyone except for my mother and me.

"We went back to Pushkin, though the news of what had happened reached home before we did. It was hard for us after that. What little work my mother could find was menial. She would not hear of putting me to work, insisting I studied. I did. I was angry with my father for what he had done, and for leaving us alone. I fed this anger into my studies. Seven years passed like this. We still had my father's sabre and I practised every day with it. I danced, I became an accomplished gymnast, my mother imparting everything she knew, I her determined and willing protégée. In the end, grief more than her labours wore her out, threadbare like an old cloak. She endured it for one more year, amassing all she had saved and selling my father's sword so that I might leave Russia and find sanctuary elsewhere. We were all but pariahs in Pushkin now for everyone knew we had somehow displeased the grand duke and did not wish to share our shadow. She died and in her final moments told me of the meagre passage she had bought for me to England. Though much time had passed, I think she feared for me, for what the grand duke or those allied to him might do, especially without anyone to protect me. Another country… it was frightening, but at least I would be far away from him. Though I still craved revenge.

"With my mother's death, I had little choice and no other relatives to shelter me. I fled, but the money she had saved was not quite enough and so my passage across the Baltic Sea was an uncomfortable one, and I arrived in London penniless. I was forced to live on the streets, but always returned to the docks as it became the closest thing I had to a home. Until Damian found me. You know the rest."

Holmes nodded. "And so you sought vengeance, to punish those who had wronged you, and the grand duke most of all."

"When I heard of his visit, I knew I had been granted a rare opportunity. Regardless of my father's part in it, blood demanded blood, and suffering demanded suffering. I have failed, but I hope retribution finds him."

"Then let the law see to it," Holmes implored, who kept his eyes on Irina as I cast mine nervously towards the edge of the bridge. "His wrongdoing shall be borne out. Be sure of that."

With a mournful look she said, "The law will see me hang for what I have done, or confine me to a gaol cell for the rest of my days. I came to England to be free."

Too fast, she leapt onto the balustrade and jumped.

Holmes sprang for her, but succeeded only in grasping a feather from her swan's garb. I ran to the balustrade and leaned over, only to be rewarded with the sight of a small white-clad body floating facedown in the water.

"It is a poor end, Watson," Holmes said, turning away to slump against the rail. "A poor and unsatisfactory end."

The snow had stopped, and the night's chill waned along with it. Flakes had begun to melt, revealing the grime of London still clinging beneath.

CHAPTER TWENTY-SEVEN

A LINGERING MYSTERY

Some time later that evening, the police dredged Irina Laznovna from the black, unforgiving waters of the Thames. Her body had all the warmth of sleet in winter, her life summarily ended, her vengeance unfulfilled.

"Any sign of Graves?" Gregson asked of one of the officers, who shook his head. "Must've been swept farther downriver," he said, stroking the stubble on his chin. "If we haven't found him by morning, he'll be somewhere in the North Sea and we'll never see him again. Wouldn't you say so, Mr Holmes?"

Holmes declined to reply. His gaze never left the river. Despite the weather, there were still boats on the water. Barges, schooners, the old ramshackle tug.

"Mr Holmes?" Gregson pressed.

"I expect you are right, Inspector," he said curtly, and turned as sharp as a grenadier guard before stalking away. "Come, Watson. The good inspector has everything in hand. There is little more for us here, shivering like waifs by the riverbank."

I followed, bidding the inspector a good night and craving a warm supper and a dry bed.

The next morning we were summoned back to the Langham by the grand duke. Despite its ill provenance, he had taken possession of the portrait and had it proudly displayed in his sitting room, confronting us upon arrival.

"It is not such a bad likeness, I think," he said airily as his burly attendants saw us to our seats. I noted he had his arm in a sling.

He regarded the piece for a few silent moments before going on. "How can I express my gratitude?" he asked sincerely, no longer the aloof Russian aristocrat but merely a father who was grateful for the service we had done for him and his son. Though the boy being unharmed was cause to rejoice, the entire matter had left something of a bitter taste.

I believe Holmes felt the same way.

"Tell us how Arkady Laznovich died," he said simply. "Irina Laznovna claims she saw you strike the killing blow."

The grand duke hid his surprise well. His mood then darkened and for a moment I thought Holmes might have overstepped. In the end, he slumped into the armchair opposite us and sighed.

"Yes, he died by my hand; I am ashamed I did not confess to it at the time. I was young, a foolish and vainglorious man. I squandered my youth on self-aggrandising pursuits and abused the privileges of my position and power. I did not know Arkady Laznovich, but I thought I knew his kind. A proletariat scholar, seeking to reach the heights of his betters or at least bring them down to his level.

"Know this," said Konstantin, pausing in his account, "I

will not admit publicly to my crimes. I won't subject Sergei to such scandal. I am a different man to the one I was, and I am trying to make amends for any past indiscretion. I beat Arkady at cards. He was not cheated, he was merely overconfident. The fact he accused me of such would have been enough for a severe remonstration, but I let it pass. I had humbled him, and this was enough for me. I told him to return to his family. This he did, for I think, even as drunk as he obviously was, he knew I had showed lenience.

"In truth, it rankled that I had been accused of cheating him, and I thought of little else the next day. When his wife came to beg for their money back and my continued mercy, I saw a chance to make her pay for her husband's behaviour. I was cruel, and it was only when I saw the girl with her that I realised what I had been about to do. I let her go, and she crawled back to her husband.

"I thought no more of it, truly. I believed the matter done with. It was later that evening, outside of a gentlemen's club, that Arkady found me again. Still drunk, though sobered by anger, he accused me of attacking his wife. This was true, though not to the extent he made out. He demanded retribution, said I was a coward and a dog for hurting a woman. I could not let that stand, for twice now he had called my honour into question. I had been fencing earlier in the day, and when he saw Grigori with my foils and sabres, he challenged me. I use real swords when I fence, and he wanted a duel," Konstantin gave a little incredulous chuckle, "can you imagine that?

"I complied. I wished to truly shame this man, to show him he had erred. I wanted to punish him, see him ridiculed. I had not thought he might actually be an accomplished swordsman. He had no blade of his own, so I loaned him the use of one of mine."

"And then what happened?" I asked, as keen as Holmes to

learn of the deed that had spurred this entire horrid affair.

"We fought. I had thought to cut him," Konstantin ran a finger across his cheek, "here perhaps, give him a scar he would not soon forget." He shook his head. "But he was… *ferocious*. Unskilled ferocity is not so hard to counter, *that* I expected, but he knew how to fight. I quickly realised he meant to kill me. Grigori saw this too and tried to intervene. Laznovich cut him," the grand duke gestured to his chest, "and I made the most of my opponent's distraction. I ran him through the heart. I did not wish for it, but I feared it would be him or me dead at the end of a sabre. What choice did I have but to conceal the matter? I returned to my hotel in need of strong vodka. Grigori, he made sure the body would be found in a less… salubrious part of the city. As soon as I had calmed my nerves, I sent a message to Pavel Zyuganov, my lawyer, who took care of the rest. I did not know the girl saw me. I thought her accusations an act of desperation.

"I became a different man after that night, Mr Holmes. I met my wife, and we had Sergei. I forgot my past and hoped it would forget me." He turned again to the portrait. "I will keep it, I think, as a reminder, though it pains me to look upon it, I will admit."

He said nothing further, and his attendants made it abundantly clear that our audience was at an end.

"We shall bid you a good morning, Grand Duke," said Holmes, rising. Konstantin nodded, but did not favour us with a look as we left him to his troubled thoughts.

"Is there nothing we can do, Holmes?" I asked as we were leaving the Langham. "A man has committed murder and is also indirectly responsible for the deaths of nearly forty innocent men and women. Yet he walks free."

"Gregson has made overtures to the Russian police, and we can only hope justice shall find the grand duke there. The scandal of it will not be something he can easily ignore. Regardless of what Gregson's efforts might yield, I feel certain the grand duke will be the maker of his own punishment, and in that at least Irina Laznovna can find some peace I hope. Guilt shall be his shackles, remorse his cell. Grand Duke Konstantin will not soon find himself free of that, I think."

"Perhaps," said I. "At least it is an end to it, I suppose."

"Not quite," Holmes said. "For there is one final thing still to be done."

It would be our last visit to Berkeley Square and the mansion of Damian Graves, presumed to have met a grim end in the darkness of the Thames.

Gregson had deployed several constables to search the house for any further evidence, though with both suspects dead, it would prove to be something of a moot gesture. Holmes and I had kindly been given licence to look over the house, perhaps in the hope of my companion revealing some hitherto overlooked scrap of evidence or possibly simply out of courtesy for the service he had rendered unto the law.

I had expected to discover nothing of import, so it was with gathering incredulity and not a little alarm that we noted several items of value we had seen on our previous visits were now, inexplicably, missing.

Holmes said nothing of this to the constables and bade me to follow his example. It was only later in the comfort of 221B Baker Street that we spoke of the matter.

"Is it possible, though, Holmes?" I asked, sitting in my favourite chair by the fire, nursing a warming brandy and smoking a cigar.

Holmes's countenance was lit only occasionally by the pale orange flame of his pipe. Night had drawn in again, the two of us having spent almost all of the day in Berkeley Square.

"A great deal, though improbable, is perfectly possible, Watson," he answered, standing ramrod straight by the window, pipe in his hand. He had no drink and I wondered if his Morocco case was nearby. "One only has to consider all of the facts."

"But to survive such a swim, and wounded to boot," said I. "Could Graves's house not have been robbed?"

Holmes took a deep pull on his pipe, and held it for a moment before releasing a thick wreath of aromatic smoke.

"A man such as Graves, in his prime, a slave to fitness and physical perfection. A man such as this could make that dive and live. As for his wounding, all we know is that he bled, and but a little. For all we know it was a graze, nothing more, allowing him to swim. His pistol, left unfired, demonstrates his unwillingness to engage in a fight. He did not, and so we are left with but one possibility—a desire to escape by feigning his own death, and what better opportunity would come his way? None, I think. This when taken together with the items removed from his home, items of rare value and small enough to be transported easily in a simple travelling case, leads me to one conclusion. Damian Graves is not dead."

"You have convinced me, Holmes," I said. "And at least the same can be said for the grand duke's son," I added. "In that the boy yet lives. A sorry business, all in all."

"Quite so, Watson, for that at least we can be thankful."

"And what of the painting then, not poisoned after all?"

"Early on I began to suspect the painting was but the means and not the method. The sheer size of the Royal Opera House and the difficulty in recreating the exact same conditions of the Grayson Gallery was, by any scientific method, a practical impossibility. My own experiments revealed as much to me. What then the purpose of it? A ruse, Watson, a lure for the trap;

death delivered by the girl's hand to Konstantin's heir. Suffering of the cruellest kind. Getting the grand duke to the Opera House required an altogether more *artful* solution." He smiled at this.

"Very droll, Holmes, very droll. But how could you be certain she was there, one of the dancers? She could have secreted herself in the audience."

"I admit that detail almost escaped me, Watson, and it was not until I placed the distinct aroma of rosin powder that I realised what our killer intended."

"The dust on her cloak and at the gallery," said I, catching hold of the thread at last.

"Quite so, Watson. I initially believed it could be chalk, used for grip." Holmes's eyes narrowed. "In that at least, I was half right. Rosin powder, however, has something of a faint pine odour, which I detected but could not rightly attribute until I saw the half-finished painting of Arkady, Varvara and young Irina Laznovich. A faded photograph, ravaged by time, obscures and omits much. Not so a rendering of the selfsame image in exacting detail upon the canvas, whereupon I saw the ballet shoes and my error. Lavender again covered the odour a little but made it distinctive enough from the other performers to betray her presence. To her disguise then, a swan amongst the flock. How to roust the bird, eh? I reasoned she would not have heard the names Arkady and Varvara in quite some time; not only that, but she would be unprepared for such an emotional jolt and hence her reaction."

"Really rather brilliant, Holmes."

"Ah, not so, Watson," said he, waving away any praise. "Merely reason and observation, the essential tools of any detective."

"Well, I believe I'm going to turn in," I said, as I finished my brandy, "it's been quite the adventure."

"Very good, Watson. I think I shall stay up awhile," he replied, turning back to the window.

"Right you are, Holmes. Good night."

"Good night, Watson," he said. His voice grew absent as the fire dwindled and the shadows deepened around him, and Sherlock Holmes looked out into the London night somewhere in the direction of the Thames and Blackfriars Bridge.

SHERLOCK HOLMES
CRY OF THE INNOCENTS
Cavan Scott

It is 1891, and a Catholic priest arrives at 221B Baker Street, only to utter the words "*il corpe*" before suddenly dropping dead.

Though the man's death is attributed to cholera, when news of another dead priest reaches Holmes, he becomes convinced that the men have been poisoned. He and Watson learn that the victims were on a mission from the Vatican to investigate a miracle; it is said that the body of eighteenth-century philanthropist and slave trader Edwyn Warwick has not decomposed. But should the Pope canonise a man who made his fortune through slavery? And when Warwick's body is stolen, it becomes clear that the priest's mission has attracted the attention of a deadly conspiracy…

PRAISE FOR CAVAN SCOTT

"Many memorable moments… excellent."
Starburst

"Utterly charming, comprehensively Sherlockian, and possessed of a wry narrator." **Criminal Element**

"Memorable and enjoyable… One of the best stories I've ever read."
Wondrous Reads

TITANBOOKS.COM

SHERLOCK HOLMES
THE PATCHWORK DEVIL
Cavan Scott

It is 1919, and while the world celebrates the signing of the Treaty of Versailles, Holmes and Watson are called to a grisly discovery.

A severed hand has been found on the bank of the Thames, a hand belonging to a soldier who supposedly died in the trenches two years previously. But the hand is fresh, and shows signs that it was recently amputated. So how has it ended up back in London two years after its owner was killed in France? Warned by Sherlock's brother Mycroft to cease their investigation, and only barely surviving an attack by a superhuman creature, Holmes and Watson begin to suspect a conspiracy at the very heart of the British government…

"Scott poses an intriguing puzzle for an older Holmes and
Watson to tackle."
Publishers Weekly

"Interesting and exciting in ways that few Holmes
stories are these days."
San Francisco Book Review

"A thrilling tale for Scott's debut in the Sherlock Holmes world."
Sci-Fi Bulletin

TITANBOOKS.COM

SHERLOCK HOLMES
THE LABYRINTH OF DEATH
James Lovegrove

It is 1895, and Sherlock Holmes's new client is a high court judge, whose free-spirited daughter has disappeared without a trace.

Holmes and Watson discover that the missing woman—Hannah Woolfson—was herself on the trail of a missing person, her close friend Sophia. Sophia was recruited to a group known as the Elysians, a quasi-religious sect obsessed with Ancient Greek myths and rituals, run by the charismatic Sir Philip Buchanan. Hannah has joined the Elysians under an assumed name, convinced that her friend has been murdered. Holmes agrees that she should continue as his agent within the secretive yet seemingly harmless cult, yet Watson is convinced Hannah is in terrible danger. For Sir Philip has dreams of improving humanity through classical ideals, and at any cost…

"A writer of real authority and one worthy of taking the reader back to the dangerous streets of Victorian London in the company of the Great Detective."
Crime Time

"Lovegrove does a convincing job of capturing Watson's voice."
Publishers Weekly

TITANBOOKS.COM

SHERLOCK HOLMES
THE THINKING ENGINE
James Lovegrove

It is 1895, and Sherlock Holmes is settling back into life as a consulting detective at 221B Baker Street, when he and Watson learn of strange goings-on amidst the dreaming spires of Oxford.

A Professor Quantock has built a wondrous computational device, which he claims is capable of analytical thought to rival the cleverest men alive. Naturally Sherlock Holmes cannot ignore this challenge. He and Watson travel to Oxford, where a battle of wits ensues between the great detective and his mechanical counterpart as they compete to see which of them can first to solve a series of crimes, from a bloody murder to a missing athlete. But as man and machine vie for supremacy, it becomes clear that the Thinking Engine has its own agenda…

"The plot, like the device, is ingenious, with a chilling twist… an entertaining, intelligent and pacy read." **The Sherlock Holmes Journal**

"Lovegrove knows his Holmes trivia and delivers a great mystery that fans will enjoy, with plenty of winks and nods to the canon." **Geek Dad**

"I think Conan Doyle would have enjoyed reading this story: the concept of an intelligent, self-aware Thinking Engine is brilliance itself." **The Book Bag**

TITANBOOKS.COM

SHERLOCK HOLMES
GODS OF WAR
James Lovegrove

It is 1913, and Dr Watson is visiting Sherlock Holmes at his retirement cottage near Eastbourne when tragedy strikes: the body of a young man, Patrick Mallinson, is found under the cliffs of Beachy Head.

The dead man's father, a wealthy businessman, engages Holmes to prove that his son committed suicide, the result of a failed love affair with an older woman. Yet the woman in question insists that there is more to Patrick's death. She has seen mysterious symbols drawn on his body, and fears that he was under the influence of a malevolent cult. When an attempt is made on Watson's life, it seems that she may be proved right. The threat of war hangs over England, and there is no telling what sinister forces are at work…

"Lovegrove has once again packed his novel with incident and suspense." **Fantasy Book Review**

"An atmospheric mystery which shows just why Lovegrove has become a force to be reckoned with in genre fiction. More, please."
Starburst

"A very entertaining read with a fast-moving, intriguing plot."
The Consulting Detective

TITANBOOKS.COM

SHERLOCK HOLMES
THE STUFF OF NIGHTMARES
James Lovegrove

A spate of bombings has hit London, causing untold damage and loss of life. Meanwhile a strangely garbed figure has been spied haunting the rooftops and grimy back alleys of the capital.

Sherlock Holmes believes this strange masked man may hold the key to the attacks. He moves with the extraordinary agility of a latter-day Spring-Heeled Jack. He possesses weaponry and armour of unprecedented sophistication. He is known only by the name Baron Cauchemar, and he appears to be a scourge of crime and villainy. But is he all that he seems? Holmes and his faithful companion Dr Watson are about to embark on one of their strangest and most exhilarating adventures yet.

"[A] tremendously accomplished thriller which leaves the reader in no doubt that they are in the hands of a confident and skilful craftsman."
Starburst

"Dramatic, gripping, exciting and respectful to its source material, I thoroughly enjoyed every surprise and twist as the story unfolded."
Fantasy Book Review

"This is delicious stuff, marrying the standard notions of Holmesiana with the kind of imagination we expect from Lovegrove."
Crime Time

TITANBOOKS.COM

SHERLOCK HOLMES
THE SPIRIT BOX
George Mann

German Zeppelins rain down death and destruction on London, and Dr Watson is grieving for his nephew, killed on the fields of France.

A cryptic summons from Mycroft Holmes reunites Watson with his one-time companion, as Sherlock comes out of retirement, tasked with solving three unexplained deaths. A politician has drowned in the Thames after giving a pro-German speech; a soldier suggests surrender before feeding himself to a tiger; and a suffragette renounces women's liberation and throws herself under a train. Are these apparent suicides something more sinister, something to do with the mysterious Spirit Box? Their investigation leads them to Ravensthorpe House, and the curious Seaton Underwood, a man whose spectrographs are said to capture men's souls…

"Arthur Conan Doyle was a master storyteller, and it takes comparable talent to give Holmes a second life… Mann is one of the few to get close to the target." **Daily Mail**

"I would highly recommend this… a fun read." **Fantasy Book Review**

"Our only complaint is that it is over too soon." **Starburst**

"An entertaining read." **Eurocrime**

TITANBOOKS.COM

SHERLOCK HOLMES
THE WILL OF THE DEAD
George Mann

A rich elderly man has fallen to his death, and his will is nowhere to be found. A tragic accident or something more sinister? The dead man's nephew comes to Baker Street to beg for Sherlock Holmes's help. Without the will he fears he will be left penniless, the entire inheritance passing to his cousin. But just as Holmes and Watson start their investigation, a mysterious new claimant to the estate appears. Does this prove that the old man was murdered?

Meanwhile Inspector Charles Bainbridge is trying to solve the case of the "iron men", mechanical steam-powered giants carrying out daring jewellery robberies. But how do you stop a machine that feels no pain and needs no rest? He too may need to call on the expertise of Sherlock Holmes.

"Mann clearly knows his Holmes, knows what works… the book is all the better for it." **Crime Fiction Lover**

"Mann writes Holmes in an eloquent way, capturing the period of the piece perfectly… this is a must read." **Cult Den**

"An amazing story… Even in the established world of Sherlock Holmes, George Mann is a strong voice and sets himself apart!" **Book Plank**

TITANBOOKS.COM

For more fantastic fiction, author events, competitions,
limited editions and more

VISIT OUR WEBSITE
titanbooks.com

LIKE US ON FACEBOOK
facebook.com/titanbooks

FOLLOW US ON TWITTER
@TitanBooks

EMAIL US
readerfeedback@titanemail.com